NOWHERE TO HIDE

Rage at her younger sister's brutal murder has nearly consumed Ellen Harris. So when her work as a psychologist wins her an appearance on the evening news, Ellen seizes the moment. Staring straight into the camera, she challenges the killer to come out of hiding. Phone calls flood the station, but all leads go nowhere. Then it happens: a note, written in red ink, slipped under the windshield wipers of her car. 'YOU'RE IT.' Ellen has stirred the monster in his lair — and the hunter has become the hunted!

Books by Joan Hall Hovey
Published by The House of Ulverscroft:

LISTEN TO THE SHADOWS

JOAN HALL HOVEY

NOWHERE
TO HIDE

Complete and Unabridged

ULVERSCROFT
Leicester

First published in the
United States of America

First Large Print Edition
published 2001

Copyright © 1993 by Joan Hall Hovey

British Library CIP Data

Hovey, Joan Hall
   Nowhere to hide.—Large print ed.—
Ulverscroft large print series: mystery
1. Detective and mystery stories
2. Large type books
I. Title
823.9'14 [F]

ISBN 0–7089–4418–3

Published by
F. A. Thorpe (Publishing)
Anstey, Leicestershire

Set by Words & Graphics Ltd.
Anstey, Leicestershire
Printed and bound in Great Britain by
T. J. International Ltd., Padstow, Cornwall

This book is printed on acid-free paper

To my grown children Gary, Brenda,
Daryl and Bill,
and to my daughters-in-law
Adeline and Lynne,
and my son-in-law, Peter
With love

1

August 6, 1979

The closet was at the top of the stairs at the end of the hall. To get to it he had to pass by two doors, one on either side, both now partly open. He could hear talking, very low. Farther away, the sound of running water. In three quick strides he was past the doors and inside the closet. He knew he was smiling. He felt excited the way he always did when he got past them. Even if anyone had got a glimpse of him, it wouldn't really matter. He was invisible. The invisible man.

The secret door was to his right, just behind the wide rack of musty-smelling winter coats in varying sizes. He ducked beneath them, and opening the door, let himself into the narrow, cave-like space.

The space separating the inside and outside walls went nearly the whole way around the third floor, stopping abruptly at the wall of the stairwell where he had to turn around and go back the way he had come. Once, this space had been used for storage — old bed springs, broken chairs, trunks — but the

1

doors, except for the one in the closet which he had come upon quite by luck, and through which he had come again and again, had long since been replaced by sheetrock and papered over with rose-patterned wallpaper.

It was pitch black in front of him and all around him, like he was all alone in the world. He had his flashlight, but didn't turn it on. He knew the way. Besides, it might shine through someplace.

As he made his way along the darkened corridor, breathing the stale, hot air, his progress slowed by the long, heavy skirt he wore, he had to stoop. At seventeen, though narrow-shouldered, he was nearly six feet tall.

Sweat was trickling down between his shoulder blades, and under the wig, his head felt squirmy, so he took the wig off and stuffed it into his pants pocket, under the skirt.

And then he was there. He could see the thin beam of light shining through, projecting a tiny star on the wall. It was coming through the place where two Sundays ago, when they were all at Chapel, he had made a peephole. He'd made it by simply pounding a nail through, then drawing it cleanly back out so that there would be nothing detectible on the other side — no more than a black dot.

A giggle floated through to him and the

```
#110  22-11-2018 10:11AM
Item(s) checked out to Neligan, Marian.

TITLE: Go ahead, secret seven.
BARCODE: 30007008789506
DUE DATE: 13-12-18

TITLE: Wish for a witch
BARCODE: 30007009598607
DUE DATE: 13-12-18

TITLE: The house with chicken legs
BARCODE: 30007009622589
DUE DATE: 13-12-18
```

smile froze on his face, his fists clenching involuntarily. *No, it can't be me they're laughing at. They can't see me. They don't know I'm here. I'm invisible, remember?* Calming himself, he slowly brought his face to the wall.

★   ★   ★

Eight narrow, iron-framed beds faced him, each covered by a thin, grey blanket with a faded red stripe across the top and bottom. Twelve beds in all, but the two at either end were cut from his view. A few religious pictures hung above the beds. The one facing him directly said 'Suffer the Little Children to Come Unto Me'. It had a picture of a lamb on it. Only three of the beds were occupied. It was still early. Some of the girls were probably downstairs watching their allotted hour of T.V. Others would still be doing kitchen duty. At least one troublemaker would be doing 'quiet time'. He grinned.

He understood now that the laughter he'd heard had come from one of the two girls sitting on the edge of the bed flipping through a teen idol magazine. He'd caught a look at the cover — some weirdo with a green punk hairdo and a guitar slung around his neck. The two sluts, heads together, were still at it, giggling, whispering, low and secretive. He felt a hot surge of hatred course through his veins. He wished SHE would walk in on them right now. He knew what they were doing. They were talking about who they liked, who they thought was 'cute,' who they would let do *it*. They were thinking and talking about that.

Two beds over, a fat girl with short brown hair that looked as if someone (guess who? Ha-ha) had cut it around a bowl, lay on her back with her hands behind her head, staring at the ceiling. A jagged scar traveled from a spot between her eyebrows right up into her hairline. He could tell she'd been crying; her raisin eyes were all red and puffy, practically disappearing in her moon face. They cried a lot in here. Mostly in the middle of the night when they thought no one could hear. It always excited him hearing their soft muffled sobs. Sometimes, though, it just made him mad like it did when they laughed. Then he wanted to fix it so they didn't make any sound at all.

His gaze wandered back to the girl who had first caught his attention, the one who sat under the lamb picture, and who he'd wanted to save for last. She was sitting cross-legged on the bed, a writing tablet balanced on her knees, her long, pale hair fallen forward,

4

though some damply dark ends curled against her neck. He watched as she scribbled a few lines, then frowning, looked over what she had written. She would chew on her yellow pencil, then write some more, the pencil making whispery sounds on the paper. He watched her for a long time, taking in the flushed, shiny cheeks that made him think, as had the darkly damp curls, that she might just have stepped out of the bath. Yes, he remembered hearing the water running. He liked to see them when they just got out of the bath — all that damp, flowing hair, pinkly scrubbed skin, soft necks. Sometimes they changed into their flannel nightgowns right there on the edge of their beds, right there in front of him — though of course they didn't know that.

That was the best part. Them not knowing. It didn't matter that they dressed so hurriedly and so slickly that he often didn't get to see much. Though occasionally there was a flash of white shoulder, a curve of breast.

I'm watching you, he thought, and had to stifle a giggle of his own.

And then she raised her head and those clear blue eyes were staring straight at him, stabbing fear into his heart. He couldn't move.

She was frowning, not in the way she did

when she was thinking of what to write, but with her head cocked to one side, as if she were listening for something. A terrible thought struck him. What if he hadn't just *almost* laughed, but actually done it, right out loud? Adrenaline pumping crazily through his body. He backed slowly away from the peephole. Standing perfectly still with his back against the wall, he waited. When after several minutes there were no screams, no sudden cries of alarm to alert the other girls — and HER, especially HER — he began to relax. His heartbeat returned to normal; once more he brought his eye to the hole. She was back to writing. Of course she was.

He smiled to himself.

He hadn't laughed out loud, after all. And she hadn't seen him. Of course she hadn't. His gaze slid down to her breasts, their shapes round and firm as little apples under the flannel nightgown.

But you will, he thought. *You will.*

2

1992

Standing on the top rung of the stepladder, Ellen raised up on her sneaker-clad toes and carefully fitted the silver angel on the top of the tree. Its shadow shivered on the ceiling, then was still. 'Hand me that blue bulb, Myra, please,' she said from her rickety perch.

'Silent Night' was playing on the stereo — a new London Philharmonic tape. It was the first Christmas Ellen Harris had celebrated in three years.

'Christ, will you be careful,' Myra said, having returned from laying another log on the fire. 'I swear, you had to be a tightrope walker in your last life, you're so damned sure-footed.' She started to set her glass of wine down on the blond coffee table, caught herself, and slid a coaster under it, which brought a faint smile from Ellen. Behind Myra, the fire crackled and leaped to life, the flames lighting the sherry in her glass a lovely ruby red.

A twin tree bedecked in colorful bulbs and tinsel was reflected in the window. Beyond the window, fat snowflakes fell softly — just like in the snow-scene painted on the Christmas bulb.

A perfect dress rehearsal for Christmas Eve, Ellen thought. And what was it they said about a good dress rehearsal? *Oh, hell, knock it off*, she told herself as Myra's hand hovered above one of the boxes lined up on the sofa, chose one.

'No, the steepled one next to it,' Ellen said. 'Yeah, that's it — thanks.' She gingerly reached for the bulb.

'Pretty,' Myra commented, handing it up to her. 'Looks old-fashioned.'

The scenic ornament was electric blue in color. Ellen held it in her upturned hand as if it were a precious jewel. 'It is.' Her smile was wistful. 'Hand-painted. It belonged to my mother, and to her mother before her.' She searched for a bare spot on the tree, found just the right one. 'Gives me a sense of continuity, I suppose,' she said, studying the effect. 'And maybe it sounds crazy, but it sort of makes me feel a small part of Mom and Dad will be here, sharing Christmas with me and Gail.' It felt so good to be finally able to say that and mean it. Her parents wouldn't be fighting, of course. They never fought in the ideal scenarios of Ellen's imagination. Well, at least she didn't hate them anymore, and that was something.

'It doesn't sound crazy at all,' Myra said, picking up her glass and taking a sip of wine. 'Maybe a little sentimental, but what the hell? Sentiment's good. Actually, I wish I could say the same about . . . ' Her words trailed off, but not before Ellen heard the old note of bitterness creep into her friend's voice.

Ellen said nothing. She knew only too well that for a lot of people, the Christmas season was not a time of good cheer, nor did it necessarily start up visions of sugar plums dancing in their heads. This, in fact, was the clinic's busiest time. People got depressed, even suicidal, during the holidays. She wouldn't be in the least surprised if the season had more than a little to do with Myra's recent nightmares. Memories of childhood horrors, more or less successfully held at bay during the rest of the year, seemed strangely to gather strength in December.

'What time does Gail's plane get in?' Myra said, deliberately changing the subject.

'Eleven-twenty in the morning. I can't wait to see her. Imagine, *my* little sister signing on with a major recording studio.' Giving a final straightening to the silver angel, Ellen climbed down from the ladder. She stood back to admire her artistry.

Myra plucked an icicle from the shoulder of her blouse and tossed it among the decorations. 'I expect any day now I'll come over here and be confronted with life-size standups of Gail all over the house — you know, the kind like the Kodak people put out of Bill Cosby.'

'I wouldn't do that to you. You'd see them on the lawn first.' Ellen grinned and left the tree to begin tidying the sofa which was strewn with paper and boxes. Myra followed, glass in hand.

'Seriously, you guys have such a super relationship. I envy you. Most sisters can barely stand to be in the same room with each other. Or so I've heard.' She finger-combed her hair over her forehead, a habit, to hide the scar that resulted from a childhood sledding accident. 'Being an only child, of course, I wouldn't know.'

Ellen was thoughtfully stacking the empty boxes out of sight on the closet shelf. It was true. She and Gail were close. Closer than any sisters she knew. She suspected it had a lot to do with growing up in a booze-fertilized battleground. Moving from the closet to the sofa and back again, she said, 'Gail and I love each other, of course, but it's more than that. There's a kind of desperation at the bottom — an 'us against the world' thing.' She gave

Myra a wry smile.

'Yeah, I know what you mean.' Myra was standing behind her at the open closet door offering the last of the boxes. 'Listen, I — I hope I didn't bring you down with my talk of nightmares.'

Ellen turned, surprised. 'No, of course not. Why would you think that?'

'I don't know. It's just that you've been acting sort of ... preoccupied, I guess. Anyway, enough of the heavy crap, okay? We're supposed to be celebrating here. Christmas is just five days away and your sister is arriving tomorrow. So lighten up, Ellen.'

'Kiss my 'you know what',' Ellen said pleasantly, taking the boxes from her.

'Ass, dear. The word is 'ass'. God, but you're a prude.'

Ellen laughed. If Myra could defy the dark, then so could she. Compared to the hell of Myra's childhood, hers and Gail's would read like the Waltons'. 'Well, what do you think of it?' she asked brightly, gazing up at the tree. 'Is that a masterpiece, or is that a masterpiece?' Just for an instant did the old pang of loss hit her. Ed had always been the one to decorate the tree, while she had been perfectly content to sit and watch the transformation, which seemed nothing short

11

of magical, take place.

But Ed had died of a heart attack three years ago at the ripe old age of thirty-six. Just the night before they had talked about adopting a child. He'd seemed fine. Just fine to her.

'He said he was cold', the assistant foreman had told her the next afternoon, as he stood shifting his feet in their big boots, his eyes tearing. 'Then he sat down on some lumber — and he was gone.'

They called it SCA — 'sudden cardiac arrest'. 'It happens,' the weary-eyed doctor had told her sadly, apologetically, as Ellen listened in disbelief. 'A seemingly healthy young man — no one really knows why. I'm so sorry, Mrs. Harris . . . so very sorry . . . '

'It's a beautiful tree, Ellen,' Myra was saying, bringing her back, fading out the remembered sounds and smells of the hospital. 'In fact, the entire house looks fabulous. Especially this room. I love it. It just seems to wrap itself around you.'

Looking around her, Ellen couldn't help feeling a warm glow of pride. The room really did look nice, kind of rustic colonial, if there was such a thing. Most of the furniture was antique, pieces she'd picked up in flea-markets and second-hand shops and refinished, working on evenings and weekends. The rich, taffy-colored tables and sideboard reflected the fire's glow.

New slipcovers in soft floral chintz revived the old sofa and chair. When she and Ed had moved into the old farmhouse, there'd been worn, ratty carpeting on the floor. To her delight, when she'd lifted one corner, she discovered hardwood flooring underneath. A good cleaning and a coat of varnish had restored it to its original beauty.

The oval braided rug on which she and Myra now stood she owed to her Sears credit card — 'owed' being the key word here. But she'd wanted everything to be perfect for Gail's visit. With Gail working in New York, they didn't get to see one another nearly often enough, and now with the promotional tour coming up after the holidays, it would be even less.

The anxious feeling was back. Even with the aromatic scent of spruce permeating the air, and Christmas music playing in the background, Ellen couldn't shake the sense of something not right. It had been with her from the moment she opened her eyes this morning, and kept coming at her all day, little spasms that made her chest feel suddenly tight and her hands get busier. Mere seasonal anxiety? Had to be. What else?

'You've got a real talent for decorating,'

Myra said, having wandered over to admire the large print hanging above the red-brick fireplace. Sepia-toned, it was of a gentle-faced woman in a long dress bathing a child in a round metal tub. The blond, curly-haired cherub had a daub of soapsuds on his softly rounded, Victorian chin. This particular treasure she'd come upon at a garage sale one Saturday morning last spring. It had been hard not to appear too eager and weaken her bargaining position.

'Almost as much as you do for helping the walking wounded,' Myra went on. 'In my house, you'd be lucky to find a chair to sit down on without having to clear it of old clothes and magazines first.'

'You've got three kids to clean up after,' Ellen said, putting an arm around her friend's shoulders. 'C'mon, let's go out to the kitchen. I need a coffee.' Catching Myra eyeing her empty glass, Ellen dropped her arm, saying, 'But you go ahead and have some more wine; it will help you sleep.'

Myra didn't need any coaxing. While she poured, Ellen couldn't resist another admiring look at the tree.

Returning the wine decanter to the sideboard, Myra said, 'You know, I always feel a little like a parasitic lush drinking your booze while you're having coffee or a coke.'

'Well, don't. Some of us can handle an occasional drink and some of us can't.' With that, she headed out to the kitchen, a suddenly silent Myra at her heels.

At the kitchen counter, Ellen plugged in the kettle, caught a distorted image of herself in the shiny chrome — dark blue eyes, tiny lines fanning out from the corners. Light auburn hair in its familiar chic new cut. The hairdresser said it would make her look younger and more 'today'. Ellen didn't know. She wasn't used to it yet. It was short at the back, longer on the sides, the ends swept toward her chin. Her neck felt oddly breezy, making her feel even taller than her five foot eight, like an ostrich with its feathers plucked.

Spooning Maxwell House instant into her cup, she could feel Myra sitting at the kitchen table waiting for further explanation. She supposed, after springing it on her like that, she owed her one. Without turning around, she began haltingly, 'I — uh, developed a bit of a problem after Ed died. Every morning I went to my job, part of which, as you know, is counseling the adult children of alcoholic parents. And every night I came home, and before I even took off my coat, fixed myself a hefty vodka and soda, light on the soda. By nine o'clock I'd be smashed and dead to the world in front of the television set.'

The water had begun to bubble, the only sound in the ensuing silence. Ellen poured it over the coffee grounds. The pleasant aroma wafted up to her. When still no response came from Myra, she glanced over her shoulder. 'Don't look so shocked,' she said quietly.

'I can't help it,' Myra said, her dark eyes big. 'I am. I knew you didn't drink, but I always figured it was because of your parents — and what happened. I thought you hated . . . '

'Don't hate it at all. Got a real taste for the stuff, in fact. I have what is known in clinical terms as 'a predisposition toward alcoholism'. In real terms, I'm a drunk waiting to happen.'

'My God, Ellen, I feel awful. You've done so much for me. You always seem so strong. I never dreamed — why didn't you say something?'

'I couldn't. I didn't tell anyone.' She came and sat down across from Myra and blew a little on the steaming coffee, sending heat up to warm her face.

Looking out the kitchen window, she saw that the snow was coming down harder. It occurred to her that it might not let up and Gail's flight would be canceled. She banished the thought.

'I was ashamed,' Ellen said after several moments. 'I, of all people, should have known

16

better. I can't begin to tell you, Myra, how many women have told me they vowed as children never to touch alcohol, and yet at some point in their adult lives find themselves . . . well, where I found myself. Alcoholism doesn't happen all at once. It's a clever disease; it creeps up on you. But I caught it in time. I was lucky, many aren't. So now you know. End of subject.' She sipped her coffee.

'But — how come you keep booze in the house?' Myra asked incredulously.

'I like a challenge,' Ellen said, and laughed, then grew serious again. 'But enough of that. I want to hear more about those nightmares you've been having lately.' It hadn't been so bad, telling, but she was definitely more comfortable in the counselor role. The old 'needing to be in control' thing.

'There's not much more to tell,' Myra said, still clearly not quite recovered from Ellen's confession. 'I wake up out of a sound sleep and there's this looming dark shadow at the foot of my bed . . . Damn, Ellen, I should have known. I'm your friend, for God's sake. I should have been there for you. I should have — '

'You couldn't. I didn't want you to,' Ellen said flatly. She laid a firm hand over Myra's. 'And you *were* there for me after Ed died. I don't know what I would have done without you. Now, enough already.' She withdrew her hand. 'So tell me — you wake up in a sweat. What else?'

Myra sighed, shrugged lightly, stared into her sherry. 'Just this awful feeling of terror. I can't move or speak.' Her voice had grown small and childlike. She was playing with her hair again. 'It fades quickly — the shadow, but I still get a feeling of someone there — in the room with me. Someone — evil. If it was part of a dream, I don't remember the dream.'

'Do you think it has anything to do with your father and — '

'No,' she cut in, shaking her mane of chestnut hair as if for emphasis. 'I knew you'd think that. I guess it's natural you would. But it has nothing to do with my father. I'm certain of that.'

Ellen nodded. 'Good. Does Carl know?'

'No. I started to tell him a couple of times, but, I don't know, something stopped me. Maybe I just didn't want him to think it was all starting up again.' She grinned dryly. 'At least I didn't wake up screaming.'

She had, in the old days. Myra had come to Ellen several years ago as a client, a victim of incest, her psyche in shreds, her self-esteem at zero point, dragged even lower by a series of self-destructive relationships.

18

With help, and Myra's own incredible strength and natural need to be happy, she'd managed to piece her life together. There was no talk, of course, of 'getting over' her horrendous childhood. It was Ellen's contention that no one ever got over anything. You just learned to come to terms with it, to stop beating up on yourself for something you had no control over. One step at a time. One forward, sometimes three backward.

By the time Myra met Carl, she was a single mother of two, clerking in a fashionable dress shop, soon to work her way up to assistant manager. Carl had proved to be her 'rock' instead of the usual quicksand type. A quiet man whose love and good humor seemed boundless, Carl treated the boys as if they were his own and they reciprocated by adoring him. Then along came Joey, a dark-eyed imp whose grin could melt the hardest heart.

Still, three boys were a handful. Myra needed her sleep. Ellen could see now the dark circles under her eyes — bruisy shadows that hadn't been visible in the soft light of the living room. So why the nightmares? Why after all this time? Had something happened recently to trigger old memories? Could it all be starting up again?

'Hey, we're supposed to be celebrating

here,' Myra said suddenly, brightly, as if reading Ellen's mind. 'So please stop looking at me like I'm a bug under a microscope.'

'Was I?'

'C'mon, Ellen, I had a couple of nightmares, so big deal. I probably won't have anymore. And why does there have to be a deep, dark reason, anyway? You told me yourself it's our night dreams that keep us from going insane. By the way, did I tell you I love your hair that way? Makes you look younger, more sophisticated. Okay if I have some more cheer?' she said, already getting to her feet.

3

New York's Shelton Room was jam-packed and noisy with excited anticipation and pre-holiday spirit. A high-ceilinged room with oak paneled walls, brass accents and plenty of exotic plants, it was dimly lit by tiny globes hanging like a hundred pale suns from the ceiling. An expanse of burgundy carpeting covered both this floor and that of the Shelton's adjoining dining room, leading just through the double oak doors at the side. Glass encased red candles centered each and every table. Christmas decorations shimmered here and there like bright surprises. There was even an enormous tree decked out in red velvet bows to greet patrons upon entering the lobby.

But the tall man with longish dark-blond hair, seated at the back of the room at one of the smaller tables, had no interest in Christmas or in the club's decor; he'd barely noticed either. Nor did he join in the enthusiastic applause that erupted the instant Gail Morgan stepped her silver-sandaled foot on stage, though he did feel the hot quickening in his loins the way he always did

21

when the hunt was successful. Though admittedly, he hadn't had to look too hard for this one.

He'd unbuttoned his dark overcoat for the benefit of the doorman, revealing the obligatory shirt and tie, though he'd been careful to avert his face, pretending to be looking for someone in the crowd. And then the doorman had gotten busy with someone else, and there was no further need for charades. He hadn't bothered to check his coat; he wasn't planning on staying long.

Taking a slow sip of his Miller Lite, he watched without expression, though not without interest, as the spotlight followed the singer in the white, strapless dress, the skirt flowing about her legs like liquid, to center stage.

In the same moment, a waitress clad in the required black slacks, white shirt and black bow tie, moving slickly through the maze of tables balancing a tray of beer and drinks in her upturned hand, hesitated at his table. Then, seeing his glass nearly full, she moved on. She'd blocked his view for only an instant, but it was enough to provoke a rush of anger in him.

Gail was beaming a dazzling, if slightly shy smile, out at her audience, who, even now, as she adjusted the microphone to suit her diminutive height, continued to applaud and cheer. She was tinier than he'd expected from seeing her picture in the paper. Hardly bigger than a kid, though she looked nothing like the snapshot in the file. He couldn't make out the color of her eyes from here, but he knew they were blue; he had her statistics. He had all their statistics. Her hair was blonder, and now instead of the short, parted-on-the-side cut, it fell softly to her bare shoulders. And she was painted up, of course. Painted up to look like a whore.

Just like his mother had painted herself up. And Debby Fuller. He had been just a kid, then. She'd thought he was some kind of fool, coming on to him the way she had, and then when he'd tried to give her what she asked for, she went all crazy on him, screaming at him, slapping his face. He'd shown her then who the *real* fool was. He'd fixed that snotty bitch — fixed her good. Maybe he ought to pay Debby a little visit one of these days. Fix her permanently. He grinned, thinking about it. And then all thoughts of Debby Fuller faded into the background as a hush fell over the room, and Gail Morgan began to sing.

She was prettier than either his mother or Debby, he had to admit that. Tiny and perfect as a doll. His gaze lingered on her bare shoulders, smooth and white as marble. He imagined how they would feel to his touch. His eyes went to her throat. He could almost feel it, warm and throbbing, and the thought started up a hot tingling in his hands.

Without taking his eyes from her, he fished a cigarette from the crumpled pack of Pall Malls on the table and put it between his thin lips. The paper had described her voice as 'bluesy' and 'bittersweet', an exciting cross between Billie Holiday's and Peggy Lee's. He didn't know who Billie Holiday was, but his mother had liked Peggy Lee, he remembered. She had all her old records and played them on an old record player — all the 'oldies but goodies' she'd say. When she got drunk, she'd play *Is That All There Is?* over and over again, dancing by herself around the kitchen floor with a sad, stupid smile on her face. 'Come dance with me, baby', she'd say, holding out her pale, slender arms to him. 'Come and dance with Mommy.'

He pushed all thoughts of his mother away and concentrated his attention to the girl on stage, to the rich, throaty voice that floated around him.

He didn't know or care much about music, but it made him feel kind of nice hearing Gail sing. Maybe she would sing just for him alone. He'd like that. He might even let her live if she did. Sing for your supper, Gail.

Sing for your life. If not, then she'd soon be singing a different tune. He smiled at his own perceived wit, a smile that did not reach the pale, cold eyes behind the glasses.

He watched as a few dreamy-eyed couples left their tables to wander onto the small, crescent-shaped dance floor near the stage. Gail was smiling down at a grey-haired woman who had deliberately maneuvered her partner so that they were directly in front of Gail, the woman beaming up at her, giving Gail the 'thumbs up' sign.

Pathetic old fool, he thought, as he removed the chimney from the lighted candle on the table and, leaning forward in his chair, touched his cigarette to the fire.

Twin orange flames danced in the dark-tinted glasses.

* * *

At intermission he slipped away, leaving a half-smoked cigarette floating in his beer, hissing softly to silence, a thread of smoke trailing upward.

Outside it was snowing and blowing, swirling white around telephone poles, pink in front of the neon lights, stinging his face, banging a sign nearby.

Hunching inside his coat collar, he waited

for a break in traffic, then dashed across the street where his brown van was parked in an out-of-business gas station. A FOR LEASE sign hung crookedly in the plate-glass window. From here, he could look across the street and see her own car parked in the club's parking lot — a red Mustang, an old model, but in good shape. A few people walked hurriedly along the sidewalk, heads lowered into the storm.

He eyed two kids huddled in a doorway, faces intent, passing what he guessed to be a toke back and forth. No one looked in his direction.

Turning back to the van, he began brushing the snow from the windows, then quickly slipped into the driver's seat and switched on the ignition. The motor purred to life. The clock on the dash said 10:18 p.m. She got home shortly after midnight. He'd followed her three nights running, staying just far enough behind the Mustang to avoid being spotted. Her routine never changed.

It would tonight. Tonight she wouldn't be coming home to just her cat. Chuckling low in his throat, he flipped on the signal light and began working his way out into the steady stream of New York traffic. A speeding taxi cut him off, horn blaring. Anger scalded through him. Easy, he thought. Plenty of time. Her building was only a twenty minute drive from here. Not a good idea to draw attention to himself.

As he drove, he began thinking about the way she'd looked on stage. She'd been looking at him, too, of course, trying to let on she wasn't. Teasing him. But he knew she wanted him. Yeah, she was hot for him, all right. He kind of liked it that she wasn't just some little nobody the way the others had been, hardly worth a mention in the paper. Hadn't he read that she'd got some big recording contract and all that? Well, tomorrow they'd be reading about her again.

But they'd be thinking about him.

4

It was just after eleven when Ellen got back from driving Myra home. Though Myra lived only a mile from her, the road was treacherous, and Ellen, never a happy winter driver, was glad to be off it. Too, Cutter's Road, (named for the logging road it once had been) while pleasant enough to walk along during the day, was dark and desolate at night. Only a few old farm houses left, most fallen into neglect and disrepair, long-abandoned.

She'd sat in the idling car until a slightly tipsy Myra was safely inside the house. Ellen felt guiltily responsible, but what harm if it would get her through at least one night without the nightmares?

Christmas lights had winked seductively at her through the curtain of snow. In an upstairs window, she thought she glimpsed Joey's face, and felt a twinge of envy. She would like to have had a child — something of Ed to help ease the loneliness. But that was another of those 'nobody knows why' situations. 'You're wallowing again,' she said aloud, unbuttoning her coat and hanging it in the closet.

She went upstairs, showered and put on her terry-cloth robe. Finding she was not in the least sleepy, she came back downstairs where she now sat with a steaming mug of cocoa, in front of the fire.

The scrapbook, bulging with clippings of Gail's each and every achievement, lay open on her lap.

She'd started keeping a scrapbook eight years ago, when Gail, barely out of high school, had gone off to New York to seek her fame and fortune. Gone with only a couple of tattered suitcases, some free publicity photos taken by a budding photographer friend who Gail promised to make famous as soon as she 'made it' and the two thousand dollars Ellen had managed to save toward her education. There'd been no talking her out of it. And perhaps, seeing how determined she was, Ellen hadn't tried as hard as she might. Besides, she believed in Gail's talent. Never mind that the thought of her little sister all alone in the big, bad city terrified her.

'I know there are grants and scholarships available if I really wanted to go,' Gail had said when Ellen tried to persuade her on the necessity of a college education. 'And I could work part-time, but that's not where I want to put my energies. All I ever wanted was to be a singer.' They were living in the small flat on Albert Street, sitting at the kitchen table when Gail had told her, 'Having something to fall back on suggests the possibility of failure, and that's a possibility I don't dare let myself even consider, else it might become a self-fulfilling prophecy. I used to lie in bed at night when I was little, Ellen, dreaming of how it would be — imagining myself on stage, hearing the applause that drowned out the sounds of Mom and Dad fighting — and other times, too.' Her big blue eyes had beseeched Ellen for understanding, for support, but they'd been unflaggingly determined, too. 'I want to be somebody, Ellen. I want my turn at the brass ring.'

Well, you've got a good grip on it, now, sweetie, Ellen thought, smiling, picking up the latest article, which included a particularly glamorous picture of Gail. She'd cut it out of the paper a couple of weeks ago, but hadn't gotten around to pasting it in the book yet. She read it for the hundredth time.

LOCAL GIRL HITS BIG TIME

Maine blues singer Gail Morgan, has landed a major recording contract with Genesis. The Genesis deal will see her recordings, including her recent independent record 'Do You Know Me?' available in the United States and Canada. She has also signed a contract with Beli International to distribute her recordings in Belgium, the Netherlands, Luxembourg, Austria and The United Kingdom.

In addition, Morgan travels to Holland in February for a five show concert tour through the Netherlands. The Evansdale, Me. native is also in pre-production for an N.B.C. special which will begin taping later this month.

Not bad, kiddo, Ellen thought. *Not bad at all*. Turning the article over, she read idly about a sale at Regan's Shoe Store over on Elm, and, not to be outdone, Welton's Pharmacy was having a 50% mark-down on Christmas wrapping. Below was a brief write-up on the now abandoned and boarded over Evansdale Home for Girls, which city council had deemed fitting, since it was both 'a blight on the land and a hazard to children,' to be torched by the fire department, thus providing them with a useful exercise in firefighting, and at the same time sparing the city the expense of having it demolished by other means.

Good riddance, Ellen thought, not missing the irony. She pasted the article onto the page with a bit more force than necessary. Just as she was returning the swollen scrapbook to its drawer in the sideboard, thinking she'd soon have to get a new one, the phone rang. The wall clock said 12:24. Smiling, Ellen picked up the receiver. 'Hi, sweetie.'

'I always knew you were psychic,' came the familiar voice. 'Then again, who else would be calling you at this time of night, right?'

'I'm glad you called. I was too excited to sleep, anyway. You just getting home from the club?'

'Yeah. The roads are a bitch-and-a-half. I practically had to crawl. Fender-benders everywhere. I was getting worried they might start canceling flights; I'd go nuts if they did. But the weatherman says sunny and clear for tomorrow, so everything's a go.'

'Great. I was getting a little concerned myself. Oh, Gail, I can't wait to see you. This is going to be the best Christmas ever. We've got so much to celebrate.'

'Yeah, the Morgan girls haven't done too bad for themselves, considering.'

'Especially Gail Morgan,' Ellen said, smiling into the phone and thinking she just might break her cardinal rule and break open a bottle of champagne so they could toast

Gail's success — maybe even a few times.

'Thanks, Ellen. I couldn't have done it without you, and I mean that. Oh, I can't wait to get there. It'll be kind of like it used to be. Remember how we used to lie in bed and talk half the night?'

'I remember.'

There was a pause. Then a solemn, quieter Gail said, 'I wasn't thinking about when we lived with Mom and Dad. I was thinking about those two rooms you rented on Albert Street so you could spring me from the home.'

'I know you were.' Ellen was flung back in time. She was seventeen again, sitting in the hard-backed chair in the visitors' room of the Evansdale Home, with its dark green tiled floor, and the air smelling of creosote and something else Ellen could not define, something that made it hard to breathe. Miss Layton, her teacher, had come for moral support, and was sitting beside her. She patted Ellen's hands, clutched in her lap, white-knuckled against her blue plaid skirt.

Ellen had barely recognized the small grey figure that stepped so tentatively into the room, eyes questioning, yet accepting. Behind her, the stern-faced matron was steeled for the first sign of trouble, ready to spring into action.

There would be no need. Gail stood before them, before those who would decide her life, hands clasped politely in front of her — a good little girl, bearing little resemblance to the sassy, spirited sister Ellen remembered. And then those blue eyes were gazing into hers, filling with a shy, cautious hope that wrenched Ellen's heart. 'Hi, Ellie,' she smiled. In the face of all that had happened, she smiled.

At first, Ellen feared they were not going to let her take Gail, but Miss Layton had vouched for her, said she was a responsible and capable young woman and both girls would be quite fine, and that, after all, was the objective, wasn't it? Unless Gail was being held prisoner for some wrong doing. In the end, they could think of none, and so they had, however reluctantly, released Gail into Ellen's care. Ellen had often wondered since if her teacher had signed something saying she would accept responsibility if anything went wrong. And yet, though they always exchanged Christmas cards, Ellen had rarely seen Miss Layton after she dropped them off in front of their building that day.

'That was such a dump,' Ellen said, when Gail brought her back to the present. 'Remember how we had to share a common bath with the rest of the tenants, and how that awful landlady was always screaming at everyone to turn off the hall lights? And, God, that awful lime-green hallway; remember how it always reeked of pee and wet plaster?'

'You made Kraft dinner that first night,' Gail said. 'It was the best meal I ever ate. And those two rooms on Albert Street were better than any mansion.'

Ellen swallowed against the lump in her throat. 'I'm so proud of you, Gail.'

'Yeah, me, too. Hey, when are you gonna make your own dream happen and open that private practice you always talk about?'

'One of these days. You'll be my inspiration.'

'You know what they're saying? They're calling me the overnight sensation. Can you believe it? Here I've been singing my little heart out for the past eight years with hardly anyone noticing, and suddenly they're talking about the new kid on the block getting the big break, like I haven't paid my dues.'

'I seriously doubt that you've ever sung with no one noticing. And keep in mind, dear sister, that some people struggle their entire lives for that big break, and it never happens. So be gracious in victory,' she admonished gently.

'Oh, I am, Sis, believe me. I'm not

complaining. Well, I suppose I am in a way, but . . . oh, you know. God, it was such a good night at the club tonight. The audience was so great. This sweet little woman actually danced her partner right up to the stage so she could give me the 'thumbs up' sign. People have been terrific. I can't describe to you the feeling I get when everything is right on — the waves of love that go back and forth — it's kind of like flying, you know?' Gail chattered on in that breathless, excited way she had even as a kid, sometimes requiring no answer at all. Ellen was smiling into the phone, enjoying Gail's own enjoyment of her success, caught off guard when Gail asked suddenly, 'So how's it going with you and Paul?'

'I'm not sure. He's gone off to Eastport to visit his parents for the holidays.' She felt a pang of guilt. He'd been gone four days now, and she'd hardly given him a thought. Maybe because she just needed a little breathing room.

'What do you mean, you're not sure?'

'He's pressing for a deeper commitment. He says my problem is I'm comparing all men to Ed. When I stop doing that I'll realize we belong together.'

'Is he right?'

'I don't know. Maybe. I'm just not sure I

want to get seriously involved with anyone right now. I'm not even sure I can.'

'So tell him that.'

'I did. He's not listening. Hey, let's not talk about Paul, anymore, okay? I want to hear more about you.'

'Never mind changing the subject. Listen, maybe you're not giving the guy a fair chance. Why don't you just flow with it, see where it goes?'

'I'll think about it.'

Not that Paul was unattractive, quite the contrary. Tall and handsome with a neatly trimmed beard that lent him an air of distinguished authority, women were drawn to him. Ellen had *not* been an exception.

Paul Henderson was one of four psychologists, including Ellen, who worked at the clinic. A colleague. She wasn't sure it was a good idea to be going out with someone she worked with. It had started out as an innocent lunch. He'd said he wanted to discuss one of his cases with her, get her opinion. And then he'd bought those tickets to see *Les Miserables*, and after he'd spent so much money, how could she possibly refuse? Not that she'd really wanted to.

Paul had a way of looking at you that made you feel you were the most important person in the world, which, of course, was partly what made him so good at his job. Yet Ellen couldn't help wondering, and not for the first time, if maybe Paul didn't encourage a little hero-worshipping in his female clients. More than once, she'd glimpsed a pretty big ego behind those intelligent eyes.

Thoughts of Paul faded as she listened to Gail telling her that her roommate, Sandi, a willowy, incredibly beautiful girl whom Ellen had met once and liked immediately, was also off visiting her parents for the holidays. Sandi was a model. 'You know,' Gail was saying, 'It's been kind of nice having the place all to myself. I can walk around in the buff if I like. I don't have to worry ab — ' She broke off in mid-sentence. 'Hello! Is someone there? Hold on a second, Ellen.'

The line went silent and alarm raced along Ellen's nerve endings. It seemed forever until Gail was back on the line, saying fondly, 'It was just Tiger — crazy cat. I forgot to feed him and he was letting me know in no uncertain terms.'

Ellen let out the breath she'd been holding. She couldn't stop herself from asking, 'Are your doors locked?' and heard the indulgent smile in her sister's answer. 'Yes, Mommy, my doors are locked — double-locked, in fact. Windows, too. But I love you for worrying.'

Upstairs, Ellen set about making up the other twin bed. This time tomorrow night, Gail would be in it. She could have waited until morning to make it up, but she was still feeling restless. She'd splurged on candy-striped sheets and pillowcases, and bought a pretty pale green satin puff to match the one on her own bed.

A bouquet of yellow roses was centered on the small, wicker table by the door. Off-white walls, soft lighting from milky globes, splashes of green provided by hanging plants and an assortment of pillows all conspired to give the room a bright, airy feel. For a long time she'd kept everything just as it was when Ed was alive. She'd found comfort in being sur-rounded by those things they'd shared together. It had made it easier to pretend he was still with her. But now she needed to create a space of her own. It was time to let go of the past.

Ellen wandered to the window, one of two overlooking the dense, piney woods behind her house. She could see only blackness beyond, a faint silhouette of the tree outside her window, and her own ghostly reflection in the glass.

Turning from the window, she stood

uncertainly. There was something she must do. Something important she'd forgotten but she couldn't think what it was. The turkey was in the freezer, all the fixings for their Christmas dinner bought. No Kraft dinner this time.

Finally, taking off her robe and stepping out of her slippers, Ellen crept between the cool sheets and waited for sleep to come. But her mind was not easy, as it had not been easy all day, and for a long time she lay listening to the house settling, to the howling wind outside, and tried to still the nagging sense of foreboding within her.

5

After hanging up the phone, Gail slipped out of her white, strapless dress. Draping it carefully over a wooden hanger and covering it with the plastic bag from the cleaners, she hung it up in the closet and closed the door.

With a little sigh, she picked up her cup of tea by the phone and took a sip. It had gone luke warm and she made a face, accompanied by a small sound of disgust. Setting the cup back down in its saucer, it rattled a little as a yawn overtook her. She was starting to wind down. Good, that meant she would sleep. She glanced down at the packed bags on the floor at the foot of the bed — a happy, reassuring sight. Her Christmas gifts to Ellen were stacked on the chair, all gaily wrapped, topped with bright, shiny bows. All but the last one, but she'd get to that in the morning.

Stifling another yawn and wondering how in hell she was going to lug all this stuff out of the house, she perched on the edge of the bed, toed off her silver, high-heeled sandals and peeled off her pantyhose. Leaving them on the floor where she'd dropped them, clad only in her strapless bra and white silk half-slip, she padded to the vanity, where she sat down and switched on the lamp. She began taking out her rhinestone — albeit 'very good' rhinestone earrings. The beige tweed carpeting felt soft and soothing under her bare feet, and she indulged them in a little massage.

And then Gail's feet grew still as she sniffed the air, thinking she smelled cigarette smoke. But since neither she nor Sandi smoked, she must be imagining it. Unless she'd brought the smell home in her clothes and hair. Gross. After a moment, she forgot about it, caught up in thoughts of her sister and the wonderful time they were going to have together.

Ellen would love what she'd gotten her, Gail thought, setting the earrings on the vanity top and picking up the brush, bringing it slowly and absently through her fair, shoulder-length hair. Especially the teal blue suit she'd spotted in Sybil's today and hadn't been able to resist. With her classy looks and those blue eyes — bluer even than Gail's, like sapphires — she'd be a knockout. Paul will be mightily impressed, she thought, grinning to herself. One thing you had to say for him, he had great taste. He sounded so different from Ed — dear, sweet Ed who had treated her as she'd always imagined a big brother would,

42

and who had clearly adored her sister. Not that they didn't have their spats. She didn't know what would happen with Paul, but for Gail, it was enough that Ellen had rejoined the human race.

Continuing to brush her hair, Gail launched into her favorite fantasy about the day she'd be in a position to buy Ellen a new white Ferrari. She'd have it delivered right up to the door, a big red bow tied on the antenna. And she had no doubt whatever that that day would come. Gail was firmly convinced that you could get whatever you wanted in this world if you wanted it badly enough and were prepared to be single-minded about it.

Even so, it was hard to believe it really was all happening for her, that finally all the dedication, all the hard work, was paying off.

Ellen's birthday was coming up in May. She was a Gemini, the sign of the twins. Maybe she'd get the car in time for Ellen's birthday, she thought, laying the brush down and smiling dreamily, imagining the joyous surprise on her sister's face at the sight of her very own showroom-new Ferrari in the drive.

Dream on, girl, she told herself, grinning at her reflection in the mirror.

Tiger padded into the room just then, stopping once to wash his face, then winding his sleek, warm body around her bare ankles, first in one direction, then the other, purring the whole time like an old washing machine.

'I owe her so much, Tiger,' Gail said, reaching down to stroke the cat's soft, glossy fur. 'If it wasn't for . . .'

Suddenly, Tiger's back arched under her hand and he hissed, making Gail's heart leap in her breast, and her hand draw back as if it had been burned. 'Shit, cat, you scared me! What the . . . ?'

But Tiger, fur standing on end, had already fled the room while his bewildered, shaken mistress turned in her chair just in time to see his electrified, retreating tail.

And then she caught a movement from the corner of her eye. Turning, she froze at the sight of the closet door slowly opening.

★　★　★

Three hundred miles away in Evansdale, Maine, Myra Thompson lay asleep in the darkened room beside her husband, Carl. Myra whimpered in her sleep, and though her husband muttered some incoherent, sympathetic response, and laid a gentle arm about her waist, he did not wake.

Ellen had been right about the wine helping Myra get to sleep, but not in

44

imagining it would hold the nightmares at bay.

*   *   *

Across town, in an old Victorian house, an old woman lay on filthy sheets, her unwashed hair spread on the pillow like gray seaweed, framing her gaunt face. Hollowed eyes gleamed in the darkness.

On the bedside table, a tray of rotting food was set just out of reach of the claw-like hand that clutched at the blanket covering her. But it was not food she wanted just now.

'A-l-v-i-n,' the raspy, witchy voice called out in the silence. Her throat was raw from calling. She'd sleep now and then, wake to call again. She'd been calling for a long time. Now, finally, her bladder let go and the stench of urine was added to the already putrid smell of the room.

Tears of rage and helplessness filled the old woman's eyes, ran down the parchment dry cheeks.

*   *   *

In the bedroom of the semi-basement New York apartment, *he* knelt over the still, white form, artist's brush in hand. Carefully, he

45

drew the red-tipped brush over her mouth, which was slightly open, revealing small, perfect teeth.

After several minutes, he settled back on his haunches to appraise his work. A few more final touches. 'There,' he said at last, pleased at the results. 'Finished. Now you look more like yourself. The *real* you.' He gave an ugly laugh. The laugh died as suddenly he became aware that his cheek was on fire where the bitch had raked him with her long nails. He put his fingertips there, and they came away with his blood.

'Bitch,' he hissed. 'Whore.' He drew his hand back and slapped her full-force across the face, a purely satisfying sound in the silence. Her head lolled to one side. But his fury was not yet abated.

Slowly, he began to undo his belt buckle.

6

The day dawned clear and sunny. Ellen was on the road by nine o'clock, more than two hours before Gail's flight was due in. She couldn't wait in the house any longer.

She glanced at the LOTS FOR SALE signs along her road as she drove. Soon, she wouldn't know this place. According to the paper, land development would begin this spring. Now, after the last night's snow, it was picture-postcard pretty. But she knew she wouldn't mind having neighbors. It would be nice to look out her window and see children flying down the hill on their sleds and toboggans, hearing their shrieks of fearful delight, bright scarves trailing like banners behind them.

It had been different when Ed was alive. Born one of seven and raised in a tenement flat, this place was his dream, and she had been more than happy to share it with him. They had gone on picnics, taken long walks through the woods, armed with cameras. She had never failed to be awed by the unexpected sight of a deer, a bushy-tailed red fox, or a rabbit quivering in their path. But she knew these were not things she would be doing on her own. Nor with anyone else, for that matter. That time belonged to her and Ed. And though she would never lose her appreciation of the beauty of the land, the isolation no longer held the same appeal for her.

★ ★ ★

The sun glinted hard off the airport window, through which, less than fifteen minutes ago, a crowd had stood watching the descent of flight 267. Now, only Ellen remained to gaze up at the vast expanse of blue sky — a sky which was empty of planes at the moment, with only wisps of dispersing jet stream to mar the blueness. She could feel the vibration of a jet engine starting up, its awesome power thrumming on the polished floor beneath her feet.

What are you waiting for, she asked herself. Gail's plane had already landed. She wasn't on it. Feeling vaguely the way she had the time she'd gotten separated from her mother in Woolworth's department store, Ellen shifted her bag to her other shoulder, glanced behind her, half-expecting to see people staring at her as they had stared then.

She had been no more than two or three at

the time. She remembered few details, just that same awful sense of panic, of being abandoned. Which was ridiculous, of course. She was no longer that child, and there were a dozen perfectly reasonable explanations why someone would miss a plane.

The big clock on the wall told her it was exactly twenty-five — no, twenty-six minutes now since Gail's plane had touched down.

In her eagerness, Ellen had gotten there more than an hour early. She'd put in the time drinking coffee in the little coffee shop and scanning through the pages of *People* magazine. At last she'd stood with the others watching excitedly as the plane emptied, anticipating her first glimpse of Gail among the passengers descending the narrow metal steps. She continued to watch for her even after it was quite clear that Gail was not on the plane. Her expectant smile had died slowly, in keeping with the sinking sensation in her stomach.

Bewildered, she'd watched friends and relatives quickly find one another. After a flurry of back-slapping, teary hugs and exchanged holiday greetings, (during which Ellen searched each and every face, hoping against hope she had somehow missed Gail) the room had cleared. Baggage claimed, some passengers drove off in waiting cars, while others piled into the taxis lined up in front of the building.

Alone now, but for the few employees and one elderly gentleman sitting across the room, perched on the edge of one of the molded plastic chairs, puffing intently on a pipe, (like her, he seemed to be waiting for someone) Ellen's disappointment was almost irrational in its intensity. She tried to think what to do.

Out in the corridor, a white-haired black man rattling past pushing an empty luggage cart glanced in and gave Ellen a friendly, if mildly curious smile, making her acutely aware that she just looked as lost and miserable as she felt.

Hesitating briefly, she left the waiting room and hurried out into the corridor toward the stairs leading down to the baggage area. Amidst a lot of amplified static and crackling, a female voice paged a Mr. Donald Ramsay, and Ellen found herself listening for her own name to issue from the sound system.

Fancying again that she had somehow managed to miss Gail, who was no doubt at this very moment collecting her luggage and wondering where in hell her big sister was, Ellen broke into a half-run, her shoulder bag slapping soundlessly against her hip, the heels of her boots clacking down the wide marble stairs, faint hope buoying her spirits.

At the bottom of the stairs, however, even as she looked frantically around, her heart sank even lower. There was no sign of Gail, as she'd known deep down there wouldn't be. In an airport as small as this one, Gail would have had to be in deep disguise for Ellen to have missed seeing her.

Gazing down at the empty, revolving carousel, it seemed strangely to mock her. On the verge of tears, she turned away, spotted a pair of pay phones beside a row of gray metal lockers, just past the gift shop. *Why don't you call her apartment? She might have gotten sick at the last minute, or maybe the Mustang broke down on the way to the airport; she's been having some trouble with it, lately.* But Ellen made no move in that direction. Suddenly burning up inside her parka, she unzipped it.

She eyed the phones a moment longer, then, as if they posed some sort of threat, she turned away and went back up the stairs.

★   ★   ★

'And what was the name again?' the pleasant young man in uniform asked, taking in the light auburn hair, the trim, sensuous figure under the off-white parka — a shade that

51

gave her complexion a flattering glow, he thought, as that shade tended to do with certain skin tones. He knew he was staring, but it was next to impossible not to with those incredible eyes looking so beseechingly into his. Cheekbones to die for. God, this one could almost make him forget he was gay.

'Morgan,' Ellen said, stepping closer to the counter. 'Gail Morgan. She's my sister. She was supposed to be on flight 267 from New York.'

The man tapped the information into the computer, waited, while Ellen began fidgeting with her purse strap, twisting it into rope.

A woman in high-topped sneakers and socks, wearing something purple tied around her hair, was half-heartedly pushing a broom across the floor, reminding Ellen of a Carol Burnett skit she'd seen on T.V. Ellen had to execute a quick move to avoid the broom that came within inches of her boots.

' 'Scuse me,' the woman mumbled. The young man rolled his eyes. 'Bertha, really!' he admonished her.

'I said, 'scuse me. Whadda ya want?' Pushing on, she stooped to retrieve a gum wrapper from under a chair, stuffed it into her sweater pocket.

'We have to make allowances for Bertha.

She had dreams of becoming a flight attendant. Is that *the* Gail Morgan? The singer?' He flashed her a toothpaste-ad smile, his eyes lighting hopefully.

Ellen said it was, and heard the clipped tightness in her words. Any other time would have found her warming instantly to the subject of Gail's career, but right now it seemed almost trivial. Sensing her impatience, he returned to the matter at hand.

'Ah, yes, here she is, all right. Gail Morgan. She was booked on flight 267, held a ticket for seat E5. Window seat.' He tapped more keys, waited. 'She never boarded, ma'am,' he said, looking up at her. 'That seat went unoccupied. And there's no record of her canceling.'

The sound system crackled to life. 'Would a Mr. Joseph Ingalls please come to the phone.' Ellen watched as the elderly man with the pipe left his seat, took the call, and hurried off toward the corridor, soon disappearing, leaving Ellen feeling somehow betrayed by him.

A memory was prodding her consciousness again, the way a tongue prods a loose tooth. She pushed it back. Beyond the window, a 747 was taking off. She watched it soar higher and higher until it was no more than a silver streak in the sky, flashing in the sun.

'Ma'am?'

Ellen turned to see the young man frowning at her. 'Yes?' The coffee she'd consumed earlier now seemed to have alchemized into a burning acid in her stomach.

'Are you all right?'

'I'm fine.'

'I was just saying you could probably call her in New York. Something must have —— '

'Yes, yes, I will. Thank you.'

'The telephones are . . . ' He'd begun to point, but Ellen was already headed in that direction, cutting him off, thanking him over her shoulder for his help.

'By the way,' he called after her. 'I think your sister's just great. I just *love* her work. My friend and I saw her in . . . '

Ellen missed where it was they saw her.

★   ★   ★

Downstairs, Ellen picked up the receiver, and, trapping it between her neck and shoulder, was rummaging around in her purse for change, when, in her peripheral vision, she saw the policeman coming toward her. Looking up, she saw that Myra was with

54

him. The heaviness in their walks might have been enough — but it was the look of pure anguish on her friend's face that laid a cold hand on Ellen's heart and made the blood drain from her body.

7

Detective Steve Shannon of N.Y.P.D. stood in the alley just outside the window of the girl's bedroom, knee-deep in snow — snow that had fallen during the night, but was undisturbed, leaving little reason to concern himself with obliterating telling footprints. Through a narrow strip of window, where the blind did not quite reach the bottom, he was able, by bending his knees and squinting, to see inside the room, to see all that the killer had seen. Twin beds, the chair, now toppled, which had been stacked with Christmas gifts, the blue leather suitcases standing at the foot of the bed awaiting a trip that would never take place. He wondered if her killer had found that bit of irony amusing.

His gaze carefully avoiding the dead girl on the floor, he raised his eyes to the publicity photos of both girls on the walls, though fewer of the victim than of her roommate, a Sandi something — a model. They were still trying to locate her.

The bedroom door was open, leading out into a narrow hallway and through to the livingroom, with its early Salvation Army furniture. His partner was still inside trying to calm the landlady, a Mrs. Bloom. She'd found the girl.

Shannon studied what was left of the wire meshing that had been nailed over the window. He figured a common pair of wire cutters had done the job. Enough rust to guess it was put on a couple of decades ago by some misguided soul who imagined it would offer adequate protection against an intruder. Well, maybe a couple of decades ago it might have, he thought. But not these days.

A hole had been punched through the glass, just big enough to allow a man to put his hand through and find the lock. The window was closed now, a red tee shirt, probably the girl's, stuffed into the hole so she wouldn't feel a draft when she came into the room. From its shape, he could tell it was put there from inside the room.

There were dried footprints on the carpet, just under the window. They went no farther. So, once inside, he'd taken off his shoes.

He'd been hiding in the house, waiting for her.

Steve wouldn't know officially the time of death until forensic got here, but he'd seen enough in his twenty-two years on the force to make an educated guess. The landlady, who lived in the next apartment, had said the victim always got home by midnight or shortly after. She knew this because she'd be up watching the news and could hear her come in, could hear her key in the lock. Except for last night. Last night, as luck would have it, Mrs. Bloom had been visiting an upstairs neighbor.

So Gail Morgan had probably been dead between ten and twelve hours. This he deduced not only from Mrs. Bloom's statement, but from the condition of the body, and because the snow outside the window had been undisturbed. He'd already confirmed with the weather office that it hadn't stopped snowing until around 3:00 a.m., erasing the killer's footprints.

★   ★   ★

Back inside the small, slightly seedy apartment, Mrs. Bloom, an ample-bosomed woman with wispy orange hair and a kindly face, stood just outside the front door recounting to his partner what she'd already told Shannon. Sheryl was listening intently, nodding, making sympathetic noises from time to time.

' . . . I just knew she wouldn't have gone away like that and left poor Tiger in the apartment alone. Not when she asked me just last week to take him while she went to visit her sister in Maine. I told her I'd be happy to do it — I already have three cats of my own, you see. Could one more make a difference?' She was gazing down tenderly at the striped cat in her arms, her plump, liver-spotted hand stroking him as she talked. A widow of many years, Mrs. Bloom wore a wide, gold band on her finger. 'Poor Tiger,' she crooned, 'when I heard you crying inside that apartment, I just knew something was terribly wrong. I just knew it.' Her eyes filled as she looked up at Shannon. 'Some say I have the gift, you know. Sometimes I just know things — ever since I was a child. Such a lovely girl she was — never had men in her apartment or anything like that. Neither of the girls did. Not like some I could name. When I went into her room and — and saw her like that — her poor face, oh, my . . . ' She pulled a hanky from the cuff of her shapeless sweater and blew loudly. 'I didn't even know her right off. I . . . '

'Did you have to use your key, Mrs. Bloom?'

'My key? Oh, no, no. That was the other thing. The girls would never leave the door unlocked like that.'

So he had simply picked up his shoes, Shannon thought, and carried them right out the front door, probably putting them on in the hallway. Obviously not too concerned about being seen. True, it would have been well after midnight and this was a relatively quiet street, but still, this was New York . . .

'Take Mrs. Bloom back to her apartment, Officer Mason,' Steve said gently. 'She's had a terrible shock. Maybe there's someone Officer Mason could telephone to come and stay with you, Mrs. Bloom — a friend or relative.'

She sniffed into her hanky. 'There's — there's just Mr. Goldberg upstairs. That's where I was when . . . it must have happened. Else I would have heard the window break, wouldn't I? I would have heard. We were having a nice, friendly game of gin, Mr. Goldberg and I. Poor man's in a wheel-chair now. His cronies who used to come and see him have all passed on. It was late when I came back down, like I said — nearly half-past one. Yesterday was Mr. Goldberg's birthday, you see. I took a small cake, nothing fancy. What can you do? So I missed my news. I don't usually . . . '

Which, unfortunately, removed Mrs. Bloom as someone who could testify to the time Gail Morgan got home last night. The tenant who lived in the apartment above the girls was, in Mrs. Bloom's words, 'deaf as a breadbox'. She would have to be, Shannon knew, because from the look of this room, there had been one hell of a racket. The apartment across the hall was vacant. So, no one heard anything; no one saw anything. If Mr. Goldberg hadn't chosen to come into the world precisely when he did all those years ago, Shannon thought, Mrs. Bloom would have been home, and, as she herself had stated, she would certainly have heard . . .

Looking down at the near-naked girl sprawled on the floor, head lolling to one side so that he could see the ugly bruises on her neck, he wondered if Mrs. Bloom's being home, or the neighbor not being deaf, would have made one iota of difference. People heard things all the time, and saw things, and looked the other way. No one wanted to get involved. Yet the landlady hadn't struck him as that sort. Maybe he was just getting cynical in his old age.

With a heavy sigh, the big, gray-haired detective knelt on one knee beside the body. New York turned up more than its share of dead girls, and the bastards who murdered them were multiplying even as he thought about it, coming up with newer and sicker ways of inflicting pain and humiliation and death.

Suddenly bone-weary right down to the

marrow, and feeling every second of his fifty-three years, the detective reached out his hand with their wide, blunt fingers and, blatantly disregarding the rules, gently drew down the girl's half-slip to cover her nakedness. The camera boys would be here any minute.

Her torn bra and panties lay beside one still, childlike foot. He looked back at her face and wished to hell he could wash that shit off before anyone else saw her, but of course he couldn't.

'That was nice, Shannon,' came a female voice from the doorway. He looked up to see Sheryl smiling fondly at him. 'What you did just then. You'd get the book thrown at you, of course, put your pension in jeopardy, and you're old enough to know better — but still, it was nice.' Stepping farther into the room, she surveyed the mess. 'Christ! She sure put up one hell of a fight for a small girl, didn't she?'

Steve's gaze followed her own — to the telephone table that lay on its side on the floor, receiver knocked from the phone's cradle, the cup and saucer a brief distance away, the cup still intact, bearing a coral lipstick print, probably the victim's. A dark tea-stain had spread on the beige tweed carpet. The vanity was swept clean of its contents — bottles, jars, brushes were strewn in every direction. The lamp cord was plugged into the wall socket, the lamp still on, dangling upside down, making a pale circle of light on the carpet.

One of the twin beds was neatly made up. The other, next to where Shannon knelt, had its dusty rose bedspread yanked out of place, one of its corners hanging just short of the victim's upturned hand. She must have clutched onto it at the end, in those final, desperate moments of her life.

After she was dead, her killer had gone to the trouble of painting her face up to look like a clown's. Shannon recognized the smell of grease-paint from his high school drama days. They actually called that shade of white 'clown' white.

He looked quickly past the wide blue eyes staring blankly up at him out of drawn, black triangles, to the silver, high-heeled sandal lying on its side beside her blond hair. The other sandal was under the bed, probably kicked there in the struggle, tangled in a pair of pantyhose. He tried to ignore the familiar burning pain in the pit of his stomach.

'The packages all say 'to Ellen' ', Sheryl said, bending down beside the up-ended chair with its scattered Christmas gifts. Something blue spilled from an unwrapped package on the floor. Sheryl hooked a finger under the cover and raised it to get a better look. 'Great taste,' she said.

'That would be the sister in Maine,' Steve said, getting to his feet, grunting a little with the effort. Had to lose twenty pounds, lay off the beer and grease. He glanced down at the packed suitcases that weren't going anywhere. 'She knows by now,' he said to no one in particular. *Merry F-ing Christmas, Ellen*, he thought.

He didn't envy the poor bugger who'd been tagged with the job of breaking the news to her, but he was damn glad it wasn't him. He was getting too old for this business. Well, three more weeks, he consoled himself, and the only thing you'll have to worry about catching is fish. Just twenty-one days until he retired. It couldn't come too soon.

Taking a handkerchief from his pocket, the detective carefully, so as not to disturb any possible prints, hung up the phone. The calls he'd needed to make he'd already made from the landlady's phone.

On the floor, beneath where the receiver had lain, was a three-strand rhinestone earring. It winked obscenely at him in the light from the dangling lamp.

8

Voices drifted up to her from downstairs, hushed voices, the sort people used when sitting in a room where the dead lay. *Don't listen to them! Shut them out!* A terrible sorrow pushed at her consciousness. Ellen squeezed her eyes shut, tried to will herself back to sleep, to sink back down into the safety of dark oblivion. It was no use. Something heavy was pressing down on her chest. She couldn't breathe.

And then she remembered. Her parents were dead. They'd been returning from an all-night party, both still drunk, (no one told her that, but she knew). Her father at the wheel. 'They struck an embankment,' an ashen-faced Miss Layton told her. Ellen's teacher had been summoned from the classroom by Mr. Reid, the principal, and Miss Layton had, in turn, called Ellen out into the hallway, closing the door on the rows of raptly curious faces. ' . . . At least they didn't suffer, dear,' she'd said, explaining through trembling lips that they had both died at the moment of impact.

Ellen's initial reaction to the news of her

parents' death had been one of relief — enormous relief. It lasted only an instant, but long enough to flood her with shame and horror, and she prayed that Miss Layton had not caught that unforgivable expression on her face — that she would never know the vile heart of her favorite student.

Lying there, tears began to stream down Ellen's face as she thought, *I really did love them. I did. They were my mother and father, for God's sake. They weren't bad people. They could be very dear, both of them, when they weren't drinking.*

Gail. She had to go be with Gail. Gail needed her. Folding back the covers, which seemed incredibly heavy, she slid her feet out onto the floor and sat up. As she did, the room tilted and went into a spin. Ellen lowered her head into her hands until the dizziness passed. At last she opened her eyes, at the same time shivering in the chill air of the room.

A room bathed in moonlight. Tree shadows swayed beyond the lacy curtains. Someone had opened one of the windows a crack and the curtain fluttered in the wind. That explained why the room was cold, but not why the air smelled of winter. Or why the windows were situated in the wrong place, and were taller than her own windows. Though the room was vaguely familiar, it was not the one of her childhood. Confused and disoriented, Ellen was struggling to stand when she saw the door slowly opening and Myra standing in the doorway, and it was the sight of her friend that brought the truth crashing in on her with the force of a tidal wave. The nightmare that had perched on the rim of her consciousness now engulfed her, and she sank back down on the bed. She was no longer seventeen years old, and it was not her parents who were the topic of the conversation that was taking place downstairs.

Oh, Gail. Oh, please, God, no.

And then she was in Myra's arms, and Myra was sobbing, saying over and over again, 'I'm so sorry, Ellen. I'm so, so sorry.'

★ ★ ★

Later, bits and pieces came back to her. Her screams of denial on the drive from the airport. At home, the sharp sting of Doctor Evans' needle as it pierced her upper arm, bringing a merciful nothingness.

★ ★ ★

With the help of the valium Doctor Evans had prescribed for her, Ellen managed for the most part to get through the funeral in a zombie-like state, barely aware of people coming up to her, dabbing their eyes with tissue, offering condolences, well-meaning platitudes. 'I'm sorry, dear . . . so sorry about your sister . . . a terrible tragedy . . . doesn't she look lovely, just like she's asleep . . . God sometimes takes the good souls young . . . ours is not to reason why . . . God moves in mysterious ways . . . '

God didn't do this, she thought, though she tried to smile her appreciation, to mumble some appropriate response. Some faces were familiar, more not. Not so surprising. Evansdale was a small town, seldom visited by murder. A little excitement was not unwelcome. It didn't matter. Nothing mattered.

Until she thought she saw Miss Layton, her old high school teacher, standing in the parlor doorway, wearing her familiar black pillbox, her purse clutched in front of her. Ellen rose unsteadily to her feet to greet her. In that same moment, a small group gathered in front of the doorway, blocking Miss Layton from view. When they moved on, she was no longer there.

Perhaps I only imagined her, Ellen thought.

Later, at the gravesite, Ellen looked for her in the crowd, but she was not there.

'You're doing just fine,' Paul whispered when she stumbled slightly at the sight of the open grave. His hand was at the small of her back, guiding her forward. His expensive lemony cologne wafted to her, mingling with the cloying scent of many flowers and the damp, upturned earth, and she was afraid she was going to be sick.

Reverend Palmer was standing patiently on the other side of the grave holding the bible open to the place from which he would read, one hand trying to still the rattling pages. His eyes, gazing into hers, were like the eyes she had seen in a portrait of Jesus. She avoided them. The wind caught and lifted the sparse hairs he'd so carefully combed over his scalp, revealing his bald pate. About his ankles, his robes fluttered like great black wings.

Above her, the skies were clouding over, threatening more snow.

All these things Ellen noticed, concentrated on, so as not to look at the coffin with its brass handles, and the single red rose she had placed on top, or think of Gail inside — which, of course, was impossible.

'You're so damn brave, Ellen,' a teary Myra

said, flanking her other side. 'I'd be falling apart if it was me.'

I am, Ellen thought, and wondered why her friend couldn't see that. Yet it was true that she had not broken down since the drive from the airport, or even shed a tear, and that must puzzle Myra. It puzzled her. It was as if something hard encased her heart. The few times she'd been sure the dam was about to burst, only a few pathetic whimpers had escaped her.

Reverend Palmer closed the bible, bowed his head in prayer. Ellen followed suit, though she did not pray. A slight shifting in the crowd, stirrings, a few murmured 'Amens', and she opened her eyes to see the coffin being slowly lowered into the ground. The onslaught of pain hit her with such savagery it took her breath and turned her legs to liquid. Still, she did not fall, but managed to remain standing until it was over. She was grateful to let herself be supported between Paul and Myra back to the car.

And then they were part of the caravan, following behind the hearse, making their way down the long, winding path that led out of the cemetery to the highway. It seemed callous to her that they should be driving so much faster now than when they had entered, as if, their duty to the dead accomplished, they were eager to be finished with it.

Sitting beside Paul, Ellen clutched her hands together, sudden panic rising in her breast as the space between herself and Gail widened. *I don't want to leave her. I have to go back. I don't want to leave my little sister in that cold, dark ground.* A dry sob broke from her. Paul reached over and squeezed her hand.

'It'll take time,' he said.

* * *

Lieutenant Mike Oldfield watched until the last of the train of cars disappeared around the bend, then he stepped out from behind the copse of trees where he'd been videotaping the solemn proceedings below. Not that he'd really expected Gail Morgan's killer to show up here, considering she'd been murdered in New York City. But you never knew. He wouldn't be the first killer to show up at his victim's burial. Must give them an extra power-rush, Mike thought, seeing all that pain and knowing they caused it.

He hadn't been exactly immune himself, though his own feeling was one of heaviness. He'd had a hard time looking at Ellen Harris through his camera lens. Watching her, he knew it was taking everything she had just to stay on her feet.

She'd looked so vibrant, so full of life when he first saw her at the airport. Right up until the moment she looked up and saw him coming toward her.

Sometimes this job sucks, he thought, setting the camera in the trunk of the car and slamming the lid shut.

In the still quiet of the cemetery the sound echoed until it died away into nothingness.

* * *

'Eat,' Myra urged. 'You'll get sick if you don't eat.' Myra set the bowl of steaming soup in front of her, placed a spoon in her hand as if Ellen were a child learning to feed herself.

'Maybe later, okay?' Ellen tried to smile, not wanting to seem ungrateful.

But Myra was not to be dissuaded. 'Just a little,' she coaxed. Having no will to resist, Ellen obeyed mechanically, setting the spoon down when she could no longer swallow.

She looked out the window. The skies had cleared. It was not going to snow after all. Sunlight lay a buttery path on the light wood table, played over the backs of her hands. It seemed a cruel betrayal that the sun should be shining, that she should be drawing warmth from its rays. Ellen placed her hands in her lap. Despite the sun, they were icy cold.

Myra came and took the bowl away. 'Good girl,' she said, though Ellen had eaten little. Water ran in the sink. Myra was doing the dishes. With a husband and three kids, God knew, she had more than enough to do at home, but Ellen was glad she was there.

A buzz of restrained conversation drifted from the living room. Some of those who had attended the funeral had come back to the house. She wondered if Paul had invited them.

Gail should be here with me now. We should be enjoying our little time together before she goes on tour. Now Ellen would never see her again. Gail was lost to her — to the world. Her beautiful song had ended.

Someone — out there — had done that.

Suddenly, she began to shake, a violent, convulsive shivering that started in her legs, swiftly gripping her entire body. She tried to make it stop, and couldn't. From somewhere, Paul appeared, stepping in front of an anxious Myra to drape a knit shawl around her shoulders. He kissed the top of her head. 'Shh,' he said. 'Breathe deeply. That's it. That's the way.'

'She ate a little soup,' Myra said in a small voice, sounding as if Ellen's present condition

73

was somehow her fault. Myra used to apologize for things that weren't her fault. But she didn't do that anymore. It was a thing they had worked on.

'Good,' Paul said coolly. To Ellen he said, smiling, 'It's important that you keep up your strength. Why don't you come upstairs and lie down for a while?' He placed gentle hands on her shoulders. 'You look so tired, dear. You really do need to rest.'

He was right. She was tired. So tired she wondered if she might die from it. Was that possible? The thought was not an unwelcome one. Yet, she didn't think she really wanted to be alone just now.

She looked up at Paul, so handsome in a charcoal grey suit, white shirt and maroon tie. She saw him in her mind's eye, moving about the parlor, extending a warm hand to one after another of those who came to pay their respects, smiling just enough. How smoothly and expertly he had handled everything. Ellen was grateful to him. Even if she'd been up to it, she was not very adept at that sort of thing.

Paul was helping her to her feet. She felt so cold — as if she might never be warm again. But the shivering had stopped.

'I'll go with her, Paul,' Myra was saying, laying the dishtowel on the counter and coming forward, wiping her hands on her apron.

But Paul was already ushering Ellen from the room. 'No, it's okay. You go on with what you were doing. And you might see if anyone would like more tea or coffee, Myra, if you don't mind.'

As they reached the stairs, Ellen glimpsed a wedge of living room, saw the tree she had so lovingly decorated. People were milling around, eating small sandwiches, holding cups of tea or coffee.

She wondered idly where all the food had come from, and then she remembered seeing all those saran-wrapped trays and plates lined up on the counter, and Myra saying she couldn't cram another thing into the fridge. Friends had brought the food, of course. Friends of hers, of Gail's, coworkers.

How kind people were. She should thank them. It was her place. This was her home, after all — and Gail her sister. *Oh, Gail. Please, dear Lord, let me wake up and all this be just some terrible dream.* The living room went out of view as Paul, his hand gently at her waist, guided her up the stairs. Ellen clutched the smooth, oak bannister for support, every step she took an enormous effort.

'It was a big funeral,' Paul said when they

reached the landing. 'Fitting for a star. Your sister would have been pleased.'

It was as if he had struck her.

★   ★   ★

She was lying on the bed with the curtains drawn against the sunlight, when someone rapped lightly on the door. She turned her head, half expecting to see Myra, hoping it was, but it was Reverend Palmer who entered her room when she said 'Come in.' Without asking her permission, he sat down on the edge of her bed and began to pray over her.

'You may not understand it now,' he said when he lifted his head, 'but some higher purpose has been served by this terrible tragedy.' His moon face glowed with pious righteousness, reminding her of some evangelist she'd seen on television. 'God never gives us more pain than we can bear, dear.'

'That's not true.'

The minister only looked pityingly at her. Ellen thought about the way the wind had lifted his hair and laid bare his bald spot. She looked into that virtuous face and thought about that, and liked thinking about it. She was glad when he left.

Paul had engaged Reverend Palmer's services. He was not someone she would have chosen. Paul had taken care of all the arrangements. She supposed she had no right to be critical. *A funeral fitting for a star. Your sister would have been pleased.*

How could he have said that to her?

She looked over at the vase of yellow roses on the wicker table. They were curled and brown.

Dead. Like Gail was dead.

★ ★ ★

In the days and nights that followed, Ellen floated in and out of a valium-induced haze, trapped in a well of blackness so deep no light could reach her. With the passing of time, her doorbell rang less and less often, though Ellen took little notice.

Gradually, she began coming downstairs, sitting in a kitchen chair, or pacing from room to room, or staring out of windows, seeing nothing. When the pain got too bad, she took to her bed.

Other times, she found she was quite able to sit and talk with Myra, or Paul, or whoever was there, functioning almost normally, just as though she were not an empty shell, with nothing left of her but severed, bleeding nerves. And at odd times a part of her seemed strangely to stand apart from whatever was taking place, to become both spectator and participant.

Paul tried to reason with her, explaining to her about the stages of grief, quoting the experts, just as if she had never heard all the psycho-babble, had not spoken it herself. She was glad he was away at a conference in California.

At some point, she noticed the tree was gone from the living room, together with her gifts to Gail. Myra, of course. Dear, thoughtful Myra.

The parade of visitors bearing food and condolences had long since dropped off, and one day Ellen shuffled into the kitchen to find Myra, wearing one of Carl's shirts over paint-spattered slacks too big for her, (though she'd been slim for years now, when Myra was feeling depressed, she returned to wearing 'fat' clothes) standing at the kitchen sink washing dishes, just as she'd been on the day of the funeral — on the day Paul remarked about the star quality of the funeral, saying how pleased Gail would be. He probably meant well enough, she thought now. It was the sort of thing people said.

A pink, plastic transistor radio sat near Myra on the counter, tuned in to her favorite country music station, but turned low so as not to disturb Ellen.

She gently took the soapy dish from Myra's hand and set it on the counter. Managing a smile, she said, 'You go on home now. I'll finish these.'

Myra stood hesitantly, her dark eyes moist with unshed tears. 'Are you sure? I really don't want to leave you alone.'

'I'm sure.' She hugged her. 'You are such a good friend, Myra. But Carl and the kids need you now. And you need to be with them. I know it's damn near impossible, but maybe you can try to salvage what's left of the holidays.' Their Christmas, of course, was clouded by Ellen's loss, spoiled. She felt badly about that, especially for the boys. She imagined they were all feeling pretty neglected by now, and right that they should.

'There's a stack of sympathy cards on top of the fridge,' Myra said, tugging on her boots, 'just in case you feel like opening them.'

'Thank you.'

'You don't *need* to open them. It might just upset you.'

Feeling a rush of affection for her friend, Ellen put her arms around her, perhaps as much for herself as for Myra. So many emotions buffeted her, so many they were impossible to separate in her mind. When she drew away, she looked squarely at Myra. 'I have to be alone sometime,' she said.

The tears Myra had been fighting now spilled over. 'It's not fair,' she sobbed. 'First your parents, then Ed, and now — '

'Whoever said life was fair?' Ellen interrupted quietly. 'You should know all about that, kid. Hey, wait a second.' She went to the closet and returned with two shopping bags bulging with gifts. 'Merry Christmas,' she smiled. 'A little late, but better late than never, huh? I got Joey some games to go with his new Nintendo. And by the way, thank you for the beautiful robe. You know that's my favorite shade of blue. I love it.'

Myra was getting teary again.

'Hey, look, if I need you, I'll call,' Ellen assured her, giving her another quick hug. 'You're just up the road, for heaven's sake.'

'Promise?' She sniffed a couple of times while reaching guiltily for her coat, her eyes never once leaving Ellen. It touched Ellen to see her friend so torn between a sense of duty toward her, and a natural, healthy desire to be with her family — to be where death had not visited.

Forcing a smile, and lightness into her movements, Ellen helped her on with her coat. Promising again to call, she ushered her out the door.

She stood in the doorway watching, as

Myra drove off up the road in her little green Honda Civic.

In every direction she looked, the view was spectacular. It was a day that sparkled. Snow-laden trees beneath enamel blue skies. A virtual winter wonderland.

Unmoved, Ellen went back inside.

★ ★ ★

Alone now, she wandered into the living room. She sagged down in the old sofa chair with its pretty new cover. When the silence grew too loud, she got up and turned on the television. She sat staring at the flickering images. *He was there. He was already there, in her apartment, hiding, when I was talking to her on the phone.* Gail's words played in her mind. ' . . . *Hold on a sec, Ellen. I think I heard something . . . It was just Tiger — crazy cat. I forgot to feed him when I came in and he was letting me know in no uncertain terms.*'

No, it wasn't Tiger she'd heard. Not Tiger at all.

Soon the pictures inside Ellen's head grew more vivid than those on the television screen, complete with sound and texture, making her want to claw them from her brain. A small, agonized moan broke from her; she bolted from the chair. Crossing to the sideboard, she poured herself a generous shot of vodka to go with the two valium she'd taken earlier, and which didn't seem to be working.

Her hands shook, and some of the vodka splashed the sideboard's lovely cherry wood surface. She didn't bother to wipe it up. The drawer was not all the way closed, and she could see one corner of the bulging scrapbook containing Gail's brief life.

No need to buy another one. Not now.

9

Other than to refill her glass, and turn the sound up a little, Ellen had not moved from in front of the television. The room had grown dark. She was on her third vodka, glass in hand, clear liquid gently swirling. She looked to see it creating a tiny whirlpool, and longed to lose herself in it.

What did it matter if she drank? What did anything matter now? She thought about the bottle of Valium on the shelf in the medicine cabinet — maybe twenty left.

Enough, she knew, to end the nightmares.

Strangely, Myra's nightmares came to mind. 'A shadowy figure at the foot of my bed,' she'd told her on the night Gail was murdered. 'I wake up in an icy sweat, terrified. What do you think it means after all this time, Ellen?'

'I don't know,' Ellen said aloud to her glass, her words slurring slightly. 'I don't know anything anymore.'

Ellen continued to stare at the screen. *Live at Five.* Only five o'clock. It got dark out so early now. The announcer's voice cut through the boozy haze. ' . . . More trouble in the

Middle East ... economists are predicting the country is headed for another depression ... a plane exploded over Bangkok ... ' The voice faded out again like a receding tide as Ellen began thinking about *him*. Was *he* too, at this very moment, sitting in some darkened room in front of a television set? Smiling perhaps, reliving his vile, brutal act with a sick pleasure? Her hand began shaking so hard, she had to set the drink down.

And suddenly Gail was smiling out at her from the television screen, sending a knife of searing pain straight through her heart. It was the picture of her they'd run with the last article.

'Police are still baffled by the recent murder of a young Evansdale woman,' the announcer read from the sheaf of papers in his hands. 'Gail Morgan's body was discovered two weeks ago today on the bedroom floor of her New York apartment, savagely beaten, raped and strangled. Ms. Morgan was a singer on the verge of her big breakthrough in the music industry. Her recording of 'Do You Know Me?', also written by Ms. Morgan, should hit the airways in a matter of weeks, reports a spokesman for Genesis recordings. Police are continuing their investigation into the murder.

'The search for a Scarsdale man missing in the Maine woods over the weekend has ended on a happier note . . .'

The announcer's voice lost to her now, Ellen leaned forward in her chair. She narrowed her eyes at the screen, focusing, concentrating all her mental energies. *Who are You? You're out there somewhere.* She tried to see him in her mind's eye, trying in desperation to tune him in. *What kind of monster are you to do what you did to my sister?*

Imagining Gail's pain, her helplessness, and the final terror of knowing she was going to die, sent a surge of rage and hatred through Ellen so powerful she felt it might suffocate her. Bile rose in her throat as wave after bitter wave took her, building in strength and intensity like dark clouds before a storm. When she could no longer contain the storm within her, in the space of a breath, she released the torrent of writhing, black emotion into the television screen, and beyond. *You'll pay, you bastard. I'll find you. And you'll pay for what you did.*

Outside, the cold January wind screamed under the eaves and snow-crusted branches bowed low under starless skies.

After several moments, drained and exhausted, Ellen went into the kitchen and poured the remainder of her drink down the sink. Quite sober now, she thought how silly it was what she'd tried to do. She wasn't even sure she really believed in E.S.P. Sure, she and Gail had often been able to tune in to one another's thoughts, and sometimes, when she'd pick up the receiver to call her, Gail would already be on the line. They would laugh about that and feel no small sense of wonder.

But even if something more than simple intuition was at work, it wouldn't happen with a stranger. And you couldn't call it up, like a witch's curse, no matter how bad you wanted to.

But she *would* find him, she thought, standing very still, holding the empty glass in her hand. She wouldn't rest until she did. And he *would* pay. Under the sudden pressure of her fingers, the glass shattered, cutting her in a dozen places. Ellen watched with an odd sense of fascination as rivulets of blood flowed over her hand in every direction, dripping steadily as a heartbeat onto the black and white floor tiles.

Gradually, she became aware of the

throbbing pain in her hand, and almost welcomed it.

Her life had purpose now.

* * *

Across town, in the darkened den of an old Victorian-style house, the tall man jerked awake, the can of Miller Lite dropping from his hand to roll across the floor, knocking up against the leg of the old Philco television set, spewing beer onto the faded rug. He jumped to retrieve the can, looked bewilderedly around him. Aunt Mattie? No, he couldn't have heard her from down here. Besides, his aunt didn't swear.

But someone had called out to him, an angry voice — calling him a bastard. Saying he'd pay.

10

Upstairs, Ellen stood holding the towel firmly around her hand to staunch the flow of blood. The towel was already reddening, though when she'd run cold water over her hand, she'd seen that none of the cuts were very deep.

In the mirror, her eyes looked haunted, sunken in her skull. Her new hairdo lay flat and greasy against her head. She looked like hell. *Get yourself together, Ellen. You've got work to do.*

She opened the medicine chest, her reflection flying out of view. Taking down the bottle of Valium, she flushed the remaining tablets down the toilet. It was important to keep her wits about her. Smelling the faint sourness coming off her body, she realized she needed a shower.

Tomorrow she would fly to New York, she thought, turning on the taps, testing the water with her good hand. She'd talk to Sandi, Gail's roommate. And the landlady. Someone must know something, must have seen something. Sandi had called one day last week, crying. Ellen couldn't remember what was said. She'd sent flowers. There'd been so many flowers. She thought of the stack of cards on the fridge. She would go through them. Perhaps Gail's killer had even sent one. She'd heard of such things.

She would take a sabbatical from work. She had nothing to give to anyone else just now. Someone else would have to take over her caseload. She wouldn't be returning for a while.

Not until she found *him*.

She was half way down the stairs when the door-bell rang. She glanced at the clock. It was five minutes past eight. Frowning, she wondered if Myra had come back.

Other than the glow from the television, the room was in darkness. Ellen switched off the television, turned on a couple of lamps, and opened the door.

It surprised her to see Miss Layton standing there, looking much as she had standing in the doorway of the funeral parlor — small black hat perched on her graying head, purse clutched in front of her. Up this close, she looked smaller somehow, and Ellen could see the deep lines etched in her face, and the way her lively blue eyes had faded. She supposed she shouldn't be surprised, after all these years, that her teacher had aged, and yet she'd foolishly imagined Miss

Layton remaining forever young, forever a formidable presence.

'I hope this isn't an intrusion, Ellen,' she said. At the sound of that clear voice, instilled with the wisdom and gentle authority Ellen remembered, the years fell away.

Ellen opened the door wider. 'Not at all, Miss Layton. I'm pleased to see you. You — you look wonderful.'

The elderly woman entered amidst a rush of cold air and the faint scent of lavender. She didn't address the compliment. 'I know one often prefers solitude at a time like this,' she said, sitting ramrod straight in the chair Ellen offered, ' . . . but you've been on my mind, Ellen. I had to come and see for myself how you were coping. I'll be leaving Evansdale at the end of the month. Perhaps before I go, there's something — something I can do for you.'

'Nothing, Miss Layton. But thank you.' She sat across from her on the sofa. 'Where will you be going?'

'I have a widowed sister who lives in Atlanta. She's been after me for some time now to come live with her. It's a gracious old home, surrounded with lawns and trees.'

'It sounds lovely.'

'Yes, it will be a pleasant arrangement, I feel. Lillian and I always got on well.'

'I'll make us some tea,' Ellen said, rising, feeling a measure of comfort in the elderly woman's presence. Perhaps because she'd been there for her at a crucial time in her life, because she knew her and Gail as children. How wonderful she had been that day they'd gone to get Gail released from the home. Just as the petite Miss Layton had always been able, with a mere look or word, to cow the biggest trouble-maker in the class, no matter his size, she had brought that tight-lipped social worker around to her way of thinking.

So many years ago. In some ways it seemed like yesterday.

'Are you sure it's no trouble, dear?' Miss Layton said, eyeing Ellen's bandaged hand. Ellen's own gaze followed. 'It's nothing serious. I broke a glass. I guess I'm a bleeder,' she added with a thin laugh.

Miss Layton didn't smile. 'I did come to the funeral parlor, you know,' she said, a little sheepishly. 'But I'm afraid my courage abandoned me. It was so reminiscent of that — other time.'

'I know,' Ellen smiled. 'I saw you there. I looked for you later. I'll just be a few minutes. The tea will warm you. Unless you'd prefer a nice glass of sherry.'

'Tea will be fine, Ellen.'

She served the tea in her best china cups

and saucers, gold-rimmed with yellow roses, and set out a plate of cookies. They sat across from one another. Miss Layton sipped her tea. 'And how *are* you getting on, Ellen?'

Ellen was forced to meet those knowing, unwavering eyes. Only their color was faded. Ellen shrugged. 'I'll survive, I suppose.'

'Yes, you will,' Miss Layton said, a direct command that would not be questioned. 'You're a survivor of the first order, a fighter. You always were, Ellen Morgan.' She'd used her maiden name, spoken to her just as if she were still sitting in her classroom, second seat, first row by the door.

'In a teacher's professional life,' she went on thoughtfully, 'there are some students who stand out, while others, I'm afraid, fade in the mind. For that, perhaps we will have to atone one day. But you, Ellen — I have often thought about over the years. Of course, I remember what a good and hard-working girl you were, always such a joy to teach. But what I remember most was your sense of fair play. You were always one to champion the underdog — the first to hold out a friendly hand to a child who did not quite fit in, and this despite your own regrettable circumstances.'

'I appreciate your saying these things to me, Miss Layton. It's really very kind of you.'

'Posh. It's not kindness at all. It's only the truth. I was not in the least surprised to hear that you went into a helping profession. It was so wise of you, Ellen, to go back to school.'

Looking at her teacher, clad in a brown crepe dress, the ivory cameo brooch at her throat, as familiar as a uniform, Ellen remembered how distraught she'd been when Ellen dropped out of school to find a job. Yet in the end she'd been there to support her decision. 'None of that seems to matter now, does it?' she said.

'Of course it matters,' Miss Layton said adamantly. 'You have nothing to berate yourself for. You always felt you could make things right, Ellen. And sometimes that simply is not possible. Sometimes terrible things happen over which we have no control. My dear, you were fiercely protective toward your family — and your little sister in particular.'

11

It was late afternoon when Ellen arrived in a gray, bitterly cold New York. When she got to the apartment, Sandi Rousseau was grimly packing her things. She hadn't taken off her coat.

'Gail didn't date,' she said in answer to Ellen's question, dashing back and forth between the dresser and the bed as she'd been doing the whole time they talked. With every turn her hair swung like a sheet of beige satin. 'She was completely devoted to her career. Oh, she was friendly enough with her pianist, Doug Neal, but not in any romantic way. Though Doug might have felt differently. I talked to him on the phone. He's devastated, poor guy.'

Sandi dropped an armload of designer sweaters into the suitcase, patted them down carelessly. Sighing, she turned to face Ellen. Her lovely eyes were red-rimmed from crying. Ellen envied her her tears. 'Why do you think it was someone she knew?'

Ellen wasn't surprised she was moving out. Another day and she might have had trouble getting in touch with Sandi.

'Maybe not someone *she* knew,' Ellen said calmly. She was sitting in the one chair in the bedroom, trying not to look at the fading chalk outline of Gail's body on the carpet. 'But someone who knew her. He was waiting for her, Sandi. He must have known who she was, that she would be coming home alone.'

The girl clutched a full-length tweed coat about her, as if she were suddenly feeling vulnerable. 'Maybe you're right. I hadn't thought of that.' She sagged down on the bed. 'She had a lot of fans. Sometimes they get — obsessed or something.' She gave Ellen a look of pure misery. 'I'm so sorry, Ellen. I wanted to come to the funeral, but I — I just couldn't.'

Ellen crossed the room and sat down beside her, touched her arm. 'I know. And I do understand. Gail would have, too.'

'Oh, God, I hope so. I can't believe she's gone.' Her voice broke. She pulled Kleenex from her pocket and wiped away a fresh welling of tears. 'Who would do such a horrible thing? What horrible fiend would do that to her? She was such a sweet person.'

'I don't know, Sandi. But I intend to find out.'

'Gail adored you, you know. She used to talk about you all the time. She told me about your parents, the drinking and all that — and

95

then that terrible accident. She said you were always there for her.'

No. Not always, Ellen thought. 'I was the oldest. I did what I had to do. Gail would have done the same for me.' *I liked it that Gail needed me. It was never a burden. I liked being the one she looked up to.*

'She was real proud that you went back and got your degree. That must be hard when you're older.'

Ellen smiled. 'Not terribly. I always liked school.' *We did make it all work out. Dammit, we did!* Her gaze wandered involuntarily to the chalk outline on the carpet. Her throat tightened. Why? Why did this happen to her? Reverend Palmer was wrong. There was no great purpose being served here.

Seeing where Ellen was looking, Sandi rose abruptly, causing the bed to squeak. The dresser drawers open and empty, she attacked the closet, tearing dresses and coats from their hangers, leaving them to rattle like old bones in her wake. 'I have to go. I'm sorry, but I have to get out of here.'

'Of course. Sandi, you mentioned obsessed fans. Did Gail ever talk about anyone who fits that picture? Some particular incident that maybe bothered her? Strange letters?'

'No. Nothing that comes to mind, anyway.'

Sandi had taken the last dress from the closet, laid it across the top of the overflowing heap of clothes, and was now trying to force the suitcase shut. Ellen leaned her weight on the top, while Sandi managed to zip it around. 'Thanks.'

'You need some help with these?'

'No, thanks anyway. I didn't bring my car. I'll call a cab.' She was about to pick up the receiver when she turned, frowning. 'You know, there was something.'

'What?'

'A phone call. She got this weird call.'

'Weird how, Sandi?'

'Well, someone who just whispered, 'Do you know me?' You know, the name of Gail's new song.'

'Yes. What else did he say?'

'That's just it. Gail wasn't even sure it was a *he*. It's hard to tell from a whisper, I guess. Anyway, whoever it was didn't say anything else. Do you know me? Then they hung up. Gail didn't freak or anything, but I remember she got kind of quiet.'

'When was this?'

'Around one in the morning. Maybe a little before. Gail hadn't been home from work very long. It was just a few nights before . . . ' She bit down on her lower lip as she glanced at the now boarded-up window. 'She was a good friend to me, always boosting me up when things weren't happening for me just the way I thought they should. Nothing ever got her down for long. She was one of the most positive people I've ever known.'

'Do many people have this number, Sandi?' Ellen asked, thinking, as she had the first time she saw her, how lovely she was. It was hard to imagine modeling agencies not clamoring for her services.

'No, not really. Just those people we needed to have it, people important to our careers. Agents, publicity people and the like. And our families, of course. The number's unlisted.'

'I don't suppose you considered having it changed.'

She looked surprised at the question. 'No. Not for one phone call. It wasn't like we were being harassed or anything.'

'Did you report the call to the police?'

'No. I didn't think of it again. Not until now. I don't think Gail did either. Just some creep with nothing better to do.'

'It doesn't sound like a random call, though, does it? Not just someone punching out numbers. He knew who she was. He knew the name of her song.'

Sandi said nothing. She'd gone very pale.

'Sandi, do you have Doug Neal's address?' Ellen asked.

She blinked as if she'd gone into a momentary trance. 'The police took Gail's address book, but, yes, I have Doug's address. His phone number, too, if you want it. Surely you don't think . . . '

'I don't think anything at this point,' Ellen said. 'I'd just like to talk to him, that's all.'

★ ★ ★

When Sandi was gone, Ellen walked down the hall and knocked on Mrs. Bloom's door. It opened almost at once as if the landlady had been waiting for her. Though Ellen had never met Mrs. Bloom, she seemed to know who Ellen was.

'Come in, dear. I've made a nice pot of tea. This must be so terrible for you. Do the police know anything yet? Have they found the man who did it?'

They talked over tea. Mrs. Bloom's apartment was cluttered with knickknacks, dusty potted plants. Yellowing lace doilies lay limply over the arms and backs of stuffed, sagging chairs. A grandfather clock stood in the corner by the window facing the street, ticking loudly, pendulum swinging. Except for the small television set at the opposite corner of the room, Ellen got the impression that the place had been decorated in the forties, and remained frozen in time. The air in the room smelled faintly of mold and cat pee, evidenced by the yellow tabby eyeing Ellen warily from one of the chairs, and another, this one smaller and black, curled up asleep on the window-sill.

'You can see I'm a cat person,' Mrs. Bloom said smiling, bending with some difficulty to pick up the orange striped cat that had padded into the room just then, and which Ellen knew had belonged to Gail. 'They're such wonderful company,' the landlady said fondly. 'They ask nothing of you but a little love and a bit of food.'

Ellen reached out her own hand and stroked the sleek head, gazed into the green, knowing eyes. Pain pierced her heart. *What did you see, Tiger? What could you tell me if only you could speak?*

Though Mrs. Bloom talked freely, she was unable to tell Ellen anything useful — only what she'd already told police. No one had seen anything. No one heard anything. Mrs. Bloom had been visiting an upstairs neighbor when it happened.

Before leaving, Ellen gave her a month's rent, and, ignoring the face filled with curiosity and not a little astonishment — never mind that she'd accepted the money quite readily, and with just the tiniest gleam in her eye — went back to the apartment.

She supposed she wasn't being entirely fair to Mrs. Bloom. You could hardly fault her for wanting to rent an apartment that might otherwise remain vacant for months. People got edgy about living in a place where a brutal murder had occurred. And this building, after all, was Mrs. Bloom's livelihood.

The landlady had been adamant about keeping Tiger. 'He was over here as often as he was home, anyway,' she'd told Ellen. 'The girls were away a lot. Tiger knows he's loved here, don't you, Tiger?'

She'd also, at Ellen's request, packed all of Gail's clothes into boxes with a promise to give them to the Salvation Army. She was really a good soul. Ellen didn't think she could have borne having to look at them.

Other than Gail's Christmas gifts to her, and the few photographs police had not confiscated from the wall, Ellen took nothing.

She already had her scrapbook. And her memories.

Far more than enough to fuel the fire of vengeance that raged within her.

12

The police had removed the tape from the door only two days ago, Mrs. Bloom had told her. She hadn't had a chance to clean up the place yet, and offered to do it while Ellen stayed for a second cup of tea. Ellen said no, just leave it.

Now, standing in the middle of the room, she could feel the violence of that night all around her. Sighing, she sat down on Gail's bed. Noticing something pea-green peeking from beneath the pillow, she withdrew it and held it up. A tee shirt. She smiled with memory. Gail was always one to sleep in big, sloppy tee shirts, even when she was a kid. Pressing the soft fabric to her face, she breathed in the light, spicy fragrance of L'Air du Temps, Gail's favorite perfume, mingled with her own natural essence.

Smells that would soon fade, she thought, like the chalk outline on the carpet. Even as Gail herself would soon fade in the minds of most of those who had attended her funeral. With the scent of the tee shirt flooding her senses, the casing around her heart finally cracked and peeled away, and the dam of pent-up tears burst forth. She sobbed into the tee shirt for a long time.

When all her tears were spent, and her eyes felt as if they'd been rubbed with sandpaper, Ellen whispered, 'Help me, Gail. Help me find whoever did this to you.'

Only the silence answered.

★　★　★

That night she slept in Gail's bed, clad in the tee shirt with SAVE OUR PLANET on the front, which was only slightly damp in spots from her tears. Before coming to bed, she'd stood before the full-length mirror in the bathroom, smiling, seeing the way the tee shirt just barely covered her bottom, knowing it would have reached nearly to Gail's knees.

Her reflection had blurred as the tears came again.

Now, lying beneath the covers, Ellen could see in the lamplight the boarded-up window and the green blind that, when she'd tried to tug it down further, resisted her efforts. Someone peering in through the unshaded strip of window could easily have made out the telephone number on the phone, which sat only a few feet away on the nightstand.

Her gaze left the window. It settled on the closet door, and fixed there. She pictured

Gail coming into the room, taking off her shoes, undressing, opening the closet door and hanging up her dress, (he'd been standing in the far corner, concealed behind the rack of clothes) maybe humming to herself, happy in the knowledge of her hard-earned success, looking forward, as Ellen had been, to their spending Christmas together.

Phoning Ellen.

She replayed their conversation in her mind. He'd been listening, too. Waiting. And then he'd inadvertently made some sort of noise, something that had alerted her. Perhaps he wanted to hear better. Or maybe he was just getting impatient.

She'd thought it was Tiger.

When did you know you were not alone, Gail?

Narrowing her eyes, Ellen imagined the closet door slowly opening. She concentrated hard, imagining it so vividly, she started when she thought she saw the door actually move outward a fraction, and felt something of the horror that must have struck Gail's heart.

She would have fought. Gail was a fighter. But she was a small girl, and in the end was helpless to save herself.

What did he look like? Was he someone

you knew? Someone whose face you recognized?

Above her head, a television suddenly blared to life. Strangely, Ellen found the sound comforting. She turned on her side and closed her eyes. Her questions stilled for a time, and she soon slept, but it was an uneasy sleep.

And she dreamed.

★　★　★

It was a warm, breezy June day and she and Gail were walking home from school, Gail's small, moist hand locked in hers. They were crossing over Smith's Bridge, gazing up at the seagulls soaring above them, at times peering over the railing at those perched on the whitewashed rocks below, filling the briny air with their squawking cries.

They walked past Melick's Barber Shop with the candy-striped pole out front, and Gail called 'Hey, kitty, kitty,' to the Siamese cat curled up asleep in the dingy plate-glass window. Then on they went past Hasson's corner grocery, with its Coca-Cola sign creaking in the wind behind them.

As they turned onto Burr Street — their street — the houses quickly grew more dilapidated. They passed sad, dark houses with some of the windows broken, replaced by rattling cardboard, doorsteps sunken into the broken pavement.

A gust of warm, smelly wind chased dirt and gum wrappers up the street toward them. An empty wine bottle rolled and clunked against a telephone pole.

As they neared their own house, a brown, three-story, wooden frame, their footsteps slowed. Loud, ugly voices reached them from behind the windows of the bottom flat — voices that shouted and cursed and threatened. You never knew what awaited you on the other side of the door. This was a place where you never took your friends, a place where shame and fear and craziness lived.

Standing outside the door, Gail's hand in hers, Ellen felt the familiar sinking in her stomach. The angry voices made her feel angry too, and miserable, and she wished she could just take Gail and run away. Maybe she just would! Then they'd be sorry.

Suddenly Gail was crying and trying to pull her hand from Ellen's. 'You said you wouldn't leave me,' she cried. 'You said you wouldn't ever leave me, Ellie.' Her cries grew louder, hysterical. 'You promised, Ellie. You promised.'

When Ellen turned to comfort her, to calm her fears and tell her everything was going to be all right, just the way she always did, it was Myra's face she saw, Myra's mouth that was open in screams, her eyes wide with terror.

Ellen shot bolt upright in the bed, the screams echoing in her mind, the tee shirt clinging wetly to her.

The first thing that met her eyes was the chalk-out-line of Gail's body on the floor. She could feel her sister's presence in the room.

13

'That's the building where that singer was murdered, isn't it?' the cab driver said without turning around. He spoke with a heavy New York accent and looked a little like an aging Al Pacino. Ellen supposed he was curious about their destination.

'Yes, yes it is,' she said, as the cab driver slammed on the brakes and gave the finger to a scurrying pedestrian. Traffic crawled. Horns bleated. Ellen sat back against the leather seat, her dream returning to her. Usually she didn't remember her dreams, but this one clung to her — so vivid, so damned real. The sights, the smells, the sounds, all exactly as she remembered from her childhood. Except for one thing. But for the voices of her parents, the street had been deserted. Like a ghost street in an old western, with little eddies of dirt and paper being blown about like bits of tumbleweed.

'Someone you knew.'

'My sister.'

'Jesus.'

There were always people on Burr Street, sitting on doorsteps, hanging out of windows, cigarettes dangling from slack mouths. Women with their hair in pink curlers screaming at their kids down in the street, shouting to one another, sometimes friendly shouts, sometimes not, wearing dresses held together by safety pins.

She closed her eyes and saw again the top of Gail's blond head, her child's face in profile, felt again that warm little hand in hers, so very trusting. It was Gail's cries, her accusations that had left Ellen so shaken. And then the way her face, when Ellen had turned to her, had become Myra's face. What did it mean? Did Gail somehow blame her? And why was it Myra's face she saw?

Maybe it didn't mean anything. Maybe it was just a dream.

But she knew better. How would she attempt to analyze such a dream if one of her clients had described it to her?

The cab screeched to a stop. 'Here we are, ma'am,' the cab driver said, getting out and holding the door open for her. 'I'm real sorry about your sister. That's a real bummer. The crazies are takin' over the freaking world.'

Ellen agreed silently, thanked him and gave him what she hoped was a proper tip. When he tipped his cap and flashed her a bit of gold tooth, she guessed she must have.

She always felt out of her element in New York, overwhelmed by the noise, the pace, the fact that you couldn't walk down the street without people brushing you on either side, hemming you in. Whoever had coined the term 'asphalt jungle' had been right on the mark. Yet, despite that, she could easily see why this place held such a fascination for Gail, and girls like her. A city teeming with dreams as tall as the sky-scrapers that blocked the sun, it had its own heartbeat, unlike that of any other city in the world.

Gail had been a New Yorker in her soul long before she ever got there, drawn to the bright lights like the proverbial moth to the flame. When Ellen tried to warn her about the dangers of the big city, she would laugh and say, 'You know, Ellen, you can get mugged in your own home town, too. Don't think I haven't met my share of weirdos in good old Evansdale.'

Ellen climbed the wide stone steps of the New York Police Department, her shadow-self gliding up the stairs ahead of her.

★   ★   ★

Detective Steve Shannon came out from behind his massive, cluttered desk and took her hand. 'Mrs. Harris. Let me offer you my

110

condolences on the loss of your sister.' He closed his door on the din outside. 'Would you like coffee?'

'Yes, please.'

The coffee maker was in the corner. He filled two Styrofoam cups. 'Cream? Sugar?'

'Black, please.'

He set the cups on the desk, Ellen's in front of her. She was still standing, unbuttoning her coat.

'I suppose you've come to collect her things from the apartment.' He could see the family resemblance, especially the eyes. But where the victim had been petite, Ellen Harris was tall. She moves like a dancer, he thought. Her hair was that color they used to call 'strawberry blond' in his day.

'No, Sergeant Shannon,' she said, draping her coat over the back of the chair and sitting down. 'That's not why I'm here.'

He took in the simply styled navy dress she wore, the strand of pearls. Belying an air of soft womanhood, Shannon sensed a fierceness about her.

Taking his cue, he went back behind his desk. He picked up his pen and began making little tapping noises on the blotter. She was obviously planning on staying awhile. Well, maybe she could help shed a little light on this case. Somehow he didn't think so. Oh, Christ, he thought miserably. I don't need this.

The strain of her sister's murder showed on her face. Her pupils were unnaturally large. Shannon had seen his share of shock victims in his time, and clearly, Ellen Harris was still in shock.

He waited.

She glanced briefly at the wanted poster on the wall behind him, then at him. Her blue gaze was penetrating, damn near unnerving. 'I want to know everything that you know about the circumstances surrounding my sister's murder,' she said, her voice strong and unwavering. 'And I want to know exactly what your department is doing to find her killer.'

★ ★ ★

It was an hour later when Ellen left the police station. The wind had picked up, accompanied by a light, freezing drizzle. Drawing up the hood of her blue London Fog, she stepped onto the sidewalk. Glancing in both directions, she intuitively turned left, becoming part of the stream of pedestrian traffic.

She'd walked two blocks before she finally spotted a small diner with the sign 'D.J.'s' over the door. It was crowded inside, but she managed to find an empty booth at the back. The decor was cream and blue — soothing colors.

They weren't working on her.

She ordered the soup of the day from the peppy, pony-tailed waitress. While she waited, she thought over all the detective had related to her, which really hadn't amounted to a whole lot. Gail had put up a hell of a fight, he said, which came as no surprise to Ellen. 'She had no chance,' the detective said. 'Only a strategically placed piece of hot lead would have stopped him.'

Gail didn't believe in guns. Neither did Ellen, though she had one. She'd almost forgotten. Ed had bought one for her when they were first married and he had to be out of town a lot. In the construction business, you went where the work was.

Would she remember how to use it?

'Forensic found fragments of skin and blood under her fingernails,' the detective told her. 'Wouldn't be at all surprised if he's walking around with some pretty nasty scratches on him right now.'

The soup came and Ellen found she wasn't hungry, after all. Sliding the bowl away from her, she unwrapped the cellophane from the pack of cigarettes she'd bought from the machine at the airport. She lit her first cigarette in more than two years.

Though the first puff made her feel light-headed, she smoked it down to the filter. Lit another one.

Conversation droned around her, dishes and flat-ware clattered. In a little while the smell of frying grease began to make her feel nauseated.

She crushed out her cigarette in the ashtray, paid her check and left the diner, not noticing the man in dark glasses who'd been sitting at the counter watching her.

He followed her outside.

★ ★ ★

When she arrived back at the apartment, the phone was ringing. To her surprise, it was Paul. At first, she felt pleasure hearing his voice, until she heard the agitation in it.

'I've been beside myself with worry. I drove over to your place last night. When I got back home, I kept dialing your number until well past midnight. I thought you might have done something crazy . . . hurt yourself. I was on the verge of calling the police.'

'Oh. Well, I'm sorry, Paul . . . '

'And this morning I called Myra and she guessed you might have flown down to New York. A shot in the dark.'

'Well, you hit your target,' she said coolly, unbuttoning her coat with one hand, tossing it on the sofa. It slid off onto the floor. She switched the receiver to her other ear, annoyed that he had tracked her down, had taken it upon himself to bother Myra. She was of age, for God's sake. She was under no obligation to report her comings and goings to Paul or anyone else.

Relenting a little, Ellen asked herself if maybe she was being unfair. He was worried about her. She supposed she should be grateful he cared that much. But it was hard to concern herself with Paul's feelings right now, hard to think of anything right now but Gail being dead, and *him* out there somewhere, stalking other women.

'I'm sorry if I worried you, Paul,' she said. 'And you're right, I should have left a note or something. How was the convention?'

'It would have been a lot more fun if you'd been there with me. I miss you, darling. You need to come back to work. I'm sure it would be the best thing for you.'

'I'm not going anywhere,' she said flatly. 'Not until her killer is found. I told you that.'

'Ellen, you have to move ahead. You — '

'Please, Paul, don't tell me what I have to do. I know you mean well, but please . . . '

He was silent.

A need to share with him what she'd learned came over her. She didn't want to shut him out, dammit. She wanted his support. 'Paul, they found a half-smoked Pall Mall cigarette on the kitchen floor. They can tell a lot from that. They can do a saliva test.'

'So? That doesn't necessarily mean it was his. A lot of people smoke that brand. It's my own, you know that.'

'Yes, I know, but there's still a good chance it is. Neither Gail nor Sandi smoked, and the landlady told me they rarely, if ever, had anyone in. Gail hated the smell of cigarette smoke. She used to nag me all the time to quit. And they found broken glass in the far corner of the closet. He put it there so she wouldn't see it when she came into the room. That's where he was hiding, Paul — in the closet. He was waiting for her in the closet when she got home.'

His sigh of impatience traveled over the line. 'Jesus, Ellen, who do you think you are, Jessica Fletcher? Sweetheart, I'm worried about you. So is Myra.'

He didn't give a damn about Myra. He was just using her to build his own case. He wanted to know when she was coming home. Ellen couldn't say with any certainty. It depended. In a few days maybe, she said. She had no intention of telling him she was going to the Shelton Room tonight, or that, with any luck, he'd be watching her on tomorrow night's news broadcast.

Hopefully, the fact that she was a psychologist would carry a little weight.

'I know how you feel,' Paul was saying, 'I know how terrible this is for you. But you must let the police do their job. It's what they get paid for, what they're trained to do. All you'll do is get in the way, and end up making yourself sick.'

My God, did he think she wasn't already sick? 'I know they're the professionals, Paul,' she said, suddenly weary of the conversation. 'But they have plenty of other cases to solve. Gail is just one more.' With that, she said good-bye, told him she'd see him later, and hung up.

He didn't really want to hear anything she had to say, so why was she forcing it on him? Paul didn't understand. He didn't understand how it had been with her and Gail. No one did.

Ed had. He would have been there for her. But Ed was gone.

There was one other person. Feeling guilty for worrying Myra, she picked up the receiver and dialed her number. As she waited for her to answer the phone, she thought: *We have to find him. We have to find him before the scratches fade.*

★   ★   ★

'I didn't like the way she sounded, Carl,' Myra said after hanging up the phone. She'd gotten little sleep last night, and after getting Joey off to kindergarten this morning, she'd gone back to bed. Which was a mistake. Now her mouth tasted woolly and she had a rotten headache. Ellen's call didn't help. Still in her robe, Myra plugged in the kettle for coffee.

'Well, honey, she's depressed,' Carl Thompson said. 'And she's probably still in shock.' A big, raw-boned man with a receding hairline, he was getting into his new brown leather jacket with the warm fleece lining, a Christmas gift from Myra — zipping it up carefully, as if fearing his clumsy fingers might damage it in some way. 'You have to expect it's going to take a long time for — '

'Carl, I know that,' she snapped. 'Do you think I don't know that? And don't you think 'depressed' is a bit of an understatement for what she's feeling right now? Don't patronize me, okay?'

Hurt clouded his face. 'I'm sorry. I didn't know that's what I was doing.'

After a pause, Myra said, 'Oh, Carl, I'm the

118

one who's sorry.' Her headache was beginning to pound with a vengeance. She raked a hand through her disheveled hair. 'I didn't mean to jump at you. I mean, I know she's in terrible pain right now, but it's not sadness I heard in her voice. She said she's sure the police are keeping something from her, that she's going back tomorrow and make them tell her what it is. She was talking real fast, sort of hyper. Like she was on something. She didn't sound like Ellen at all.'

Carl tilted his head at her, frowned. 'You're getting another one of your headaches, aren't you?' he asked quietly.

'What?' Her hands went automatically to her temples. 'Getting' was hardly the word. 'It's nothing, just a . . . Joey, don't eat so fast, you'll get cramps.'

The small towhead turned in his chair, setting big, brown eyes on her. 'No, I won't. You always say that, and I don't get cramps. Me and Jimmy's going sliding. He's waiting for me.' With that, he stuffed the last of his cheeseburger into his mouth and scrambled from his chair, nearly upending it in his rush to get to his jacket, hanging on a hook on the back door.

Myra was across the room in two strides. 'Oh, no you don't, young man,' she said, snatching the jacket from his hand, ignoring the surprised hurt that leaped into his eyes. 'You change your clothes first. You know you don't wear your kindergarten clothes out to play. And it's Jimmy and *I*.'

'Aw, Mom . . . '

'And don't 'Aw, Mom' me. You — '

'Just do it, okay, Tiger?' Carl interceded, tousling Joey's hair. Without another word of protest, he was bounding up the stairs to obey, his small feet thumping on each step, and inside Myra's head, as he went.

'Honey, why don't you take a couple of Tylenol and lie down for a while this afternoon?' Carl said.

Meekly, Myra answered, 'I just got up.'

He took her face in his hands and kissed her on the mouth. Tenderly. 'I'll call you later, okay?' he smiled. A smile that could always melt her anger.

Joey had Carl's smile. Poor Joey, she thought guiltily. He's got a harpy for a mother. 'You deserve a medal for putting up with me lately, Carl.' Maybe she'd make an appointment with Doctor Hoffman. It had been a while since she had a checkup.

Hearing the van's motor idling out in the driveway, she said, kissing him lightly, nudging him toward the door, 'You'd better get going. You don't want to be running late with your calls.'

'Yeah, you're right. I've got a couple of phones to install in one of the offices over at the McLeod building this afternoon. Naturally, they wanted it done yesterday.'

She listened to the van backing out of the drive, wheels crunching on the hard snow.

Carl had been working for the phone company for the last twenty years, landing a job right out of high school. A couple of times, he'd been offered the supervisor's job, but turned it down because he couldn't stand the thought of being stuck in an office all day, handing out orders to others. While they weren't rolling in dough, they were doing okay.

She'd done the career thing. It was where she'd met Carl, in that little boutique where she worked as assistant manager. He'd come to repair a faulty phone. And returned a couple of times on the pretense of checking it out, sealing their fates. She could always go back to work, probably would eventually, but for now she liked being a mom, she liked making a home for her family. A place where they could feel loved and *safe*.

Something Myra had never known.

She didn't have to close her eyes to see herself lying in the darkness in her little bed, listening with growing dread and heaviness for her father's footsteps outside her door, to hear it open, to feel her bed sag with his weight. 'Don't tell anyone, Myra, honey. This is our little secret. No one will believe you, anyway.'

And he was right; they hadn't

She'd been a basket case when she went to Ellen for counseling. Ellen had given her back her life. And now her friend was in trouble, and there was nothing she could do to help. She'd sounded so weird on the phone, talking about the blood and skin under Gail's fingernails. It had made Myra's own skin crawl, she hardly knew what to say. When she asked her how she could be so objective, Ellen had replied simply, 'I have to be.' Then she told her she was going to that place where Gail had worked, the Shelton Room, and asking questions. She wished she could fly to New York and be with her, but it was impossible.

She looked around at her cozy yellow and white, if slightly messy, kitchen. It was Ellen who was directly responsible for them having this place. It was an old, fix-it-upper they'd snapped up at once. Myra had been pregnant with Joey at the time. The retired couple who'd owned it were spending their declining years in Florida.

She began clearing the table. Taking the carton of milk to the fridge, she was met with

Joey's artwork papering the door. No sign here of the black-crayoned, disturbing works of her own childhood, but houses with smoke curling from chimneys, trees in full bloom, bright suns smiling down. Joey leaned toward reds and yellows. A couple of the pictures had stick figures standing in the yard — five in all. Joey's family.

She was putting the milk in the fridge as Joey came bounding down the stairs and into the kitchen. He stopped when he saw her. The wary look he gave her made her heart clench with guilt.

'I'm so sorry I was rough on you, sweetie,' she said, helping him zip up his snowsuit, smoothing the red and blue knitted toque over his ears.

'That's okay, Mom,' he said, standing still for her fussing, hugging her back when she hugged him. 'Aunt Ellen is sad because the bad man kilt her sister, isn't she, Mom?' Joey said quietly.

Kneeling, Myra hugged him more closely to her, feeling his slight, little-boy frame snug inside the snowsuit. He smelled of soap and cheeseburger. 'Yes, Joey, she is.'

'I would be sad if Todd or Kevin got kilt,' he said, his voice muffled against her shoulder. 'I would cry.'

'So would I, baby,' she said, feeling a cold

panic at the thought of anything happening to any of them. 'So would I.' That's how it is with Ellen, she thought. Gail had been every bit as much Ellen's child as Joey was hers. Giving birth had little to do with it.

'I gotta go now, Mom,' Joey said, squirming out of her too-tight embrace.

★ ★ ★

Within twenty minutes of backing out of his drive, Carl Thompson arrived at the McLeod building, a six-story, faded brick on King Street. Glancing at the name on the order form, he took the ancient elevator up to the fourth floor. Turning left, he strode down the corridor to the office of Anderson Insurance.

A young blond girl teetering on spiked heels, wearing a short, black leather skirt and dangling horseshoe earrings the size of saucers, distractedly showed him where they wanted the phones. (There were two new people starting on Monday, she said) and left him to join the small group already gathered around the man in the fishnet sweater who was down on one knee beside a stack of canvasses.

'We've got a real good buy on this one,' he said, referring to a seascape, assuring them that this was one of his most 'popular' works.

When he got no takers he moved on to the next, turning back the canvasses, one by one, like he was selling wallpaper. Most of the interest seemed to be coming from the women in the office while the men were standing around with their hands in their pockets, looking 'cool', but not entirely unimpressed, Carl noted.

'Got anything with a barn in it?' the girl with the earrings piped up, and Carl had to suppress a grin. He set his tool kit on the gray carpet beside him and settled down to work, now and then glancing up with mild interest at the proceedings.

He knew a guy once who did this for a living. He said the broker had a studio where he employed young, talented and starving artists who had a knack for copying the work of the masters, who could work fast, and to order. A little change here and there, a cloud added, an extra rooftop, just to keep things on the up and up. They were original oils, just the same, and sold like hotcakes all across the country.

'I do have a lovely farm scene,' the salesman said, and the girl with the earrings crouched low in her bottom-hugging skirt, and the earrings swung, making Carl think amusedly of a poor old horse out there somewhere walking around barefoot.

'I can tell you have a real eye for art, Miss . . . '

'Cindy,' she said. 'Cindy Miller.' She smiled, clearly pleased at his astute observation of her good taste.

The guy was good. He knew how to play his audience. Carl went back to work, work he'd been at so long he could do it with his eyes shut, and thought about Myra. She'd cried out in her sleep again last night. And the headaches were getting worse. He was worried about her. He wasn't at all convinced, even though she and Ellen were close, that it was all to do with Gail's murder.

Maybe a little vacation was in order. Just the two of them. He had some time coming. The boys could stay with his mother. She'd grab at the chance to spoil them rotten, and they loved being with her.

'That's some dandy scratch you got there, fella,' one of the older men commented, causing Carl to look up. 'Get in a scrap with your girlfriend, did you?'

This was met with a few snickers.

Carl's attention was drawn to the puffy gouge that started just under the man's left eye and traveled down to the corner of his mouth. The dark makeup didn't begin to hide it.

Looking momentarily bewildered, the salesman touched a hand to his face, then let out a low chuckle. 'A favorite aunt — at least, she used to be — gave me a Siamese cat for my birthday. I don't think it's going to work out,' he joked.

★ ★ ★

There'd been a cancellation, and the receptionist had called her back in the afternoon to tell her if she could get there in the next half hour, the doctor would see her.

Now, sitting in a room with others who also waited, she picked up a dated *Reader's Digest* and began thumbing through the pages, trying unsuccessfully to ignore her pounding head. She stopped at an article titled 'Helping Friends Who Grieve.' She began to read, and it was then that she had her first blackout.

She didn't know that's what it was, of course, couldn't know that her body had jerked spasmodically in the chair, causing heads to turn in her direction, or that the magazine had slipped from her grasp and fallen to the floor.

The episode lasted mere seconds.

'Are you all right, dear?' the elderly woman sitting in the chair next to her said, leaning toward her, laying a blue-veined hand on

Myra's. Her thready voice was filled with concern and not a little nervousness.

'What?'

'You looked like — something frightened you very badly just now.'

'Oh. No, I — I'm fine, thank you.' Seeing the *Reader's Digest* at her feet, Myra bent to pick it up. As she straightened, the room went out of focus, beige walls hanging with framed degrees, diplomas and medical illustrations tilting crazily. Spots danced before her eyes.

After a moment, the awful sensations left her. Her hands were clammy and trembling as she gripped the magazine.

What's happening to me?

She was afraid to look up, afraid to see everyone staring at her. Dropping her eyes, she began again turning the pages in the magazine, pretending to read.

She was grateful when her name was called.

14

'Angela, honey, don't you think that sweater's just a tad too small for you?' Lieutenant Mike Oldfield said, sitting at the formica kitchen table, drinking his second cup of coffee of the morning. He watched his sleepy-eyed daughter scurrying about the room, taking a quick gulp of milk in lieu of breakfast, gathering up her books and stuffing them into her bookbag.

Though she was only eleven, she was already starting to develop breasts, little buds that pushed at the yellow fabric of her sweater, hinting at the lovely young woman, that, as far as Mike was concerned, she was too-fast becoming. It scared the hell out of him.

The vision exploded when she wiped the milk mustache from her upper lip with the back of her hand. 'Oh, Daddy, I like this sweater, it's warm.' Giving a swish of her caramel-colored, slightly scraggly hair, she awkwardly shoved her arms into the orange sleeves of her neon green jacket. 'I gotta go,' she said. She planted a kiss on his cheek, simultaneously plucking a half-slice of toast from the plate. 'I'll miss my bus.' She gave him a dimpled grin. 'You need a shave, Daddy. Your face feels scratchy.'

He heard the door slam. It was all Mike could do not to go after her and make her go back upstairs and change into something baggy and unattractive.

Outside, the voices of children rang out like happy geese. A moment later he heard the rumble of the school bus arriving, the hiss of airbrakes, and moments after that, silence.

Why couldn't she just remain his little girl, always? He understood her as a child. He could deal with that. He could protect her. Sometimes he felt so damned inadequate. A girl needed a mother. But Karen had abandoned them when Angela was only two; she barely remembered her mother, though she kept the picture Mike had given her on her nightstand, and tried to understand.

He wondered if Karen had ever become the actress she'd wanted to be. He'd never seen her in anything.

He was thinking about this, putting the video he'd made at the cemetery in its plastic case, when the phone rang.

He took the call in the livingroom. It was long distance, from a Detective Shannon at N.Y.P.D. He was sorry to call him at home, he said, but he was having a little problem that maybe Mike could help him out with.

Mike picked up the blue mixing bowl from the sofa and set it on the floor. A few uncooked kernels of corn rolled around on the bottom of the bowl. He settled himself on the sofa. 'Whatever I can do, Sergeant,' he said.

Before getting to the crux of the call, the detective tossed Mike a few crumbs, related to him the grotesque fact that Gail Morgan's killer had painted her face up to look like a clown's as a parting gesture. It was the one piece of evidence they were keeping under wraps, the detective said. The one detail that might help them nail the bastard. The sister was in New York, he said, had dug herself in at the victim's apartment, was going around asking questions.

So there was the problem, Mike thought.

'I'm expecting her any minute now,' Shannon said. 'I can set my watch. The woman is obsessed.'

'The landlady found the victim, didn't she?'

'We've sworn her to secrecy.'

'And you think it'll take.'

'Who knows? Let's hope so.' Not that he wasn't sympathetic, of course he was, but there was nothing more they could tell her. What the hell did she think she could do that they weren't already doing? Never mind that they weren't already up to their eyeballs in unsolved killings. 'She doesn't even know her way around the city, for Christ's sake,' the detective barked. 'She'll only end up getting herself hurt. Or worse, ending up another statistic, like her sister.'

Clearly, Shannon wanted Mike to get her off his back. Because Mike had been the one to have to tell her that her sister wasn't coming home this Christmas, she had somehow become his responsibility. He felt a stirring of resentment.

'You asking me to travel to New York and bring her back here, Sergeant?' Mike asked, not bothering to keep the sarcasm from his voice. 'What should I charge her with? Harassment?'

'That won't be necessary, Lieutenant.' Mike heard the grin in his voice. 'I think she's planning on going home tomorrow, anyway — not that I'm kidding myself we've seen the last of her. She's one driven lady. With a little luck, though, maybe I pushed her in a different direction.'

'What do you mean?'

'I told her her sister's killer wasn't necessarily one of our own resident wackos. He could just as easily be someone from your neck of the woods — no pun intended. What is it — an hour's flight from there? Even if he drove, it's no big deal. An old disgruntled boyfriend, maybe, ticked off at her success, feeling thrown aside. So he follows her to New York. Or maybe it was just some nutso fan. Look at that nut who shot the president because he wanted to impress Jodie Foster. And look at what happened to John Lennon. It wasn't any secret, Lieutenant, that the girl was singing at the Shelton Room. She'd had plenty of media play.'

He promised to talk to Ellen Harris when she returned, which had been his intention anyway. He hung up slowly, a frown furrowing his dark brows.

He hadn't thought of that. Hadn't considered that the killer might be someone living right here in Evansdale.

15

Under dusky, purple skies, the old Victorian house sat well back from the road, all but hidden by tall, foreboding pines. The house might have appeared vacant but for one lone light in an upstairs window.

The man stared angrily at his reflection in the bath-room mirror, examining the infected wound on his face. The mirror was small and cracked, and his narrow face looked as if it had been sliced down the middle and put back together just a fraction off center, like a face in a Picasso painting.

'Bitch,' he muttered, squeezing a little of the ointment from the tube onto his finger, then gingerly dabbing it on the raised, puckered flesh that ran from just under his left eye down to one corner of his mouth.

The wound was hot and throbbing to his touch. He shouldn't have put makeup on it.

Debby Fuller had left her own, similar mark on him. 'Oh, my God, honey,' his mother had cried when he got home that night, 'Whatever happened to your poor face?' He fed her some story involving barbed wire and a football while she fluttered about him, washing away the dried blood, applying antiseptic. He could still feel her cool, gentle hands on his face.

Later, when she found out what had happened, she'd turned on him, banished him from her life. She sent him here. 'Let Mattie handle you,' she'd said, tossing his clothes into a cardboard suitcase. 'I can't anymore.'

He knew she was glad to be rid of him, that he cramped her style. He also knew she'd begun to be afraid of him; he could see it in her eyes. It pleased him that she was.

Only the thought of prison had made him go. He could almost hear the steel doors clanging closed on him, shutting him in, and he knew he could never, ever handle being caged up like that, like an animal. So he'd gone without much of a fight, fully intending on returning as soon as things died down a little.

He could see his mother now, sitting at the vanity, sliding the tube of ruby red lipstick over her full lips, smacking them together softly in the mirror. Before leaving the house, she would bend down and kiss his cheek lightly so as not to smudge her makeup. Her perfume would linger inside his head long after she was gone. 'How do I look, sweetie?' she always asked him, her hand going coquettishly to the soft fluff of blond hair that framed her pretty face.

That was when he was a little kid. She didn't ask later. Sometimes he could make her screw up her makeup just by staring at her in the mirror.

His mother was a fool, a painted whore who allowed men to use her. Sometimes he could hear the ugly sounds of their lovemaking through his thin bedroom wall. His hands balled into fists with the memory, his eyes darkening in the cracked mirror.

Debby Fuller was like his mother — except that she thought *he* was the fool. Teasing him, coming on to him the way she had, hips swaying, breasts jiggling under the thin pink tee shirt. 'Hi, Alvin,' she sang that day he'd been standing in the school parking lot beside his car — an old, blue Ford Comet Lili had bought him. 'I wish it could be a Porsche, baby,' she'd said as they stood together on the sidewalk looking at it. 'But at least it'll get you around until we can afford something better.' She had a new boyfriend and this was her way of asking him to lay off — a bribe. *Don't ruin this one for me, okay, baby? Don't scare this one off.*

The car was okay — rusting and noisy as hell, but it ran, and his mother could always be counted on to come up with a few bucks from her tips for gas. She was right — it did get him around. It got him around that snot, Debby Fuller. He'd fixed that little tease. Maybe he ought to pay her another visit, he thought, not for the first time. He grinned, thinking about it, forgetting for the moment the scratch on his face, wondering if sweet Debby would recognize him after all these years. Maybe she'd even be glad to see him.

His grin froze as a high, thin moan reached him. He turned from the mirror and stepped into the hallway, his eyes narrowing with hate and fear. He stared at the closed door at the end of the hall.

'B-o-o-y,' the feeble voice called out, and his face flamed. *Boy.* What she'd always called him. Never by his real name. He took a single step toward the closed door. *Shut up, you old bag, just shut the hell up!* He'd go in there, go in there right now and finish her off — except he didn't want to see her eyes. They frightened him. They always had.

He knew that's what she was trying to do — make him go to her so she could set her evil gaze on him and bring him down. Well, it wasn't going to work.

He was in control now.

Stepping back into the bathroom, with its filthy, rust-stained facilities, he opened the small drawer built into the sink enclosure.

Gazing down at his growing collection of souvenirs, he picked up a rhinestone earring from among the mound of trinkets, fondled it, then exchanged it for a slim, silver bracelet, then for a locket with a picture of a man and a little boy inside, and finally for a pretty, red plastic hairclip. There were a couple of watches, some rings, a beaded bow he'd torn from a shoe.

His little trophies, his treasures.

They helped to calm him.

★ ★ ★

Alvin closed the drawer and took the red wig from the counter and fitted it over his own thinning hair. Patting it smooth, he reached for the tube of lipstick.

He needed a new Debby. Now. Tonight. A sense of urgency filled him, an urgency so strong it made him ignore the inner voice that warned him of the danger of hunting so close to home.

Downstairs, he thumbed through the phone book, dialed a number. Hanging up, he smiled to himself. He'd hit it on the first try.

Luck was with him.

16

The instant Doug Neal opened his door to her, Ellen knew he was well on his way to drunken oblivion. When she told him who she was, he practically fell on her. 'Have a drink with me, Ellen,' he said, his voice thick with booze and emotion. 'Have a drink in memory of poor, li'l Gail.'

'No thanks,' she said, stepping past him into the apartment. 'But you go ahead.'

A grand piano dominated the room. Music books and sheet music were strewn everywhere piled on chairs and a table against the far wall. On the floor, beside a rumpled cot where he'd obviously been lying before she disturbed him, sat an overflowing ashtray and a near-empty whiskey bottle, both within easy reach.

Ellen's gaze lingered momentarily on the pale amber liquid in the bottle. She imagined how it would burn going down, soon spreading through her, flooding her senses with a lovely numbness. She resisted the temptation and put the thought firmly from her mind.

Doug sat heavily on the cot and lowered his

head to his hands. 'I loved her, you know. I really loved her. Do you think she knows, Ellen?' He looked up at her in confused torment.

'I'm sure she does, Doug,' Ellen said, sitting down beside him, knowing intuitively that Doug Neal was not the man she was looking for. Nor would he be able to shed any light on who that man might be.

Ellen stayed a while, talking, but mostly listening until the bottle was empty, and gradually his words drifted into an incoherent mumble. When she left, he was sound asleep, snoring loudly, his mouth fallen open. Ellen covered him with a blanket, and for safety's sake put his cigarette and matches out of harm's way on the mantel. At least he'd have to sober up enough to go looking for them, she thought as she returned to the apartment to dress for an evening at the Shelton.

17

'Thank you, Jesus,' Cindy Miller said aloud as the nerve-grating, torturous whine and wheeze of the vacuum cleaner was abruptly cut off. She wished it would take its last gasp so they'd buy a new one. They were so damn cheap around here. That machine was probably as old as the building. Even when Edie turned the thing off you went on hearing it inside your head for the next fifteen minutes.

In reality, other than the soft buzz of the overhead fluorescent lights and the rustling of paper as Cindy sat at her desk stuffing dunning letters into envelopes, the building was silent — until seconds later, when she heard the shuffling of feet, and the *clunk*, *clunk* of the vacuum being shoved into the broom-closet.

'Taking off, are you, Edie?' Cindy called out, taking a quick drag off her cigarette, resting it in the ashtray's groove to reach for more of the window envelopes.

A smiling Edie came into the office, shrugging into her shapeless cloth coat. Edie Carr, a small, slightly stooped woman, had been cleaning these offices since long before Cindy was born. Cindy knew Edie had it tough, yet she was always quick with a smile. Always so darned nice.

'Yes, dear, Harry is coming to pick me up,' she said, tugging an olive green knit hat over her graying dark hair.

'Lucky you.' Cindy set the envelope down and propped her chin in her hands. 'I have to take the bus.'

'Oh, dear, it's much too cold to stand around waiting for a bus. We can give you a lift if you like. Harry won't mind,' she added uncertainly.

Cindy took her off the hook. 'No, thanks, anyway, Edie. I have to get these bills out. I'm a little behind. We've been pretty busy lately, and I'm going on vacation next week.'

'Good for you. You work too hard, anyway. A pretty young girl like you ought to be having a bit of fun for herself.' Edie still had a hint of Scottish accent, even after all these years. She'd come from Glasgow, she'd told Cindy, when she was just sixteen. From time to time she talked about going back for a visit — she still had friends and relatives back home — but she'd been saying that for the five years Cindy had worked here, and God knew how long before that, and she hadn't gotten there yet. Probably never would. Harry sounded like a jerk.

'I'm taking Jody to Disneyland,' Cindy blurted. Just hearing herself say it sent a rush of excitement coursing through her. She'd never been out of Evansdale, not even as far as Bangor. 'I've been saving all year. It'll give Mom a little break, too,' she added, like she needed to justify such an extravagance.

'That it will,' Edie said, her smile widening, revealing a dark space where her tooth used to be. 'It sounds like a wonderful trip for both of you. How is the wee lad?'

'Great. He's three now and into everything. Mom can hardly keep up to him.' Her mother had taken care of Jody practically from the day Cindy brought him home from the hospital. Though she knew her mom was crazy about Jody, he was still a handful, and her mom wasn't getting any younger. It made Cindy feel guilty sometimes, especially when her mom's arthritis got to acting up, but she didn't have a hell of a lot of choice. She had to make a living. She hadn't laid eyes on Jody's father since she'd sprung the news on him that she was three months pregnant.

'I'll bet he's a wonderful little lad,' Edie said. 'A child is so precious. And your mom?'

'Good, too, except for a touch of arthritis in her shoulders. Tomorrow's her birthday. I bought her a painting. A beautiful farm scene. Mom used to live on a farm when she was a kid, you know. I'd show you, Edie, but it's all wrapped.' She gestured toward the photocopier against which the painting stood, lovingly gift-wrapped, topped with a big blue and silver bow. 'You want some coffee, Edie? There's still some left in the pot.'

'No, thank you, dear. No time.' She patted Cindy's arm. 'I just know she'll love her gift. You're real lucky to have your mom, Cindy. And she's lucky to have you. Now, don't stay too late, dear. There'll be work when you're dead and gone, as me own mom used to say.' She was moving toward the door, working her reddened hands into knitted gloves with blue and red striped cuffs, like children's gloves. 'Good night, now. Harry doesn't like me to keep him waiting.'

'Night, Edie. Take it easy,' Cindy called to her.

With Edie gone, the building seemed to drop into a deeper silence. Not that it bothered Cindy. She liked to work late. She always got more done after the others were gone. She grinned to herself and reached for another cigarette. Besides, it was the only time she got to smoke at her desk. Old Alice would have a fit if she knew.

For the next hour, while cigarettes mostly burned themselves out in the ashtray, Cindy worked steadily, her honey-blond head bent over the growing stack of stuffed envelopes to her right, practiced hands flying. But her thoughts were far away, drifting pleasantly to visions of castles, fairy tale jungles, warm, sandy beaches, and Jody's face lit up in wonder and delight.

Once, hearing the faint hitch and grumble of the elevator down in the bowels of the building, her head went up. Someone else working late, she thought as the elevator continued its climb up through the building, groaning noisily on metal cables.

It surprised Cindy to hear it stop on her own floor, to hear the doors slide open. Shit! She grabbed up the ashtray and slipped it into her desk drawer while trying to fan away the smoke. She waited to hear the inevitable footsteps approaching, but there was no further sound.

Must be *some* light walker, Cindy thought, but at least it wasn't battle-axe Alice, whose step was as heavy as her way. Cindy got up from her chair and went to stand in the doorway, half expecting to see someone in the corridor, but it was empty. She peered down the hallway in the direction of the elevator, her horseshoe earrings swaying with the turn of her head.

The hallway was dimly lit and steeped in

shadow, due to a couple of burned-out fluorescent lights the management had never bothered to replace. Kind of spooky, Cindy thought, though it had never struck her that way before. A small trickle of unease stirred in her stomach. Someone *had* to have gotten off that elevator. It didn't damn well come up here on its own. It didn't push its own buttons.

To Cindy's left was one other office (a cubbyhole, really) rented by a private eye, a sleezy type who had a fondness for brown polyester and slicked-back hair. He leered at her whenever they met in the halls. He gave her the creeps. Al Matchett, his name was.

When she complained about his behavior to Alice, her supervisor said, 'What do you expect, dressing the way you do?' But just because she liked wearing sexy clothes, that didn't give anyone the right to hassle her. Not that he actually had.

Well, it obviously wasn't dear old Al who got out of the elevator. He would have had to pass by her door to get to his office. She might not have minded so much if he was more of a James Garner type who was sort of old but very appealing.

The office to her right was vacant, had been for a month now. Probably wanted too much rent. Shrugging, Cindy went back to her desk. Must have been some smart-ass kids playing around down in the basement, pushing the elevator buttons, then jumping back. Big joke. Or else some kind of malfunction.

She sat unmoving for several seconds, head cocked, listening. Then she retrieved the ashtray from the drawer, lit another cigarette, and went back to work.

Ten minutes later, she crushed the cigarette out and stood up. She began winding elastics double around the stacks of envelopes now ready for stamping. Setting them on the desk, she dug her fingers into the back of her neck, massaged, trying to work out the knots. Her shoulders ached, and her stomach was crying out for nourishment; she decided to wait until morning to put the letters through the machine.

She dialed the familiar number, waited. 'Hi, Mom. Just wanted to let you know I'm just about finished up here. I'll be home shortly.' Looking out at the darkness beyond the window, she decided to hell with the expense, she'd take a cab home. 'Jody being good?'

'An angel,' her mother said cheerfully. 'He's waiting up for you. All bathed and in his jammies. I've made your favorite — lasagna.'

'Great. I'm starved.' Edie's right, she thought. I am lucky. So very lucky. 'I love you, Mom.'

Her mother laughed, but she sounded pleased. 'Maybe you better wait till you taste the lasagna, honey. Oh, by the way, you had a phone call. Some man — didn't leave his name. I told him you were working late.'

There were a few guys it could have been — no one special. Once bitten, twice shy, as they say. She didn't speculate. She set the envelopes on the table beside the postage meter.

And had a sudden, overpowering sense of someone behind her. She whirled around.

No one there. She was quite alone.

Suddenly Cindy wanted nothing so much as to be out of here, to be at home with her mom and Jody, sitting in their bright, cozy kitchen eating lasagna. Snapping up her coat from the rack, she put it on, slipped her stockinged feet into her high, yellow suede boots, then phoned for a cab. Finally, gathering up her purse and the painting, and, taking one last glance behind her at the waiting desks, the silent typewriters, the beige-colored divider, behind which Mr. Anderson's own office was located, she switched off the lights and closed the door. She was just about to lock it when she remembered the ashtray. Wouldn't do to leave that there for old Alice to find when she came in in the morning. She could practically hear the mutterings that would follow about 'Cindy's filthy habit,' and the windows being raised to the hilt, subjecting everyone to the cold, so they would all be mad at Cindy, too. She wished she *could* quit smoking. She'd tried a bunch of times. She guessed she was just too hyper.

Well, she'd wash out the damned ashtray, but first things first, she thought, crossing the hall to the washroom. Standing the painting against the wall by the sink, she entered one of two tiny cubicles. The place smelled of Lysol, blown even stronger by the heat pouring through the vents. Either you suffocated in this mausoleum, or you froze.

She thought how nice it would be to work in a modern, air-conditioned office, with carpets you sank into, exotic plants, and, of course, computers. Welcome to the nineties. But good jobs were hard to come by, she thought, setting her purse on the toilet-tank, hitching her skirt up and her panties and pantyhose down. She guessed she was lucky to have this one. The money wasn't so great, but they were a good bunch to work with — even Alice Fisher was mostly okay, as long as you didn't get on her bad side.

Sitting there, the quiet crowded in on her.

'Knock it off,' she said aloud, putting herself back together hastily, flushing, hearing the rush of water clanking and grumbling down through the plumbing system. 'You're spooking yourself.' It was probably all that talk about that singer getting murdered, especially from her mom, that was freaking her out. You couldn't turn on the T.V. without hearing something about it. That it happened miles away in New York City didn't seem to matter. It was enough to know she had been from around here.

Cindy had her hand on the door when she heard the outside washroom door groan slowly open, saw the swath of darkness slide across the floor at her feet. The darkness fell away as the door closed.

Her hand shot back, touched her blouse. *Stop it! So, someone else is working late. Big deal! You heard them yourself come up in the elevator. No, Cindy. What you heard was the elevator stop on this floor. You didn't see anyone.*

Cindy licked her lips, cocked her head at the floor, listened. Then, 'Edie, that you?'

No answer.

She could hear the dripping of a tap. And the hiss of hot air escaping the vents seemed louder, even over the drumming in her ears.

150

When the woman's legs came into view in the space under the door, Cindy went weak with relief. She almost laughed at her foolishness.

What she actually managed was a nervous grin.

She couldn't see much of the woman's legs, just enough to see they were thick and muscled, the feet clad in God-awful black, laced shoes, the kind her grandma used to wear. No one on this floor wore shoes that ugly, not even Alice. Even Edie's floppy loafers were more attractive.

No, it wasn't Edie out there.

Then who?

Maybe Al Matchett hired himself a new secretary. Hardly seemed his type, with those legs.

Unexpectedly, the shoes began turning in her direction until whoever it was was facing her, standing toe to toe, just as if the door were not between them.

'The other one's free,' Cindy called out, her eyes riveted on the shoes. For several long seconds they did not move. Then they went out of view, each footfall soft and deliberate. Now quiet.

But she was still out there. She wasn't using the can or washing up, so what was she doing? What was she waiting for? And why the hell doesn't she say something?

Cindy's heart was beating in earnest now, her palms sweaty. She tried to calm down. *You're being nuts! You can't stay in this john forever. Besides, you're going to miss your cab if you haven't already, and all because you're an idiot.* But all her self-chastising didn't stop her from holding her breath as she warily pushed the door open, a tentative smile of greeting on her face. 'Hi,' she said, too brightly, 'I thought I was the only one working late ton . . . ' Cindy's words trailed off as she looked up at the red-haired woman in the long, black trench coat standing at the mirror. Her head was turned slightly away, but Cindy could see her profile in the glass, could see the raised, angry scratch that ran down one side of her face.

Something familiar about that.

She had a sudden urge to grab the painting and run, but something held her there. Then, slowly, the woman turned from the mirror. She smiled. 'Hello, Cindy.'

Her voice sounded kind of odd for a woman, sort of like Dustin Hoffman's in *Tootsie*, only darker. And Cindy wasn't laughing. *How does she know my name? Such weird eyes, the color of weak tea, glittering as they took her in.* 'I — I don't think we've met. Are you new here?' Cindy's own smile wavered. She glanced involuntarily at the painting standing against the wall, took a backward step. 'Who — who are you?'

But she knew. She knew. And he recognized that she did, and the smile widened, blood-red lips extending over predatory teeth, so chilling, so utterly devoid of warmth or mercy, it made Cindy's mouth go dry as dust, and her heart wither with terror.

'I'm the big, bad wolf, Cindy,' he said. 'I'm the bogeyman in your worst nightmares.'

And then he came at her.

★ ★ ★

Over the next two hours, the phone rang intermittently in the office of Anderson Insurance. At twenty past midnight, a distraught Ruth Miller telephoned police to report her daughter missing. 'She didn't come home from work,' she cried. 'That's not like Cindy. She would have called back if she was going anywhere afterward.'

'How old is your daughter, ma'am?'

'Twenty-three.'

There was a pause, then Ruth heard the boredom she'd half-expected creep into the policeman's voice. 'I'm sorry, ma'am, but there's really nothing we can do at this point. Your daughter's of age, and if she decides not to come straight home from work, that's her prerogative. I'm sorry. I'm sure you'll be hearing from her. She's probably trying to call you right . . . '

'But you don't understand, officer,' Ruth cut in, trying to keep the hysteria from her voice, even while her frustration and fear mounted. 'Cindy did call me,' she said. 'She was on her way home. I made lasagna. I told her — '

'She must have met up with friends,' he said with studied patience. 'Look, Mrs. Miller, I know you're worried about your daughter, but from experience I can almost promise you she'll come strolling in in the next hour or two with a perfectly reasonable explanation. Just calm yourself and try to get some rest, okay?'

'It's my birthday tomorrow,' she said foolishly.

'Happy birthday, ma'am. Got another line ringing. Got to go. If she still hasn't returned home by this time tomorrow night, give us a call back.'

The line went dead.

18

Ellen had been sitting at a small table in the Shelton Room for the last hour, sipping on a club soda and people-watching — purposeful people-watching. She'd worn the teal blue knit suit Gail had bought her for Christmas, choosing silver chains and matching earrings to complete the ensemble. Standing before the full-length mirror back at the apartment, she'd thought of herself in battle-dress.

Up on stage, a jazz combo played energetically for the small crowd who had shown up to hear them. Ordinarily, Ellen liked good jazz, but tonight it was no more than background noise, mingling with the subdued drone of conversation, the tinkling of glasses around her as she again scanned the room, discreetly but intently studying the faces of the men for the one that did not quite fit in, for the one that might be 'marked'.

She knew it wasn't likely she'd spot him so easily, or even that he'd show up here, yet each time the door behind her opened to let in more customers, Ellen turned in her chair to look.

'Not a bad crowd for a week night,' the darkly attractive waitress said pleasantly. 'Can I get you anything else?'

Looking down at her empty glass, Ellen felt obliged to order another high-priced club soda she didn't want. 'Miss,' she said, as the waitress started to move away, 'could I speak to you for a moment?'

The girl turned back, her eyes questioning. 'Sure,' she answered.

'I'm Ellen Harris. Gail Morgan was my sister. I'd like to ask you a couple of questions, if you don't mind. I won't take long. I know you're busy.'

The girl's hand had gone to her mouth. 'Oh, God, I'm so sorry. It's just so horrible what happened to her. I haven't been able to sleep since. All the girls are afraid to go to their cars at night.'

Ellen nodded. 'It's a good idea to be careful. May I ask your name?'

'Mary. Mary Dewer.'

'Mary, do you remember seeing anyone, well, who was strange, in here that night. Someone alone, probably. Maybe he's been in here before — more than once — watching Gail perform.'

'No,' she said, she didn't recall anyone like that. The police had already asked her. 'I was probably far too busy to notice anything but frantic hands waving for more drinks, anyway.' The same went for the other waitresses, she said. 'Saturday nights are crazy in here. I'm sorry. Really. I wish I could be more help.'

'So do I, Mary,' Ellen replied, thinking if it were a woman alone someone would have noticed, considering the sidelong glances and outright stares she'd been attracting from the moment she sat down. 'But thanks anyway,' she smiled.

'No problem.'

'You take care now, Mary,' Ellen said. She imagined she saw the girl shiver.

★ ★ ★

At intermission, Ellen spotted Bob Feldon, the manager standing at the bar. Gail had introduced him to her once. A portly man, Feldon was elegantly attired in an Italian silk and wool blend suit, and black bow tie. Even as he was speaking to a male customer seated at the bar, his shrewd eye wandered over his domain, flickered past her. *He knows I'm here*, Ellen thought. *He's trying to decide how best to handle the situation*. Ellen left her table, removing his dilemma.

As she approached the bar, he put his hand out to her immediately, trying for just the right tone of sadness and surprise. 'Mrs. Harris, I didn't know you were in New York. I wish it could be under different circumstances.' He was effusive in his offer of condolences, kind to a fault, even insisting on picking up the tab for all her meals while she was in New York. Yet beneath it all, Ellen sensed a certain stiffness and knew he really didn't want her here. She supposed she served as an unpleasant reminder of what had happened to their star performer, and no one wanted to be reminded. Bad for business. As if she gave a damn.

At the far end of the long oak bar, the bartender was studiously polishing a glass, but listening, his image reflected in the smoky mirror behind him. Ellen made a mental note to speak with him before she left.

'I never saw her with anyone,' Bob Feldon was saying in reply to her question, 'Miss Morgan always went straight home after her performance, as far as I know. She was the consummate professional. Oh, there were a few hopefuls who would send notes or flowers to her dressing room from time to time, wanting her to join them for drinks and whatnot, but that goes with the territory. Miss Morgan always ignored that sort of thing. Though she did make herself available to *genuine* fans, signing autographs, holding still for pictures, and the like. What she did on her own time, Ellen — may I call you Ellen? — I couldn't say.' He then went on to explain, as had the waitress, that the police were already here, had already questioned everyone, including, he added with a wince, some of the Saturday night regulars. This last, Ellen knew, was meant to discourage any further annoyances she might have in mind and send her on her way.

Let the police handle it, she heard Paul's voice echo in her mind. *Let them do their job*. She pushed the voice away.

Ellen didn't think Feldon would actually go so far as to throw her out. Wouldn't look too good in the papers, which was actually where she would go if he presented himself as any serious obstacle in her search for Gail's killer.

Letting none of this show on her face, she thanked him for his time and his kindness and wandered down to the end of the bar. After several minutes in fruitless discussion with the bartender, she went back to her table, and thought about the phone call Sandi had told her about. 'Do you know me?' the caller had said, reciting the title of Gail's new song, using it in a symbolic, ominous way.

The song itself held no clue for her. Though the melody was haunting and poignant, the story itself was simply of a

159

young woman in love with a man who she is sure doesn't know she's alive. A familiar, bittersweet story, the words and sentiment simple, yet, told in Gail's unique style with all the richness of her talent, it had touched hearts.

Could the story have been Doug Neal's in reverse? Ellen wondered. Was it possible she'd been too quick in dismissing him as a suspect? She pictured him as he'd been sitting with his head in his hands, vowing his love for Gail.

Had he perhaps loved her too much?

He wouldn't be the first man to fall obsessively for a woman, then, when she could not return his feelings, resort to madness, to evil. And Ellen had gotten the distinct impression that Doug Neal's feelings for Gail went far beyond friendship.

Hadn't Sandi suggested as much?

And then Ellen remembered Doug asking her if she thought Gail knew that he loved her. Surely, if the pianist was her killer, it was not a question he would have needed to ask. For Gail would have known, wouldn't she?

Round and round her thoughts went, like mice on a treadmill, going nowhere.

The music had stopped without her noticing, the instruments now abandoned to the empty stage. Customers were leaving. A few glanced her way as they passed her table. The place was closing.

Gathering up her purse, Ellen got her coat from the coat-check girl. She took her time putting it on, buttoning it. When, finally, she was the only customer left in the place, she went over to talk to the doorman. She had nothing to lose. So far she'd batted exactly zero.

He'd been made aware of who she was; Ellen wasn't surprised. A. J. Brooker looked like an ex-football player miscast in formal clothes, and Ellen guessed if it became necessary, he would have little trouble doubling as a bouncer, which was probably the idea. He was friendly enough, though, and didn't seem to mind talking to her. Seemed eager, in fact.

Yes, he told her, he was on the door on the night in question. 'I've had a little time to mull things over since the cops were in here questioning everyone, and you know, Ellen, there *was* someone in here that night who caught my attention.'

'Oh?' That single word held all the hope that was sustaining her.

'Yeah. Not that I knew the guy. He wasn't one of our regulars. And it might not mean anything.' A.J. buried his hands in his pockets, glanced at the floor and then at Ellen. 'I figured the guy must have had some kind of emergency. Gail Morgan could hold an audience in the palm of her hand. I never saw anyone walk out on her show before.'

'He did that.'

'Yeah. Could be he just wanted to get home. You know, we had quite a storm that night.'

Despite the excitement that was coursing through her, Ellen forced her voice calm. 'Could you describe him, A.J.?'

'Well, other than when he left, I really didn't pay him all that much attention. We were pretty rushed. But I do remember his hair was kind of longish, brown or dark blond, I think. And he wore dark glasses. I might not have noticed him at all if it wasn't for that and the fact that he was alone. We don't get too many loners in here.

'He was sitting right over there,' he said, gesturing toward the table a few feet from them, close to the door.

Close, so he could slip out unnoticed, Ellen thought.

Continuing to stare at the table A.J. had pointed out, Ellen felt a chill pass through her as she tried to envision the stranger he described. A stranger who sat, and watched, and planned.

'Couldn't tell you what he wore, though he must have worn a tie. You can't get in here without a tie.'

Ellen turned back to him. 'Would you go with me in the morning to the police station, A.J.? Tell them what you told me? Maybe they could do a — a composite.'

The doorman frowned, studied his feet. With his head bent toward her, Ellen could see his scalp beneath the crew cut. His head was cut in the same square mold as his body. 'I don't know, Ellen,' he said, looking up at her, 'I would think the eyes are pretty important for that sort of thing' He gave her an apologetic grin. 'You know how they always say the eyes are the windows of a man's soul.'

'This bastard hasn't got any soul,' Ellen said.

Though she'd spoken softly, something in her tone made the doorman blink and shift his feet. 'Maybe you're right, Ellen. All I'm saying is, it would be pretty damn hard for them to come up with a decent likeness when I can't even describe the eyes.'

'We have to try, A.J. Please.'

He shrugged lightly. 'Sure. No problem. I just wasn't sure it was all that important, that's all. Like I said, it might not mean anything.'

'But it might.'

He nodded, conceding the point. 'Listen, Ellen, I'm real, real sorry about what happened to your sister. This has gotta be awful rough on you. She was a great girl. Miss Morgan was special.'

'Yes. Yes, she was.' Ellen's gaze had returned to the chair where Gail's killer had sat — for she was certain now that's who it had been — a monster hidden behind a face undistinguished except for its ordinariness.

'Yes, Ellen, yes,' came the softest whisper at her shoulder, yet so clear she fully expected to see her sister standing there when she swung her head to look. But it was Bob Feldon she saw; he was walking toward them, weaving his way through the maze of tables. 'Just about ready to lock 'er up, are we, A.J.?' he said pointedly. Favoring Ellen with a practiced smile, he moved off.

'Sorry,' A.J. said, glaring contemptuously at his employer's retreating back. 'Have you got your car with you, Ellen?'

'I came in a cab. Maybe you wouldn't mind calling one for me, A.J.'

'I'll do better than that,' he said, taking a

ring of keys from his pocket. 'I'll drop you off. That way I won't have any trouble finding your place in the morning.'

* * *

Ellen was fitting her key into the lock when Mrs. Bloom came padding out into the hallway, belting an old plaid robe around her ample middle. 'I tidied things up some, dear,' she said. 'I hope you don't mind my letting myself in. It wasn't right that you should have to do that.'

The chalk outline of Gail's body was gone from the carpet, leaving in its place only a dark, damp stain. The black magnetic fingerprint powder had all been dusted away, and the bedroom 'put to rights.'

An odd phrase, that, she thought, in the light (or darkness) of things. She supposed it had been unconsciously deliberate on her part that she'd left things as they were. With the evidence of the violence Gail suffered wiped clean, some of the energy of that night had dissipated as well. However well-meaning, Ellen found herself resenting the landlady's interference.

'Thank you, Mrs. Bloom,' she said. 'That was kind of you.'

'No trouble, dear. Oh, by the way you

had a caller earlier.'

'Oh? Who?'

'He wouldn't give his name. He just said he wanted to talk to you. Said he'd catch up with you later.'

'What did he look like?'

'He wore one of them trenchcoats,' the landlady said. 'And dark glasses.'

19

Though the doorman had promised to pick her up at ten, it was eleven when his silver Honda finally pulled up in front of the building, and nearly noon when they arrived at the police station.

Other than some of the players, little had changed about the scene since yesterday, or the day before that. The place was a bedlam. Phones clamoring, men shouting to one another. From somewhere came the tap-tapping of a typewriter Ellen couldn't see. Laughter rang out from the far corner of the room where a black woman sat on the edge of a desk, showing off long, shapely legs clad in net stockings for the benefit of the policeman who was admiring the view with hard, bemused eyes. As if sensing competition, the woman turned and gave Ellen a slow once-over. The policeman's eyes followed.

They passed by a girl of about twelve sitting slouched on a bench, her arms crossed defiantly over her adolescent chest, an expression of surliness on her face.

Beside her, a dark-haired woman who might once have been pretty sat stiffly, her own face impassive. The place smelled of sweat, stale cigarettes, and human desperation. She looked around at the greasy walls hung with yellowing wanted posters, sprawling maps stuck with blue-headed pins. It was like a scene out of some forties' cop movie.

Sergeant Shannon sighed perceptibly as she entered his office, A.J. in tow. He gave the doorman a cursory glance. He looked at his watch. 'You're late, Mrs. Harris.'

'Heavy traffic,' she joked, surprising herself that she still could. She introduced the doorman.

Shannon nodded. Turning a long-suffering, though not unsympathetic smile on Ellen, he said, 'Obviously, you had a change of heart about going home today. No doubt you had a good reason.'

His expression told her he didn't for a second expect one, so it gave her a measure of satisfaction to see his interest perk considerably when she told him why they were here.

Hefting his bulky frame from behind the desk, the detective crossed the room and closed the door on the din outside, leaving only muffled sounds to be heard, and moving shadows to be seen through the opaque glass.

The doorman's growing unease made Ellen wonder for the first time if he'd always operated on the right side of the law. Her gaze traveled to his hands — big hands — quite capable of bouncing an unruly drunk from the premises of the Shelton Room. Or strangling a small woman to death.

Had she really heard Gail whisper, 'Yes, Ellen, yes,' at her shoulder? Or had she imagined it? if she hadn't, could it have been the doorman she was accusing, rather than some mysterious stranger he'd made up?

Stop it! My God, she was beginning to suspect every man she came in contact with. Surely A.J. wouldn't be here with her if he was Gail's killer. Yet, hadn't she heard of murderers who actually took part in the search for their victims?

She wondered again who the man was who came to the apartment last night, the man who refused to give Mrs. Bloom his name. She hadn't mentioned him to A.J, or Sergeant Shannon. There seemed little point. Since the man planned to 'catch up' with her, she would know soon enough. Plenty of people wore dark glasses, didn't they?

'Mr. Brooker is quite right, of course,' the detective was saying, leaning his weight against his desk, beating out a slow tattoo on its edge with his pen, ' . . . about the glasses presenting something of an obstacle in coming up with a good likeness. But since it's all we have at the moment, naturally we'll go with it.' He looked vaguely sympathetic at Ellen, who sank weakly into a chair. 'You never know,' he said, 'could be they're prescription glasses. Maybe someone will recognize him and call in.'

But Ellen knew he thought she was grasping at straws. She didn't care; at least he was going to follow up on it. 'That's the general idea, Sergeant,' she said.

Soon after, leaving A.J. in the hands of the police sketch artist, Ellen took a cab to the CBS studios on Fifty-seventh Street, near Eleventh Avenue.

20

Two hours later, a young girl wearing granny glasses was clipping a microphone to the lapel of Ellen's blue wool jacket. 'If you wouldn't mind just snaking that wire down the inside,' she smiled, rolling the wad of gum she was chewing over in her mouth, giving off a faint scent of Juicy Fruit.

If not for the tangle of cables, the cameras, lights and technicians, Ellen might have been sitting in someone's den or library. Two big, comfy chairs angled toward one another, fronted by a long coffee table with a bowl of silk daisies in the center. To complete the illusion, shelves of books rose up behind her.

The camera rose and dollied in like some strange robot, posturing, seeking her out. Catching a glimpse of herself in the monitor, it startled her to see how pale and drawn she looked, despite the heavy makeup.

Carol Braddock had been standing talking to one of the cameramen. Now she approached Ellen, smiling warmly. As she positioned herself in the other chair, clipping on her own microphone, Ellen could see her mentally preparing herself, buckling in like a seasoned pilot, waiting for the signal for take-off.

She seemed to be lit from the inside, sleek platinum hair coming just to the tops of her bejeweled ears, a froth of peach scarf at her throat, brows expertly arched over clear, green eyes.

Ellen had been deliberately focusing her attention on the interviewer. Now, seeing the cameraman's hand go up, she felt trapped by more than just the heat and glare of the studio lights. Her heart was hammering and her palms were slick with sweat. 'Just follow the red light,' the interviewer had coached her. Ellen wanted to run. *What the hell am I doing here? I'm a private person. I hate being 'out there.' Gail is the performer in the family.* No, Gail *was* the performer, she reminded herself. Just hold that thought. Hold onto it tight.

'Okay?' the interviewer asked, smiling at her with some concern.

Ellen nodded weakly.

'No need to be nervous.' She gave Ellen's hand a reassuring squeeze. Her emerald ring flashed under the lights. 'You'll do just fine. This is your chance, Ellen,' she said, her voice as intimate as if they were old school chums. 'Someone may have seen something. Someone may know something.'

Someone does, she thought. And he just might be watching. She was counting on it. It was part of the reason she was here.

'Remember, Ellen,' the woman said, lowering her voice conspiratorially, 'this madman took something very precious from you. Concentrate on that. Your sister's life is over, and your own will never be the same. Isn't that what you told me?'

'Yes,' Ellen said, sensing an air of unholy excitement in the woman. Not that she was complaining. It was her own decision to do this. No one had forced her. She'd been, in fact, quite prepared to plead to go on. Fortunately, it hadn't been necessary.

Ellen adjusted her jacket, being careful not to dislodge the microphone. Feeling clammy inside her clothes, she let out a long, shuddery breath as the cameraman held up four fingers, then three, two, one . . .

'Good evening. I'm Carol Braddock.' The newswoman's green gaze was steady in the monitor, her voice clear and resonant. 'It has been twelve days now since Gail Morgan's nude body was discovered by her landlady in the bedroom of her semi-basement apartment on New York's East Side. The singer was raped, beaten and strangled.' Each word was a tiny hammer blow against Ellen's heart. 'Police are saying little . . . '

Ellen watched part of the interview with Sergeant Shannon in which he grimly told reporters there were no new leads in the case, but that the investigation was continuing. There was a brief shot of Gail on stage at the Shelton, shifting quickly to the building where she'd lived, zooming in on the window in the alley through which her killer had gained entry. Then Gail's body, draped with a sheet, being solemnly carried from the building on a stretcher, being lifted into the waiting ambulance, while on the snow-packed sidewalk a small crowed looked on. The ambulance pulling away, not speeding, (no need now) sirens silent. A strange dream-like quality to the scene.

The next clip was one Ellen had not seen before, of Mrs. Bloom, orange hair wisping out from beneath her scarf, standing on the steps of her apartment building, wringing her hands, a dozen microphones shoved in her face. ' . . . such a lovely girl . . . everyone loved her . . . no trouble . . . '

Ellen heard her own name spoken as if through a howling wind-tunnel.

'One can't begin to know the degree of suffering Miss Morgan experienced at the hands of her fiendish killer,' Carol Braddock said, her voice emanating with talk-show sensitivity. 'But one thing we do know: her suffering is over now. Gail Morgan is at rest. Unfortunately, the same cannot be said for psychologist Ellen Harris, an only sister of the victim. For Ellen, the tragedy lives on.' Carol Braddock shifted expertly in her chair to face Ellen.

'Ellen, I know this is a difficult time for you, to say the least, but can you share with our viewers what you're feeling right now. I know this must seem an absurd question when the answer should be so obvious, and yet perhaps it will help her killer to understand the terrible pain he has caused you, will help him to — '

'He doesn't care about that,' Ellen said incredulously, snapping a look at her, forgetting for an instant she was being seen by millions of people.

Carol Braddock went perfectly still, silent.

The camera moved in for a close-up, filling the screen with Ellen's face.

'If you could look into his eyes right now, Ellen ... ' — manner and voice intense, persuasive — ' . . . what would you say? What do you want him to know?'

As Ellen shifted her own gaze to look directly into the camera, all her nervousness gradually seeped away. He *was* watching. She didn't know how she knew that, but she did. She knew it with an absolute certainty. In that moment, the cables, the technicians, even the woman beside her, receded to some far place in her mind. There was just her and Gail's killer.

Out there. Watching. Listening.

She spoke slowly, deliberately, in a voice so icy calm she almost didn't recognize it as her own. 'You think you are God,' she began, ' . . . with power over life and death. But you are less than nothing. Deep down, you know that, don't you? My sister wasn't expecting you. You were hiding in her closet. Coiled there, like the cowardly, slithering thing you are. Why don't you come after me, you bastard? I'll be waiting for you.'

★   ★   ★

'I didn't know you were going to do that,' Carol Braddock said tightly as Ellen was getting into her coat. 'I wouldn't have agreed to let you go on if I'd known.'

She was clearly agitated. *She's frightened for me*, Ellen thought, and realized she had misjudged her. 'I know,' she said, remembering that she had told the production assistant that she wanted only to make a special appeal for Gail's killer to come forward, or for assistance from anyone out there who might

176

have seen something, who might know something.

'You're in no way responsible, Ms. Braddock,' Ellen said. 'Nor is your station. I didn't know I was going to say what I did, either.' She didn't know if that was true or not. Either way, it didn't matter. It was done.

On her way out, she heard someone behind her say with a grin in his voice that the phones lines were lit up brighter than the Times Square Christmas tree.

Totally drained and exhausted, Ellen left the building. Darkness had fallen while she was inside. The street lights had come on, casting eerie shadows along the sidewalk. Fewer people were on the street now, their breaths visible in the cold, night air as they hurried to their destinations.

As she stood on the steps, Ellen found herself tensing as each person approached, relaxing again when they passed on by.

She felt vulnerable and alone. And afraid. Like a child who had scared itself, who had gone too far. She felt as she had when she was nine years old, lying in her small bed, hearing Gail's even breathing from across the room, while she waited for the sound of their parents' key in the lock which meant they were home from one more party.

She would squeeze her eyes shut against

the demons that lay in wait in the darkness. She would draw her feet well up under the covers so no cold hand could find them. When the need to pee betrayed her, she would finally shiver from her bed, jumping at her own reflection in the mirror.

I'm not brave, she thought. *Dear Jesus, you know I'm not brave at all. I never was.*

Hugging her coat more tightly about her, Ellen started down the stairs. She had just stepped onto the sidewalk when a car suddenly lurched to a stop at the curb and a man jumped out — a man wearing dark glasses and a trenchcoat. He rushed toward Ellen. She froze. There was no time to think. Instinctively, her hands shot out, catching him full in the chest, sending him sprawling backward on the sidewalk with a grunt. She heard his head hit hard, and the groan of pain that followed.

'Jeez, lady, what did you do that for?' The whine that came through the gasping for breath diminished some of her fear. She approached him warily. 'Who are you?'

'Hartley Greenborn,' he labored. 'I'm a writer with the National Enquirer. Is it okay if I get up now? Or will you hit me again?'

'Yes, you can get up. I'm sorry. Are you all right?'

'Yeah,' he grunted, struggling to his feet,

readjusting his glasses, brushing himself off. 'I think so. I just wanted to ask you a couple of questions, that's all,' he managed, still having a little trouble with his breathing. Obviously, she'd knocked the wind from him.

He was a good six inches shorter than herself, she noted, and wore a fur cap with eartabs. Something Mrs. Bloom hadn't thought to mention.

'I have nothing to say to you,' Ellen said, her heart-beat slowly returning to normal. 'You shouldn't rush at people like that, Mr. Greenborn. You could get hurt. You were at my building last night, weren't you? You spoke to the landlady.'

'Yeah,' he answered, trying not to look pleased with himself, but failing. 'I've been tailing you since you got here. My paper can help you find your sister's killer.'

'How do you know me? And how did you find out I was here?'

'C'mon, Mrs. Harris,' he smiled, a smile meant to ingratiate himself with her, 'give me a little credit for being good at my job, okay?'

It was all she gave him.

While Ellen wanted more than anything to have Gail's killer found, she didn't want her death exploited, or her life dirtied. She supposed he would write whatever struck his fancy, in the end, but he would do it without her help.

⋆ ⋆ ⋆

Alvin was sitting in a bar called Papa Bear's on Evansdale's west side when the news came on the television set that angled down at him from high up on the wall. Before that, there'd been a hockey game on. He couldn't have told you who was playing. Unlike the other patrons in Papa Bear's, Alvin had no interest in sports.

When the interview with Ellen Harris was over, Alvin ordered another beer. He had to will his hand steady before picking it up. After that, he had several more beers, which was unusual for him.

Alvin was quite drunk when he finally left the bar.

21

With nothing left to do in New York, Ellen took a late flight home. After securing the house, she went upstairs on leaden legs, undressed, and slipped under the covers. She was asleep almost at once.

She slept soundly. For once, there were no dreams.

The jangling of the telephone woke her. Her hand fumbled for the receiver, found it. 'Yes,' she muttered thickly, refusing to open her eyes.

'What are you trying to do, Ellen? Get yourself killed? Make yourself his next victim?'

Oh, God, she groaned inwardly. *I don't need this.* She blinked one eye open. Sun was streaming through the curtains, throwing lacy patterns on the floor. 'I'm not dressed yet, Paul,' she said, 'I'll talk to you later, okay?'

'The station was irresponsible in running that,' he went on, as if she hadn't spoken. 'You were led like the proverbial lamb to the slaughter. Don't you see what you're doing, Ellen?'

'No, Paul,' she said woodenly, rising up on

181

one elbow in the bed. Might as well let him have his say. There didn't seem to be much chance of stopping him. 'What am I doing?'

'You're casting yourself in the hero role again. But you can't rescue your little sister this time, dear. It's too late.'

The bitter truth of his words slammed against her heart, bringing her actual, physical pain. She fought back tears. He was right, of course. About both situations. It *was* true she'd always assumed the hero role in the family, dumping booze down the sink in an attempt to get her parents to stop drinking, bringing home straight 'A's, taking on the role of mother to Gail. In short, trying through her own meager efforts to gain back respect for the family. She could intellectualize and analyze with the best of them. It didn't change anything. Her story was one variation of many she'd heard from the other side of her desk.

One which, in a moment of weakness, she'd revealed to Paul. And now he was using her words against her. She'd handed him a new button to push.

As if reading her thoughts, Paul's voice took on a gentler note. 'I know this is terrible for you, Ellen, and I don't mean to hurt you any more than you're already hurting. I just want you to see things more clearly, that's all.

And right now, you're not.'

'She was my sister, Paul. Why can't you understand? I have no intention of letting him get away with — '

'Has it occurred to you,' he cut in, ' . . . that maybe Gail was involved with, well . . . you don't know what she was into, Ellen.'

'Into?' She was fully awake now. It took a moment to understand. Cold anger seeped through her. 'What do you mean, 'into,' Paul?' Her voice was deceptively calm.

'I'm not saying she *was*, of course, but you know what the music business is — prostitution, drugs . . . My God, Ellen, the tabloids are full of . . . you want to find yourself in the middle of . . . ?'

He was still raving when she said 'Go to hell, Paul,' and slammed down the receiver. She was trembling, unable to believe what he'd implied — that Gail was somehow to blame for her own murder.

The phone rang several times over the next hour. Ellen ignored it, finally taking the receiver off the hook. When a little while later she heard the doorbell ring, and looked out the window to see Paul's car in her drive, she went upstairs to take a shower.

★ ★ ★

183

Myra came to the door wearing an oversized, mauve jogging suit. She stared at Ellen standing in her doorway as if she were seeing a ghost. Kenny's and Dolly's 'Islands in the Stream' drifted from the kitchen, along with the tantalizing aroma of turkey soup.

'I've got to get away from here for a while,' Ellen said. 'Can you come with me? I'll wait with you till Joey gets home from school. We can all go to McDonald's for lunch. My treat. Big deal, huh?'

The startled expression left Myra's face as she drew her inside, hugging her like she'd been gone for a year instead of the few days it had actually been. 'Oh, I'm so damn glad to see you. Are you all right?'

'Fine.'

Myra held her at arm's length. 'Like hell you are. You look awful.'

'Thanks.'

'You're welcome. I saw you on the news last night, and I don't mind telling you, I didn't close my eyes till the sun came up.'

'Sorry. I slept like a baby myself. Damned if I know why.' She gave a small, nervous laugh.

The boys were staying with Grandma Thompson, Myra told her. 'Carl thinks we need a vacation by ourselves. Of course, there's no way I'm going anywhere. Not after . . . '

'Don't be silly. Of course you're going. Carl's right. You do need time alone together. It will do you both the world of good. I'll be fine. Really, Myra. You're not to worry.'

'Easy for you to say. Give me five minutes, okay? I'll just run a rake through this mop and dab on some lipstick. I've got coffee on, help yourself. Oh, Ellen, turn the stove off for me, will you?' she called out halfway up the stairs. Then she turned. 'When did you get home, anyway?'

'Last night. Too late to call you. You sure I'm not taking you away from anything?'

'Well, I was feeling a mad compulsion to scrub out the toilet bowl,' Myra grinned, ' . . . but I think if I really put my mind to it, I can walk away.'

They drove in Ellen's blue Sunbird to the McDonald's out near Queen's Park. Passing the clinic, Ellen thought of the clients she'd left in mid-stream and felt a twinge of guilt. But there was nothing she could do about it now — if ever.

Standing at the counter, Myra said, 'Paul called me. He wants me to talk to you. One large fries and a Pepsi, please.' Her voice dropping, she said, 'What if he comes after you, Ellen?'

Ellen knew she was no longer talking about Paul. 'That's the general idea. Don't worry — I'm not without an equalizer.'

Myra's eyes widened. 'Oh, God. You've got a — don't tell me. I don't want to know.'

'Okay.'

The place was deserted but for one man in a business suit and a couple of teenage girls wolfing down Big Macs, exploding into giggles between bites. Ellen smiled to herself, envying them their innocence. *Enjoy it while you can, kids.* A sudden vision of their young faces smiling up at her from a newspaper came unbidden into her mind. A chill went through her and she shook her head to clear the thought.

Setting her tray on the table, Ellen slid into the molded plastic chair. 'I'm really sorry about Paul bothering you, Myra. He's got a lot of nerve.' She watched her friend pry the lid off the Styrofoam cup and pop in a straw. Myra liked to see what she was drinking.

'You won't get an argument from me there,' she said quietly.

Outside the window, a yellow school bus rumbled past, a blur of small faces in the row of windows. Across the road in the park, the bare branches of trees looked stark against the winter sky, as did St. George's church steeple in the distance.

The park benches were empty. Too cold for sitting, especially if you were afflicted with arthritis or rheumatism. Ellen often walked over from the clinic and ate her lunch in the park, and she thought now of the man she'd often seen there feeding the pigeons, his crutches propped against the bench, a faraway smile on his weathered face. She thought too of the elderly woman who sat engrossed in her knitting, chatting animatedly to herself.

Ellen wondered if she would live so long. For despite the sometimes unbearable pain, she apparently didn't really want to die. She'd learned that much standing outside the CBS studios. She must remember to tell Myra about the guy from the National Enquirer. They could both use a laugh. She continued to look over into the park, watching the pigeons waddle about, poking their little beaks at the hard snow, testily competing for whatever scraps could be found.

Hearing Myra's chant: 'Calling Ellen ... earth to Ellen,' she turned from the window. 'Sorry,' she smiled. 'Were you saying something?'

'I asked you what happened between you and Paul.'

'I'd rather not talk about him, Myra — okay? If he calls you again, just hang up.'

'Sure,' Myra said, sounding hurt.

Ellen sighed. 'Okay. He suggested Gail might have been involved with drugs or prostitution, and maybe that's why she's dead.'

Myra held her french fry in midair. Finally, she said, 'My God. What an asshole.'

Ellen grinned. 'You don't like Paul, do you?'

'I think he's a control freak.' She bit off the end of her french fry. 'Sorry. I had no right to say that.'

'Of course you did. You have a right to say whatever you believe.'

Myra stuffed the rest of the french fry into her mouth, reached for another, swished it round in the pool of ketchup on her plate. 'Maybe,' she said without conviction, ' . . . he's just afraid for you. I know I was — am — after hearing you on the news last night baiting that maniac . . . '

Ellen soon turned the discussion around to Myra. She was still having the nightmares, she said, and the headaches. She told Ellen about the blackout she'd had in Dr. Hoffman's office. 'It was the first time anything like that's ever happened to me. To just lose time like that. It's so weird. Dr. Hoffman said it's my nerves. She gave me a prescription for something I can't remember.

188

I don't think it's helping.'

Ellen nodded, not at all sure it wasn't something more serious than nerves causing Myra's problems. 'The vacation will help,' she said, sounding more convinced than she felt.

When Ellen wasn't looking, Myra slickly brought the conversation back to Paul. 'You're probably feeling grateful to him for taking care of the funeral the way he did,' she said. 'But that's his thing, Ellen. He was in his element. You shouldn't feel guilty. Carl and I would have been more than happy to do . . . whatever, but Paul wouldn't let anyone else in.'

'I know,' Ellen said, vaguely remembering the cold, condescending way Paul had treated Myra. What kind of friend was she to let that happen? And now he was using her. 'Myra, thanks for removing the sense of obligation I was still obviously feeling toward Paul.'

'You're welcome. Do you really think he'll give up that easily?'

'I don't know. I hope so. I've got more important things to think about.' With that, she took the pack of cigarettes from her purse. Might as well come out of the closet, so to speak. Watching the look of surprise on Myra's face, she lit up. 'I bought them at the airport coffee shop last night,' she said sheepishly, foolishly implying it was the first she'd smoked, as if it mattered. She blew out the match and set it in the foil ashtray. 'What can I say?'

'It must be two years since you quit.'

'Two and a half, but who's counting?'

'Well, what the hell if it helps.'

'Thanks for not lecturing.'

'Never. And anyway, I'm no one to talk. I've been stuffing my face like I'm planning a major hibernation. I've put on a good ten pounds.'

'It doesn't show.'

'Yeah, right.'

'Well, maybe a little. Tell me about the nightmares.'

'They keep changing. Last night I dreamed I was back in the home and Miss Baddie had me tied to a chair, all 200 pounds of me, and she was gleefully chopping off all my hair. I could see great chunks of it falling on the green tile. I kept trying to catch it. It was awful, just so damned real, Ellen. I was half afraid to look in the mirror when I got up.'

Ellen could see the fear behind her eyes now, a haunting fear. She knew only too well how real dreams could seem. But this was more than just a dream for Myra. It was a memory. A memory of a terrible cruelty inflicted on her in childhood, one that had etched itself forever in her mind.

'I guess I'm doomed to relive it into all eternity, huh?' Myra said, as if reading Ellen's thoughts. 'Funny, though, I haven't for a long time. Though I do have to admit, I've often wondered whatever happened to that miserable old witch since they closed the place down. Did Gail ever talk about her? I mean, I know she went there long after I was out, but . . .'

Ellen didn't mind answering the question, though she could hear in Myra's voice she was sorry she'd asked it. 'No, we hardly ever spoke about the six months she spent in the Evansdale Home. She wanted to put it behind hind her, and that was fine with me. I didn't like thinking about it, either.'

Gail had ended up in the home because of a traffic accident. Myra was there because of her father, who, after molesting her from the time she was eight years old, had gone to his grave denying everything. She knew that that was the hardest for Myra. That, and the fact of her mother calling her a dirty-minded little trouble-maker when she finally did tell. It was why she'd kept running away, and why, when her own body was the only place left to hide, she'd kept on eating.

'Would you girls like this paper?' the man in the business suit said, smiling down at them, setting the folded paper on the table

191

next to them. They thanked him, returning the smile.

'How old would she have been, then?' Ellen asked, when he was gone.

'Who?'

'Miss Baddie. Isn't that what you called her?'

'Oh. Yeah. I don't really know. She always looked old to me. You know, like people do when you're a kid. Yet, in another way, she seemed ageless, like that guy in Oscar Wilde's novel'

'Dorian Gray,' Ellen offered. 'He made a pact with the devil to remain young, while his picture aged.'

'Sounds about right.'

Ellen grinned. 'Well, maybe she's long dead by now. What was her real name? Do you remember?'

'We were always instructed to call her Miss Mattie.' She frowned. 'Matilda, I think. Yeah, it was probably short for Matilda. Her last name was Chapman . . . Shipley . . . something like that. Bald as an eagle, she was. I remember she always wore a red wig, one of those cheap jobs. One day, we were all at supper, seated round the long table in the dining hall, and one of the kids tore it off. The look on Miss Baddie's face was enough to jell your blood. We were all afraid to breathe. Do you know how hard it is for a bunch of kids who are halfway to hysterical anyway not to go nuts laughing at a sight like that?'

'But you didn't.'

'You got that right.'

'What happened to the girl?' Ellen asked quietly, unable to stop herself from wondering what atrocities Gail may have suffered in that place.

'One of the dykes dragged her away kicking and screaming. She was a much mellower girl when I saw her again.'

They didn't speak for several seconds. Then Ellen said, 'People like that are bound straight for hell!'

'Or are sent from there to put in an apprenticeship for officer's training,' Myra quipped. 'We didn't call her Miss Baddie for nothing. And only then behind her back, of course. She was one calculating woman. A devil when only we girls were there for witness, but on visiting days, or when someone from the welfare department showed up, God, Ellen, even you would have believed it; she was Mother Theresa herself.'

'Didn't anyone ever complain?'

'Are you kidding? We knew better than to threaten or undermine Miss Baddie's position in the community in any way.' Myra tore a strip off her napkin, rolled it into a ball between her thumb and forefinger, dropped it into the ashtray. 'Anyway, who believes a kid?'

Hearing the pain in the question, Ellen knew they were no longer talking just about the home.

'Things are a lot better today,' she said gently.

'Are they?'

'Yes, I — oh, I don't know, Myra. I like to think so.'

'You know, thinking about Miss Baddie,' Myra said, gazing past Ellen, at that distant, awful time, 'I can only recall one foster mother who even came close to her. Most of them were okay, you know? They really tried. But I'd gotten to be quite a piece of work myself by then.' She suddenly snapped herself back, looked apologetically at Ellen. 'And why the hell am I going on and on about this? As if you don't have enough on your mind. Besides, you've heard countless hours of this garbage already. It's your ticket into heaven.' She slid out of the chair and buttoned her coat. 'C'mon, let's get out of here. Let's get some buns and go over and feed the pigeons.'

As they were leaving, Ellen glanced down at the folded newspaper the man had left them, read: LOCAL WOMAN MISSING. The picture above the caption was of a pretty blond girl wearing drop horseshoe earrings. Her name was Cindy Miller. No one Ellen knew.

★　★　★

The clock on the gray stone building facing them from across the park said 3:24 p.m. Next to it, separated by a narrow alley, was the Paramount Theater. *Silence of the Lambs* was playing.

As they were crossing the road to the park entrance, Myra said uncertainly, 'It was only the older girls, you know, Ellen, who were singled out for . . . well, I don't want you to think Gail . . . '

'Gail was twelve,' Ellen said woodenly. 'Nearly thirteen. It doesn't matter now, Myra. Don't feel bad. There's nothing to be done about it — about any of it.'

Just past the bandstand, which was heaped with snow and resembled a giant wedding cake, they found a bench in a sunny spot and sat down. On the ground, naked trees cast long shadow branches.

Myra barely had time to open the bag of hamburger buns when the pigeons swooped down on them, coming from every direction, cooing, fluttering, crowding at their feet, the bits of bread vanishing almost faster than they could scatter them.

Laughing at the birds' antics, enjoying a rare, pleasant moment in which the darkness was dispelled, neither woman noticed the brown van cruising past McDonald's, slowly circling the park for the third time, nor the red-haired man behind the wheel who stared out at them.

★　★　★

He could see them laughing and knew they were laughing at him, making jokes about him. His eyes passed over the dark-haired woman, fixed on the one in the white parka, whose hair gleamed red-gold in the sun. He knew she was Gail Morgan's sister.

Seeing her in person like this sent the blood coursing through him like molten lava. He liked this game she'd arranged between them. But he also knew she could be dangerous to him. He would have to proceed with the utmost caution.

Hearing her speak so directly to him the way she had, her lovely face filling the screen, her blue eyes penetrating, just like she was right there in the bar with him, like she could just reach through and grab him, had held him frozen. It had made him feel small and afraid.

196

It was her voice that had frightened him most. It was not the first time he'd heard it. Once, that voice had wakened him while he slept in his chair in the den. He'd thought after that he'd been dreaming, but he knew now that he hadn't been.

This one was different from the others, Alvin thought. He picked up a little speed, reluctantly leaving the park area, (someone might later remember a brown van circling the park) and headed north toward the highway. Ellen Harris was a child of Satan — a witch. She had special powers.

But Alvin had powers of his own. He knew how to take care of her.

In the meantime, he hoped she would enjoy the little gift he'd left for her in her mailbox.

Alvin smiled.

22

Wishing Myra a 'bon voyage,' Ellen dropped her off at her house and drove on home. She felt mild surprise seeing a police car parked in her driveway. She pulled up alongside it and got out.

'I'm Lieutenant Mike Oldfield,' the policeman said, crossing to her, his hand outstretched. 'How are you holding up, Mrs. Harris?' The sincerity of the question was in his voice, in the warm pressure of his hand. She recognized him as the policeman who had come with Myra to the airport.

'Managing. Thank you.' She saw in his face there was no point in asking if he had any news for her.

He didn't. He wanted only to talk to her, to ask her a few questions about her sister. Also, he had a video of the funeral he wanted her to look at.

'I hate to put you through it, but I thought there just might be an outside chance you'd see someone — someone who shouldn't be there.'

'I'm more than willing to look at it, Lieutenant, but there were a lot of people there I didn't know. Fans of my sister, curiosity seekers. But please, come inside.'

Except to wring more pain from her, the video proved fruitless, as she'd expected it would. There was no lurking stranger standing apart from the crowd, no menacing figure she could point a finger at.

She made them coffee, sat across from him on the sofa. Mike set his coffee on the end-table beside him. After a pause, he said, 'That was a brave thing you did last night.'

'The interview.' Her smile was at once weary and defiant. 'I expect you really mean foolhardy, don't you?'

'No. That's not what I mean at all. You did what you had to do. I think that's what real courage is — doing what we have to do in spite of our fears.'

'Thanks. You're in the minority.' She lowered her eyes to her coffee. 'And you're right. I am scared. I'm scared as hell.'

'Good. It means you'll be careful.' Studying her, Mike thought how well she fit in with her surroundings. Despite a definite inner toughness, there was an ethereal quality about her. He could easily imagine her on the cover of one of those romantic novels his mother used to read. Or perhaps, he thought, gazing up at the painting above the fireplace, she was more like the woman in that picture, able to find a quiet joy in the simple task of bathing a child.

'Lieutenant Oldfield?'

He snapped his head around. 'Yes? Oh, I'm sorry. I was just admir — '

'You said you had some questions. I *am* a little tired.'

'Of course.' Clearing his throat, he took a notepad from his breast pocket. He felt more than a little ridiculous, not to mention chauvinistic. It wasn't like him to go off on romantic flights of fancy. At least, not for longer than he cared to remember. Nor was Ellen Harris in any state even remotely resembling serenity, quiet or otherwise.

'We've already posted an unmarked vehicle close by,' he said. 'I don't suppose you could be persuaded to stay with family — or friends? What about your friend up the road?' He gestured in the direction of Myra's house.

'That would be defeating the purpose, wouldn't it? I did what I did, Lieutenant, because the police don't seem to be having much success. And don't they say a trail goes cold after twenty-four hours?'

'That doesn't necessarily mean — '

'Well, it's been a lot longer than that since my sister's life was so brutally torn from her,' she cut in, leaning forward, rage flashing from her blue eyes.

Mike could only nod mutely. She was right.

Chances they'd find Gail Morgan's killer *were* bleak, and growing bleaker with each passing day. Serial killings, if that's what it was, were damn near impossible to solve. Mainly because there was no motive, no connection to the victim. He thought of all the Ted Bundys, Hillside stranglers and Leslie Allan Williams still out there, still stalking and murdering innocent women. He wished he *could* nail the son of a bitch. Yet a part of him hoped to God he was miles away from here, somewhere where they didn't have television.

Somehow he didn't believe that was the case.

'Sergeant Shannon thinks you've been way out in left field with this,' he said.

'I know. He tried to convince *me* the killer is someone living right here in Evansdale. I think he just wants to rid himself of the case, dump it on the Evansdale Police Department.'

'Maybe,' he smiled thinly. 'Though I don't know what he'd have to gain. He's retired from the force as of yesterday.'

She registered surprise at the news. 'He never gave me any concrete reason for his theory.'

'It's mainly a hunch.'

'A hunch? You've got to be kidding.'

'I wouldn't dismiss it out of hand. Crimes are often solved on little more than a gut feeling. Shannon's a good cop; he's been on the job most of his adult life. He did think you might have something with the composite, though. They're running it on the evening news.'

She settled back on the sofa. 'Well, that's something.' Visibly trying to calm herself, she said, 'Look. I'm not saying the police aren't trying, but Gail is just one more murdered girl to you people. No one knew her, or loved her like I did — do — no one misses her . . .' She batted impatiently at her tears. 'Damn! Sorry . . .'

'Don't be.' Mike rose and handed her the box of tissues from the sideboard. She blew her nose, an unladylike honk that, though it shattered his gothic image of a moment ago, Mike found oddly endearing.

Ellen walked him out to his car. Seeing the flag up on her mailbox, she picked up her mail which had been collecting over several days.

'Call me,' he said, before closing the car door. 'Day or night. Even if you just feel like talking.' He scribbled his home number on a scrap of paper and handed it to her. 'In case you can't reach me at the station.'

'That's very kind of you,' Ellen said. 'I'm

202

not sure your wife would appreciate it, though.'

He smiled. 'I don't have a wife. Haven't for a very long time.'

'Oh. Sorry, I didn't mean to pry.'

'You weren't. The only woman in my life is my little girl, Angela. She's eleven, nearly twelve.'

Ellen couldn't help noticing his pride when he spoke of his daughter.

23

As soon as Lieutenant Oldfield drove away, Ellen went inside and locked the door, then, tossing the mail on the sideboard without looking at it, she went through the rest of the house checking the locks on doors and windows. Not that that would stop him. A madman with a purpose would find a way to get to her, just as he had gotten to Gail.

'Well, I'll be ready for you,' she said aloud.

In the kitchen, Ellen squirted detergent in the sink, ran the hot water over the few dishes. Was it possible the killer really was someone from right here in Evansdale, as Sergeant Shannon believed? And didn't Gail once say to her, 'Don't think I haven't met my share of weirdos in good old Evansdale'?

She was drying her hands, examining the tiny white spots, scarrings from where she'd cut herself on the glass. Looking down, she saw she'd not gotten all the blood off the floor; a line of it had crusted darkly in the groove between the two tiles at her feet.

She was down on her hands and knees, rummaging under the sink for a rag, when she heard a pattering sound, as if someone had tossed a handful of pebbles at the window. She swung her head around, striking it on the corner of the cupboard door.

Ignoring the flare of pain, her heart beating wildly, Ellen slowly straightened. Seeing it was just the wind whipping icy pellets against the glass, she relaxed. She delicately massaged the fiery spot above her right eye, feeling the indentation where the corner of the door had struck. The area around it seemed to be swelling under her touch. She felt nauseated. If she didn't get a grip on her nerves, it was entirely possible she'd do herself in, without anyone's help.

What she needed, she thought, was a drink.

Peering out the window, she tried unsuccessfully to search out the unmarked car Lieutenant Oldfield had said was parked nearby. They probably pulled into one of the little side roads, she thought, in full view of the house. If she couldn't see it, then neither could *he*.

Within seconds, the rain was coming down in torrents, as if the sky had split apart, sounding eerily to Ellen like ghostly applause.

★   ★   ★

Upstairs in her bedroom, Ellen stood on the stepladder, the same one she'd stood on just three weeks earlier to straighten the angel on the Christmas tree in preparation for Gail's visit. It seemed a lifetime ago, and at the same time, only yesterday.

Pushing aside boxes, albums, a couple of old purses, hats she no longer wore, Ellen quickly found what she was looking for — a plain white shoebox tied with green string.

Taking it down gingerly, as though something were alive inside she went to sit on the edge of her bed, the box resting in her lap. With the rain drumming on the roof, rattling the windows, she stared at it for several long minutes. Then she began to undo the string.

There it was. The gun Ed had bought for her. Once, the mere sight of the weapon had repelled and angered her. Ironically, it had been raining that day, too. Except it was a spring rain. Ed was away on a construction job when a rash of break-ins occurred in town. One woman who lived alone, Ellen remembered, was beaten so badly she had to be rushed to the hospital. When Ed returned, he had the gun with him. 'Just in case,' he'd said.

She'd fought him on it, but he'd been insistent, and in the end she gave in. Once she learned how to use it, she put the gun in this box and shoved it to the back of the closet shelf. She'd never expected to have to look at it again.

The gun was small enough to fit neatly in the palm of her hand. Its pearl handle gleamed in the glow from the lamp. Rather than revulsion, she now felt a measure of satisfaction in its cool heft. The gun gave her a sense of control.

She snapped in the magazine the way Ed had shown her, released the safety. She'd forgotten nothing. 'It's a .25-caliber automatic,' he'd told her. 'Holds ten rounds.' In spite of the seriousness of the moment, he'd grinned. 'In case you miss.'

Her hand deadly steady, Ellen pointed the barrel at an imagined intruder in her bedroom doorway, her finger resting lightly on the trigger. 'I won't,' she half-whispered. 'I won't miss.'

* * *

Angela was bent over her homework at the kitchen table, wearing headphones and munching on a Granny Smith apple. 'Hi, princess,' Mike said, ruffling her hair. She smiled up at him.

He sat down at the opposite end of the table and opened the file folder Shannon had sent him marked MORGAN, GAIL MARIE.

Copies of the photographs taken at the murder scene were locked away in his briefcase.

Mike began to read.

Some time later, he closed the file. He slipped off his reading glasses and massaged the bridge of his nose with his thumb and forefinger. Angela was practically asleep at the table. He hustled her off to bed. Then he went into the livingroom to watch the evening news.

24

During the eleven o'clock news, the composite drawing of the man A. J. Brooker said he saw leaving the Shelton Room on the night Gail Morgan was murdered was seen in living rooms across the country.

One of those living rooms was located in a modest A-frame in Dedham, Massachusetts, where Debby Fuller Allan lived with her auto mechanic husband, Dwight, and their teenage son. Dwight was in the shower, and Kevin was in his room talking on the phone — had been for over an hour now. If there was ever a telephone marathon held, Debby would put him up against anyone's daughter.

The cup was halfway to her lips when they flashed the composite. Her hand froze in midair, her mouth remaining slightly open, as though she were cast in wax. For despite the dark glasses and phony hair, Debby knew at once who it was.

She would never forget that face. Especially his thin, cruel mouth. The last time she saw that mouth it hovered above her, inches from her face, twisted in an ugly sneer as he spat filthy names at her. She could feel herself, even now, pinned beneath him. She had cried and pleaded with him to let her go, but he only laughed at her. Then he raped her. The last thing Debby remembered seeing that night was his fist coming at her.

She woke up in a ditch. Somehow she managed to crawl home without anyone seeing her, ducking into the woods each time she saw car lights approaching. She had begged her mother not to call the police, threatening to kill herself if anyone found out. She felt dirty and ashamed. She had liked him. He seemed older and more exciting than the other boys at school. She didn't care that everyone else said he was weird. She had willingly gotten into his car. It was her fault.

Her mother had finally, tearfully, given in, keeping her home from school, nursing her bruises until they had faded sufficiently for her to return.

The bruises on her soul would never fade.

The news commentator was asking anyone who recognized the man in the drawing to please call their local police department, or the 800 number flashing across the bottom of the screen.

Debby didn't bother to write it down. She knew she wouldn't ever call. They would want to know her name. They would want to know how she knew him. And no one must ever find out her dirty, shameful secret.

'Deb?'

'What?' Her hand jerked and some of the tea splashed on her leg. 'Damn!' Luckily, it wasn't too hot.

Dwight took the cup from her hand and set it on the end-table. 'Honey, what's the matter?' he frowned, belting his robe. His dark hair was damp from the shower. 'You look like you saw a ghost.'

She merely shook her head and changed the channel on the T.V.

Others were not so reticent. Calls flooded police stations across the country.

25

'Anyone you recognize?' Mike asked, calling Ellen as soon as the broadcast was over.

'No.'

Lately, news of the murder had dwindled to barely a mention, but tonight they'd done a complete recap, running Ellen's interview along with the composite.

'The sketch might just be of some poor slob out for an evening on his own,' the policeman said. 'He'll likely call in unless he told his wife he was somewhere else. That's if he doesn't panic seeing himself on T.V., especially in connection with a murder.

'Mrs. Harris, you're a psychologist. Why don't you sit down and see if you can't come up with a profile of this guy. Do you think you can be objective?'

'I don't know. Maybe.' Busy work, she thought. He's humoring me. But at least she'd be doing something.

Sitting on the sofa with the yellow legal pad on her lap, Ellen carefully penned *Serial Killers* at the top of the page. Then she drew a line down the center, headed up one column, 'disorganized', and the other

212

'organized'. On the next page she began to jot down everything she could recall about what she knew of serial killers, assuming it was such a person who had murdered Gail — you had to jump off at some point.

Four pages later, Ellen jerked the pen across the page when the phone rang. She snapped up the receiver on the second ring. Glanced at the clock. It was twenty-five past one.

'Hello?'

No answer. But someone was on the line. She could hear breathing. 'Hello,' she said again.

'Is this Ellen Harris?' A woman's voice, very soft, very low. She sounds afraid, Ellen thought.

'Yes, this is Ellen Harris. Who is this, please?'

'It doesn't matter. You don't know me.' The voice had dropped even lower, and Ellen had to press the receiver closer to her ear to hear. 'I just wanted to tell you, I know — I know who killed your sister.'

Her heart leaped. 'Who is this, please? Who . . . ?'

'I'm sorry. I can't tell you . . . I have to go . . . I'm sorry . . . '

'No, please don't hang up.' Panic filled her. 'You're right, I don't need to know who you are. Just tell me . . . ' But it was already too late. She'd hung up. Ellen had frightened her off. She held the receiver to her ear for several seconds before finally replacing it in its cradle.

Maybe she'll call back, she thought, without much optimism.

Angry with herself, hand shaking, she lit a cigarette and went to stand at the window. A police car drove slowly past the house, dome light whirling, throwing bloody color into the woods. Damn them! He won't come if he sees that.

She had Lieutenant Oldfield's home number, but there was really no reason to bother him. He couldn't do much about a phone call, even if Ellen did sense that the caller was genuine.

She sat back down on the sofa, not bothering even to glance at the yellow legal pad beside her. Crushing her cigarette out in the ashtray, she felt under the cushion for the gun. She held it in her hand for a few minutes, then, feeling reassured, put it back.

★   ★   ★

In the morning she woke up on the sofa, her body cramped and unrested, her mind heavy with unremembered dreams. The phone was

214

ringing. With a silent prayer, she snatched up the receiver, but it was Myra. They'd decided not to go away, after all, she said. 'We're coming up to stay with you, Ellen. Both Carl and I decided. We're not leaving — '

'Please, Myra, I don't want you to do that,' Ellen said, her voice tight. 'He'll know if there's someone here with me and he won't make contact. I'm okay, really. Lieutenant Oldfield's watching out for me. And I told you, I have — '

'I know. An equalizer.' For a few seconds she was silent. Then, 'I saw the police cruiser drive by last night.'

'There you go.'

'I'm here if you need me.'

'No, Myra. I want you to go on your vacation just like you planned.'

'Would you if it was me?' Myra asked quietly.

Ellen paused. 'I'll only feel guilty if you don't go.'

'Don't be silly. We'll have our vacation right here. It'll be nice not having the kids for a few days.'

There was no talking her out of it. Ellen hung up feeling a confusing blend of gratitude and exasperation.

She glanced at the pile of mail on the sideboard. She'd go through it later. Bills still had to be paid. What she needed right now, she thought, as she headed out to the kitchen, was a good, strong cup of coffee.

* * *

Edie was down on her hands and knees washing the floor in one of the washroom cubicles, her forehead shiny with perspiration. She used to get down at least twice a week, but now her knees bothered her, and the heat, so she'd stretched it out to once a week, just damp-mopping in between.

Edie took pride in her work, in the fact that there was not one speck of dirt to be found in the corners. Still, she had to admit she wasn't as young as she used to be, and lately she found herself thinking how nice it would be to be able to retire. But with Harry only driving taxi part-time, they needed her money. Maybe she wouldn't mind so much if he would talk nice to her, or smile once in a while. But she guessed that he wouldn't be Harry if he did. If he was ever any different, Edie no longer remembered or cared. Maybe one of these days she'd just up and leave him, just pack up her bags and fly off to Glasgow and live out her days in the fair land of her youth.

They hadn't lived right in the city itself,

but in a little green place just outside, where a sweet brook ran behind the house. Clara said it was all different now, that she wouldn't know the place, but Edie didn't like thinking about that.

Edie dipped her cloth into the bucket of hot, soapy water, wrung it lightly, then, smiling to herself, fantasized how lovely it would be to be reunited with the sister she hadn't seen in years, to chat with old school chums, to meet with the cheery cousins Clara talked about in her letters. She reached with her cloth into the tight space behind the toilet bowl. Maybe she'd rent a little place with a backyard, she thought, where they could all sit outside at one of those round garden tables with a pretty, striped parasol to shade them from the sun.

The fantasy set aside, she stared at the pretty blue and silver bow that her cloth had pushed into view.

Edie's smile faded.

It was the bow that had been on the present Edie had seen standing against the photocopier, the one Cindy had told her she bought for her mom's birthday — a painting, she'd said.

'What's it doing here?' Edie muttered to herself, but she was already getting a bad feeling. She'd tried to tell the others that

Cindy didn't run away with no fellow, but no one wanted to listen to a cleaning lady.

Especially that Alice Fisher, who had a royal fit just because Cindy left a dirty ashtray behind. Of course, she was always complaining about something. Lately, it was about 'that ghastly smell' in the elevator.

26

Debby Fuller Allan had slipped quietly out of bed after her husband was asleep and made the call on the downstairs phone. Her mother was gone now, taken by cancer two years earlier, carrying her daughter's secret to her grave. But lying in bed, Debby had heard her voice clearly: *You have to tell, Debby. You don't have to call the police. You could call the sister. You don't have to give your name. But you have to tell, Debby. If he's out there killing women, you have to tell someone.*

Well, she'd tried. But her mother was wrong. The Harris woman had insisted on knowing her name.

Still, that didn't mean she had to give it, did it? She could just have given her *his* name and hung up.

After Dwight left for work, and Kevin for school, Debby went to the phone again. Once, she got so far as to partly dialing the number. But she hung up quickly, too afraid they'd somehow find out who she was. What if they could trace the call? Maybe Ellen Harris even had one of those phone setups that recorded the numbers of incoming calls.

Or maybe *he'd* find out she'd called and come after her.

Most importantly, she thought of the love she saw in Dwight's eyes when he looked at her.

What would she see there if he knew?

27

Lloyd Anderson of Anderson Insurance arrived back from a business trip mid-morning of the next day, which was Tuesday, January 26th. Mr. Anderson had been in Vietnam, and recognized 'that ghastly smell' the others had been complaining about the instant he stepped into the elevator. It was one he'd hoped never to smell again.

The police came and sprayed with something that spread a sweetness to cover the odor, and pushed up the emergency door in the ceiling. Something weighed against it, but at last it gave, and a pale, slender arm dropped down. The two policemen lifted the body down, laid it gently on the floor. Mr. Anderson, whose face had gone as white as his hair, identified the dead woman as one Cindy Miller, the employee who had been reported missing.

The news traveled throughout the building as though with a life of its own, and soon the corridor outside the elevator was crowded with shaken and weeping people who had to be gently persuaded back to their own offices. Many went on home, to be questioned later.

Noticing the horseshoe earring on the dead woman's ear, and the other ear dotted with dried blood where an earring had been torn out, one of the policemen commented dryly, 'Didn't bring her much luck, did they?'

★　★　★

Ellen generally preferred showers, but with the shower scene from *Psycho* taunting her, she opted instead for a bath. She wouldn't hear an intruder with the water running, and she had no intention of being taken by surprise.

The gun was on the floor beside the tub, within easy reach.

After dressing in a soft blue lambswool sweater, cream-colored slacks and her parka, she dropped the gun in her bag, (don't leave home without it) and slipped the folded sheets of yellow legal paper filled with her scribblings in an envelope and put it in a zippered compartment on the outside of her bag.

She was just pulling out of the driveway when the phone in the house began to ring. It rang ten times before falling silent.

★　★　★

Replacing the receiver, Debby Fuller Allan thought, There, I called! It's not my fault no one answered. She was standing at a pay phone in a downtown shopping mall in East Dedham. In a way, she was relieved Ellen Harris wasn't home. In fact, she took it as a clear sign from God that he meant her to stay out of it.

★ ★ ★

It was still dark outside when Alvin slipped out of bed. He went out to the kitchen and got a beer out of the fridge. He snapped the tab open. It had unnerved him a little seeing the composite of himself on T.V., though not enough to panic him. As far as he was concerned, the drawing looked nothing like him. Still, he didn't like it that the doorman had gotten that good a look at him.

It wasn't the only thing bothering him these past couple of days. Slapping his now empty beer can down on the table, Alvin shrugged grimly into his red plaid jacket and went out the door.

Reaching his van, he slid the doors open.

The ruined painting lay on the floor. The Miller bitch had put her foot through it in the struggle. He shouldn't have taken it, though. That had been a mistake. He wasn't quite sure why, but he knew it was. He should have put the painting with her just like he had her purse.

Now he gathered it up and took it inside. When he had a fire going in the monstrous woodstove, he lifted the lid and stuffed in the painting, along with its broken frame. Standing with the lid off the stove, he watched as the flames caught, as the canvas curled and browned, and the paint melted and ran together.

His eyes glittering in the fire's glow, his face growing hot, he thought of Ellen Harris. It was all her fault. She had cast some kind of curse on him, making him do things wrong, getting his mind confused. Once he took care of her, everything would be fine again.

Soon, the heat from the flames together with the beer he'd consumed began to relax him. When the painting was reduced to ashes, he settled the lid back on the stove, threw on some dark clothes and drove the van into town.

* * *

Each time the old woman in the upstairs bedroom would hear the van leave the drive she would silently curse her nephew. The van, which had once belonged to her weak-kneed,

224

sniveling husband Henry Bishop, was now hers. But that evil boy had taken it over, just as he'd taken over her checkbook and anything else he could lay his filthy hands on.

But now Matilda was beyond hearing anything at all — had been since exactly 3:11, that morning when her soul departed her ravaged, skeletal body.

Alvin had extracted his own revenge against the despised woman.

She had not gone quietly into that good night, however, but in a rage, vowing vengeance against the nephew she'd taken in when even his own mother had abandoned him.

Alvin would yet feel her wrath.

★   ★   ★

Last night's rain had made the road slippery and Ellen was forced to crawl along. As she drove, she found herself looking again for the unmarked car, and this time was rewarded by the glint of dark green metal just off to her left, in the brush.

Satisfied, even impressed, she drove on. Strange that the road seemed narrower, somehow — a grey, lonely corridor with deep woods hemming her in, now and then a branch reaching out for her, brushing against the car. She passed several LOTS FOR SALE signs along the way. Soon, she wouldn't know this place.

Seeing Myra's little Honda Civic in the drive gave her a heavy feeling. She'd ruined their Christmas and now their vacation. She must be very popular with Carl. Somehow, she'd make it up to them.

Once Ellen reached the main road, the driving improved considerably, and ten minutes later she was pulling up in front of the police station.

'Sorry, Ma'am,' the heavily mustached officer at the desk said, 'the lieutenant was called out a while ago. I can get him to give you a call when he gets back if you like.'

'No, that won't be necessary.'

'Is there anything I can do for you?'

'Actually, there is. Thank you.' Retrieving the envelope from her bag, she scribbled Mike's name on the front and handed it to him. 'Just tell him Ellen — '

'Harris,' he finished. 'I — uh, recognized you from the television. No problem. How are things going for you, Mrs. Harris?'

'As well as you might expect, Officer . . . '

'Branscombe. Sergeant Branscombe.' He smiled sympathetically. 'Tough break about your sister.'

'Yes. I'm hoping you people can find her killer.'

'We're trying. In the meantime, you ought to get yourself a damn good watchdog living way out there on Cutter's Road where you do — maybe a Shepherd or a Doberman.'

'I'll give it some thought,' she said. Ellen sensed rather than actually noticed a flurry of activity around her. Hearing someone say 'missing woman,' she turned around in time to see two policemen, heads bent in animated discussion, walking past, and immediately she remembered reading in the paper about a missing woman when she was in McDonald's with Myra. 'Did they find her?' she asked, turning back to Sergeant Branscombe. 'The woman who was missing? Miller, wasn't that her name?'

He nodded. 'Oh, yeah, they found her all right.'

It was clear to Ellen by his tone they hadn't found her under very pleasant circumstances. Knowing he wasn't likely to be more specific, Ellen didn't press him for further answers.

As she neared her car, she saw what appeared to be a parking ticket under her wiper, and felt a surge of annoyance. *I put more than enough money in that damn meter for the little time I was in there. I know I did.* The phrase 'rubbing salt on the wound' came to mind. But as Ellen drew closer, she realized it was not a parking ticket at all rattling under her windshield, but an ordinary sheet of white paper, the sort that might have been torn from a writing tablet. It was folded in two.

Her steps slowed. Her heart racing as if it already knew something she did not, Ellen slid the note from under the wiper. Hesitated. Opened it. Written in neat, block letters in red ink, it said simply, YOU'RE IT! Nothing else. Just, YOU'RE IT!

It was from *him*. She had stirred the monster in his lair.

28

As she stood on the sidewalk holding the note in her hand, alternate waves of triumph and sheer terror washed over her. Her eyes darted round, but no passersby, except for one old man who nodded politely as he limped past with his cane, looked at her. A woman toting a sleeping child on a backpack hurried on past him.

Across the street, a young boy, his arms weighted down with books, came out of the library. He waited for a white bread truck to speed by before crossing.

Ellen looked back at the note. I can't be 'it,' she thought foolishly, as if this were a child's game they were playing. You haven't tagged me yet.

She knew, of course, she should take the note directly into the police station and leave it for Mike, yet she made no move in that direction. Instead she put the note in her bag and drove on home.

She'd barely got her coat off when the phone rang. 'Hello.'

No answer.

'Hello. Who is this, please?' Maybe it was

the girl who called before. Her hopes soared. Maybe she had a change of . . .

Before Ellen could complete the thought, came a chilling whisper in her ear, 'Do you know me?'

Her heart slammed against her ribs. Her legs turned to rubber. It was *him*. Ellen tried to speak, to challenge him, but her terror betrayed her, and she could only listen helplessly as a low chuckle traveled to her ear, a laugh so evil, so insane, it seemed to reach inside her very soul.

'Not so brave now, are you, witch?' he whispered again. 'See you soon.'

There was a click and the line went dead.

For several minutes Ellen stood holding the receiver in her hand, listening to the dial tone, like someone under hypnosis. Finally, she hung up. Her hand was still on the receiver when the phone rang again, vibrating against her palm. She inadvertantly knocked it out of its cradle. It clattered to the floor. Ellen jumped back, stared at it.

'Ellen? Ellen, are you there?' came Mike's anxious voice by her feet. 'Are you all right? Ellen . . . ?'

She picked up the receiver off the floor. Closing her eyes, she held it momentarily to her heart, then to her ear. 'Mike, hello,' she said brightly. 'Sorry about that. I dropped the phone.'

'Are you okay?'

'I'm fine,' she lied.

'Good,' he said, sounding relieved. 'I got the profile you left. I'm sorry I missed you.'

'No problem. I doubt it will be of much help, though. Serial killers aren't exactly my specialty.'

'I'm not sure they're anyone's,' he said, with a trace of anger, and Ellen remembered the missing woman who was now found.

'Was she murdered?' Ellen asked quietly. 'The Miller girl?'

There was a pause, then, 'Yes, I'm afraid so.'

'Do you think it's the same man who . . . ?'

'Ellen, we really can't be certain of anything at this point. But, of course, it's possible. Anything's possible.'

'Will you tell me if it is the . . . ?'

'Of course I will,' he said, before she could finish. 'You know that. Listen, Ellen, there's something I have to tell you. I don't want to alarm you, but the two detectives who were watching your house have been pulled off the case. With this new case, we can't spare the manpower. I'm sorry. It wasn't my decision to make.'

'You don't have to explain. I understand.'

'Damned if I do. We'll still get a squad car out there, though, as often as possible.'

'Good.'

'Look, I — uh, can get away from here in an hour or so. My daughter Angela is attending a pajama party tonight. I was wondering — well, could you use the company?'

Oh, God, could I? She wondered idly when they had gotten on a first name basis. She couldn't seem to remember. Tell him about the note, about the phone call, a small inner voice urged her. She denied the voice. Police cars would swarm the area — maybe even helicopters. Even if they used the utmost discretion, *he* would know.

He'd slip away into the night, and then he would be lost to them forever.

Gail's murder would go unavenged.

And when the time was right, the killing would begin again. Other women, in other places.

As frightened as she was, there was no way on earth she was going to let that happen.

'Ellen, are you still there?'

'Yes, I'm here. Thanks for the offer, Mike, but I think I'll make it an early night tonight. I'm a little tired.'

'I'm not surprised. Well, you try to get a good night's sleep, then. I'll call you.'

Ellen thought she detected a note of hurt in his voice. It took all her will power not to call him back.

* * *

When Alvin left Papa Bear's, he was still wearing the white wig, still limping along with the cane. Sliding behind the wheel of the van, he smiled to himself. It amused him that no one in the tavern had recognized him. Even Jake, the bartender, who certainly saw him often enough, had said, 'What'll it be, Pop?'

29

The silence of the house pressed in on her. She went through the rooms checking the locks on doors and windows. She watched television with the sound turned low. Then she checked the locks again.

The next three days and nights brought more of the same. Ellen didn't leave the house.

The media was now flooded with the news of Cindy Miller's murder, and though her heart went out to Cindy's mother and her little boy, she couldn't help feeling resentful that Gail's murder had been pushed aside. Old news, yesterday's news.

She had a constant feeling of being watched, and took to wandering the house at night, going from window to window, peering out at the shadows for the one that moved, the one that did not belong. She jumped at the slightest sound, her eyes darting at imaginary shapes in her peripheral vision. Every creak and groan of the house, the wind, even the hum of the refrigerator all took on ominous meaning.

Why doesn't he come? she thought for the

millionth time as she consumed one more of the endless cups of coffee, chain-smoked and eyed the liquor cabinet with weakening resolve. But she knew it was part of the plan to wear her down. He would come for her when she least expected it.

The gun was never far from her hand.

Several times in the night when she finally did manage to doze off on the sofa, the phone would jar her awake, whoever it was hanging up as soon as she picked up the receiver. Probably crank calls, she tried to tell herself. She'd had more than a few. But she didn't for a minute believe that.

On the fourth day, Mike came and insisted on taking her out to lunch. He looked startled when she opened the door to him, and she knew she must look the total wreck she was.

'I'm not hungry.'

'Nevertheless, you have to eat.'

It didn't take too much persuasion to get her to go.

They drove to a small restaurant in town, found a table at the back. He ordered for both of them. No one had done that since Ed. It felt comforting to have someone make even that small decision for her. She hoped no radical feminists were within hearing distance, but she found she really didn't care.

'Are you okay?' he asked when the waitress

left them. His deep-set sherry-colored eyes were intent on hers. It wasn't an idle question. He really wanted to know.

'Surviving,' she said off-handedly. The word made her think of Miss Layton, who had called her a survivor. She'd like to believe it was true.

She looked around at the paneled walls hung with posters of Jimmy and Marilyn and Elvis. A jukebox played in the corner.

'This is an interesting place,' she said absently. 'I've never been here.'

He smiled at her and she noticed how tired he looked himself. The fine lines at the corners of his eyes seemed deeper. He even seemed to have acquired a few more grey hairs. He was probably working around the clock. She also noticed he had a trace of a cleft in his chin. He was really quite nice looking. Not as handsome, perhaps, as Paul, but something better, deeper, more enduring. She realized she liked being with him. 'Are you making any headway in the Miller case?' she asked.

'That's — uh, something I wanted to discuss with you.'

'You think he's the same man who murdered Gail, don't you?'

Her perception caught him by surprise. 'It looks that way, except . . . ' He stopped himself in time, remembering there was one detail about her sister's murder she was unaware of.

'Except what?'

Her blue gaze seemed to penetrate his deepest thoughts, and he had to look away. He plucked a tooth-pick from its container and snapped it in two. 'Except she was murdered here, in Evansdale,' he said easily, hating himself for his deception. He would have to tell her, and soon. Just not now, not here. There were a few pertinent facts they'd uncovered recently he wouldn't be able to share with her until she knew. They were in the process of rounding up all known sex offenders in the area, and there was a private eye who rented an office in the McLeod building, right next door to Anderson Insurance, who was getting his share of attention, and whining about his civil rights all the way. While it was true the guy had a reputation as a down-in-the-dirt sleeze, somehow Mike didn't think he was a killer. At least not by his own hand.

'We think the guy is right here in town, Ellen.'

'So do I.' With that, she took the note out of her purse and handed it to him. 'I found this under my windshield wiper when I came out of the police station last week.'

He read it. His color drained. 'My God, Ellen, why didn't you tell me? I would never have let them pull those guys off surveillance if I'd known.'

'I know. I'm sorry. I guess I should have. It was just that I was afraid you'd scare him off. That's not all, Mike.' She told him about the phone call. 'Do you Know Me?' is the name of Gail's new song. Her roommate told me Gail got a similar call a few nights before she was murdered.'

The waitress came with their order. Broiled salmon, buttered carrots and baked potato with sour cream. It looked and smelled delicious. Ellen found she was hungry after all.

'By the way,' Mike said, holding a forkful of salmon halfway to his mouth, ' . . . you did a great job on the profile. I was impressed. You're pretty knowledgeable on the subject.'

'Thanks.' Her professional pride made her warm at the compliment. 'But will it help you to find him?'

'Let's hope so. Ellen, I'm going to request a female officer to come and stay with you for a few days.'

'I'll be content if you just put the car back on.'

'We'll do that, of course, but — '

'No, Mike. I won't be held prisoner in my own home. I'm sorry, but I just won't. What's the good of all your fancy computers?' she snapped suddenly, laying her fork down, attracting the attention of the couple seated across from them. 'Why can't you just hook up with the other police departments, compare notes, use the process of elimination?' She was floundering. Not only was she computer illiterate, she knew nothing about police work. But there was no trace of condescension in Mike's expression or his reply.

'We can and we are,' he said. 'But it's possible this guy's never had a conviction or even been brought up on charges. In that case, he wouldn't be on anyone's file.'

She said nothing.

'And, by the way, that gun in your bag won't do you much good if you're asleep when he decides to make his move. And you have to sleep sometime. He will come after you, Ellen. Of that much I'm absolutely sure.'

Hearing the conviction in his voice, Ellen shivered inwardly. 'It's what I want,' she said quietly. 'It's why I went on television.'

'I understand that. And I think a female officer is the answer. Will you at least think about it?' He'd only guessed about the gun, but he knew he'd guessed right. He wasn't surprised. She wasn't about to be anyone's passive victim.

'All right,' she said after a moment. 'I'll think about it.'

'Good girl.' He smiled. 'She'll be the soul of discretion, I promise — there's no way he'll suspect you're not alone. And we'll nail the creep.'

'I haven't agreed, Mike. I said I'd think about it.'

The waitress came with their coffee. When she turned away, Mike said quietly, eyeing her leather bag hanging on her chair, 'Can I assume you know how to use what you've got in there?'

She smiled dryly. 'Yes, Lieutenant, you can. It's not that difficult.'

'I suppose not. What did you use for target practice?'

'Tin cans. My husband taught me. In back of the house.'

Mike sipped his coffee.

★   ★   ★

On their way out, they ran into Paul Henderson with a pretty, young redhead hanging on his arm. His eyes flickered briefly over Mike, and she saw his mouth tighten just

240

a fraction before the old charm went into automatic.

'Ellen, how nice to see you. We miss you at the clinic. Some of your clients have been asking for you. Absolutely won't see anyone else.'

Hearing the underlying note of criticism, she made some vague response and went on, Mike trailing behind.

Paul knew all the right buttons to push. But along with the feelings of guilt he'd aroused in her, was a sense of relief. At least he wouldn't be bothering her anymore.

During the drive home, Mike said unexpectedly beside her, 'Tin cans don't bleed, you know, Ellen?'

She looked at him. 'What?'

Not taking his eyes from the road, he said, 'I was just wondering, well, if you could actually shoot a man. You're a person who analyzes people, who reasons things through. Have you ever seen the damage a bullet can cause? Do you have any idea what a bullet sounds like smashing through flesh and bone?'

'I know what you're trying to do, Mike. But you needn't worry. All I have to remember is what he did to my sister.'

Taking his hand off the wheel, he laid it over hers. The electricity in his touch surprised her, flustered her a little. 'This has been hell for you,' he said softly. 'We're going to find him. I promise you that.'

At the door, he leaned over and kissed her gently on the mouth. Feelings she'd thought long dead in her flooded throughout her body like a warm wave.

'I've been wanting to do that for a long time,' he said. 'Make sure your doors are locked, and think over what I said about assigning a police woman to stay with you.'

'I will.'

'I'll call you tonight.'

* * *

Inside, Ellen took off her coat, gathered up the mail from the sideboard and floated out to the kitchen. His kiss was still sweet on her mouth. For once, fear wasn't the reason for her racing heart.

Making herself a cup of tea, Ellen sat down at the table. The mail was mostly junk mail, as far as she could see, and a few bills. Noticing in the pile a letter postmarked Atlanta, GA., she opened it eagerly. Inside was a single page scripted in Miss Layton's beautiful handwriting, the kind of penmanship you didn't see too often these days.

She was settling in nicely, she wrote, and

thought she would get on fine in Atlanta, although she did miss the ocean and the few dear friends she'd made over the years. 'I go to sleep each night with the perfume of the lovely magnolia trees wafting through my window. The good Lord *does* compensate, Ellen,' she wrote, 'although sometimes our losses are so difficult to bear, we fail to notice His new and special gifts to us. Please take care of yourself, dear.'

Warmly,
Margaret Layton

Smiling fondly to herself, Ellen began to sift through the rest of the mail. An instant later, her smile vanished as she looked down at her name printed in red block letters on the manila envelope.

There was no postmark. It had been hand-delivered.

Her moment of pleasure flown, she slowly opened the envelope. She felt inside for a note; there was none. She held the envelope upside down and shook it. A glossy Polaroid snapshot slid out into her hand.

At first, she wasn't sure what it was she was seeing. It appeared to be a picture of a nude clown doll, arms out-stretched, legs bent at an odd angle.

Holding the snapshot closer, a buzzing started up in the air above her head as recognition struck. Beneath the grotesque, painted-on clown's mouth, she could now make out Gail's natural lipline, the edge of her small, white teeth between parted lips. Her blue eyes stared blankly up at her out of drawn, black triangles.

A small cry escaped her. The photograph slid from her hand onto the floor. She stood up, as if to run from the horror of what she'd seen, and had to fight to keep from fainting. She gripped the edge of the table.

Sagging back down into the chair, harsh sobs took her, sobs that convulsed her body as they tore up from the very depths of her soul.

When, at last, her sobs subsided, all fear of him was replaced by raw fury. It hadn't been enough to rape and murder Gail. He had to further degrade and humiliate her.

Dear Jesus, how you must hate women!

Damn you, Mike! Why didn't you tell me? How could you have let me find out like this?

Even when she was in New York, she'd sensed the unspoken words. The secrecy. Sensed something was being deliberately kept from her, and today in the restaurant when Mike was talking about Cindy Miller's murder, saying it appeared that her and Gail's killer was one and the same, except that Cindy had been murdered here in Evansdale, he'd been lying to her. True, a lie of omission, but a lie just the same.

It wasn't what he'd been about to say. She realized now he'd been about to tell her that Cindy, unlike Gail, hadn't been used as that sick maniac's canvas. Mike caught himself before he did.

She didn't believe it was simply to spare her feelings.

Upstairs, she splashed cold water on her face, quickly refreshed her makeup.

* * *

An hour later, she telephoned Mike from town. 'You don't have to bother about a police woman, after all,' she said, barely able to keep herself sounding civil. 'I have a very good friend who's going to stay with me for a few days.'

'Well, that's great. Is that your friend from down the road? Myra?'

'No. His name is Sam.' Let him think what he would. Ellen cut the conversation short before he could ask any more questions.

No longer would she be satisfied with merely bringing Gail's killer to justice. She fully intended to mete it out personally. Mike was wrong about one thing. It wouldn't bother her even a little bit to shoot him. In fact, hearing a bullet from her gun smash through that bastard's flesh and bone, would give her the greatest pleasure.

★ ★ ★

'Well, fella,' Ellen said, turning on the ignition, then reaching over to stroke the lab's sleek, gold head, ' . . . it's just you and me, now.' As if in answer, Sam, who was now curled up on the passenger seat just as if he'd always been there, laid a gentle paw on her leg.

Ellen hadn't had a hard time making her choice. It was as if Sam had been waiting for her. He'd eyed her expectantly from behind the wire mesh of his cramped cage out of intelligent brown eyes. He gave a short bark, thumped his tail on the floor, and Ellen had said to the bald, overalled man, 'This one. I'll take this one.'

Sam was much smaller than a purebred lab, (hardly the sort of dog Sergeant Branscombe had had in mind for her) and Ellen suspected a strain of terrier. Which was probably why poor old Sam hadn't readily found a home, and why he was scheduled to be 'put down' in the morning. The man explained they could only hold the dogs for so long, that the city didn't want to spend the money it took to feed and care for them. He seemed genuinely pleased Sam had found someone to take him.

Other than not having enough flesh on his bones, and being in bad need of some soap and water, he looked healthy enough to her.

'I'm something of a mongrel, myself,' she said, 'French Canadian on my mother's side, Irish on my father's.' The dog was looking at her as if he understood every word. 'You'll let me know if anyone tries to get in the house, won't you, Sam? You'll wake me if I'm asleep?'

Sam barked once.

Ellen laughed. 'How about a little music? Maybe it will soothe the savage beast in both of us. The good Lord only knows what *you've* been through.' She turned on the radio, and instantly Gail was in the car with them, her clear, familiar voice sending shockwaves of pain through Ellen, taking her breath. Her hand shot out to turn it off, but she found she couldn't. In the song, Gail was alive, and Ellen listened through to the end, savoring each nuance, every breath, every word, until the final note faded. Then, exhausted by the continuing assault on her emotions, she pulled the car off onto the shoulder of the road, laid her head on the steering wheel, and quietly wept.

In a little while, she felt a warm, rough tongue lick the back of her hand, and Sam's head nestled gently in her lap.

30

'I'm sorry, Carl.'

Though it was late afternoon, Carl and Myra were still in their robes, playing Scrabble at the kitchen table. 'About what?' Carl was holding two tiles in his hand, trying to come up with a word.

'C'mon, honey, I know you were looking forward to a little fun in the sun. God knows you earned it.'

'What I was looking forward to, actually, was a little time alone with my wife. And I have that. Look, it was just lousy timing on my part. Of course you should be here for Ellen.' He placed his two tiles on the board, horizontally spelling out 'page,' earning himself seven points. 'I just don't see how we're helping her sitting here, that's all.'

'I just feel better knowing we can be there in less than five minutes if we need to.'

An old Beatles tune drifted from the radio on the counter. Moments before, they'd sat silently through Gail's 'Do You Know Me?' It was the first time Myra had heard the song. Though it was very pretty, it had been hard to listen to. She wondered if Ellen had been listening. She hoped not.

'She could stay here with us if she wanted,' Carl said.

'I already asked — and she doesn't want anyone staying with her, either. She's afraid he won't crawl out from under his rock if she's not alone. She's got a gun, Carl.'

Seeing the fear on her face, hearing it in her voice, he said easily, 'I feel a whole lot better knowing she's got some protection. As long as she doesn't panic and shoot some poor vacuum cleaner salesman or a Jehovah's Witness.'

'That's not funny, Carl.'

'Sorry. Just trying to insert a little levity. Anyway, the police seem to be keeping a pretty close eye on her. I saw the cruiser drive by this morning.'

Myra said nothing. She pretended to study the tiles in her hand.

He got the message. 'Listen, why don't you give her a call? Later, we can go on up if you want. I don't think she'd object to a little company.'

'I love you, Carl.'

'Of course you do. That's cause I'm so lovable.'

She affectionately mumbled something about him being a jerk, and went into the living room. She dialed Ellen's number, but there was no answer.

'She must have gone out,' she said, returning. 'I'll try later.'

Carl reached for a celery stick from the pink-flowered bowl. When Myra was on a diet, so was he. Not that he couldn't stand to shed a few pounds. It was just that his jaw ached from all the chewing.

Myra was placing an 'e' under the 'p' in page, following quickly with two 'r's and a 'y'.

'Perry,' Carl said, his voice teasing. 'Can't use a proper name. Against the rules.'

As Myra continued to stare at the name on the board, the room seemed to darken. A vision of flailing, clawing hands leaped into her mind's eye. She went absolutely dead white.

'Myra, what is it?' Carl said anxiously, all playfulness gone from his voice. 'What's the matter?'

She told him what she'd seen.

'It's because of Ellen's sister,' he said. 'You're imagining the scene of her murder.'

'I don't know, Carl. I'm not sure that's it at all.' She continued to look down at the name she'd unconsciously spelled out. PERRY. The name meant something to her. Something horrible.

Carl laid his big, square hand over hers.

'Why don't you take one of your pills,' he said softly.

'No. They don't help. All they do is make me sleepy.' She was remembering being with Ellen in McDonald's, telling her about the girl who had yanked Miss Baddie's wig off, but it wasn't that girl's face that flashed in her mind now, but a pretty blond girl with kind blue eyes who had befriended her on that first night Myra spent in the home. *I was crying. The girl was writing in her diary. She laid the pencil down and came to sit on my bed. She didn't care that I was fat and ugly. 'Don't cry,' she'd said. 'I'll be your friend if you want. My name's Jeannie. What's yours?'*

It was as far as Myra's memory would take her.

* * *

Alvin worked his way cautiously along the edge of the woods. The back of her house was no more than fifty feet from him. Still, he'd have to be careful. The police were probably watching the place. He checked the pockets of the camouflage coveralls he'd bought at Army surplus. All set. The van was parked in a small clearing in the woods, out of sight.

Crouching low, he scurried as fast as he could, stopping only when he reached the house. Heart racing, he listened. But there were only the usual night sounds.

He hadn't even needed to use his flashlight. She'd left a bedroom light on. She always did. The tree was perfect. She wasn't as smart as she thought.

Climbing the tree proved not as easy as Alvin had thought. Twice, his foot slipped on an icy limb, momentarily panicking him. He could feel the cold rough bark through his thin gloves.

But at last he was there. He'd figured the window would be locked. He was right. Taking the screwdriver from his pocket, he wedged the end under the frame, and pushed down.

The lock snapped easily.

The floorboards creaked as he stepped over the sill into the room.

Closing the window, he walked about the room, touching things, running his gloved fingers over the satin puffs and pillows, and felt anger burn in his gut. He'd never slept in a room like this. He picked up a nightie lying on the foot of her bed. It slid through his hands. Expensive. The sort of nightie a woman like her would never wear for him. He held it against his face, could smell her perfume. It made his head swim. She was like all those girls in school who looked down their noses at him, thought they were too good for him. Acting like he wasn't alive.

Well, she was the one who wouldn't be alive.

Not for long.

31

Ellen had been on her way home, but now, with Sam curled up asleep beside her, she was heading back into town, back to the old neighborhood where she and Gail had grown up, as if drawn there by her sister's voice.

Driving past their faded brick school, she remembered how, more than once, they had tiptoed hand-in-hand down its polished corridor, late and frightened, hearing the voices of the teachers behind their closed doors. They would sneak past the principal's office, their own breathing and footsteps echoing as if they were inside a church.

The car bumped lightly over Smith's Bridge. Above her, seagulls still soared and wheeled and cried out. She remembered how she used to envy them their wings.

Nearing her own street, she cracked the window open, and the familiar smells of salt air mingling with those of poverty and neglect sent her spinning back in time.

She drove past Melick's Barber Shop. Bars now covered the plate glass window where the Siamese cat used to sleep curled up in the sun. A padlock hung on the door. The barber pole was gone.

She rounded the corner past what had been Hason's Grocery store, and was mildly surprised to see that it was still in business, the rusting Coca Cola sign still swaying above the door.

Finally, she turned onto Burr Street — their street. She slowed the car. The houses she passed looked sadder even than she remembered, smashed-out windows still being replaced by cardboard, doorsteps sinking ever deeper into the broken pavement.

She noticed two boys shoving a smaller one, and gave a blast on the horn. Sam woke to add a short, scolding bark. While the two boys glared after her, the younger one made his escape.

As she neared the house where they had lived in the bottom flat, Ellen saw a small, fair-haired girl standing forlornly on the sidewalk, her hands drawn up inside the sleeves of her green, skimpy jacket for warmth, and for one heart-stopping second, it was Gail standing there.

She drove to the end of the street, rounded the block and drove back the way she had come, through the center of town, past the police station, down King, from where she could see the ocean against the grey horizon.

Her gaze was drawn briefly to the McLeod Building, her thoughts to Cindy Miller. To the terrible sorrow of those who'd loved her. Myra told her Carl had been in Anderson Insurance installing phones on the day she was missing. He remembered her.

On Ellen drove, until the city sped away behind her, growing smaller and smaller in her rear-view mirror, until finally all signs of civilization gave way to trees and fields, and the road narrowed.

And suddenly there it was. The Evansdale Home for Girls. Grey and bleak, it loomed on the crest of the hill to her left. Behind the prison-like structure, Ellen could see the expanse of field where Myra had once told her they grew their own vegetables, the girls themselves doing the planting and tending. The field was grown over now, backed by dense woods.

Some of the wire fencing that had surrounded the grounds was still in evidence, though most of it appeared to have been pulled down, most likely by kids who came out here to party. She couldn't imagine some poor derelict seeking only a night's refuge going to so much trouble.

Gazing up at the boarded-up doors and lower windows, Ellen couldn't help wondering how many girls had suffered the torments of hell inside those cold, grey walls. You couldn't grow up in Evansdale without hearing whispers of mistreatment. 'The home' represented a bad place where you could be sent if you didn't behave. Though nothing concrete had ever surfaced so far as she knew, officials must have at least suspected the sort of abuses Myra confided to her. They hadn't closed the place down for no reason.

The small, urgent whine drew her attention. 'Sorry, Sam.' She went around to the passenger side and let him out, holding fast to the leash. They didn't know one another all that well, yet; no point in taking chances. But Sam seemed quite content to simply do his business and hop back in the car.

Why am I here, Ellen wondered. *Why did I make this journey into the past today? Did I expect to find Gail sitting on the step of our old house? Or do I imagine she's up there still — a small, pale figure waiting inside for me to come and rescue her.*

It's too late, Ellen. The moment when rescue was possible is gone. And you can't bring it back. The truth she'd been refusing to look at now rushed to the surface of her consciousness, too clear to deny. If I had warned Gail to get out of that apartment, or even if I'd telephoned 911 the instant I hung up from talking to her, she would still be alive.

She and Gail had always been able to tune into one another. She'd always known when things were not right with her little sister. Just as she'd had a sense of foreboding that day — all day. Long before they spoke on the phone, and after. Well into the night. She remembered how hard it had been to fall asleep. Even while she waited for Gail's plane to arrive, she knew.

She'd received the messages loud and clear. She just hadn't listened.

No, Gail wasn't here. She wasn't anywhere to be found. Ellen let out a long, shuddering sigh, and took a final look at the building. 'Might as well go home, huh, Sam? No point in hanging around here. We'll get you some grub on the way. You must be starved. Maybe a box of treats for all your patience.'

Sam cocked an ear. She could have sworn he smiled at her.

Driving a little further along, Ellen turned up a narrow road, backed out again, and, taking little notice of the weather-beaten sign nailed to a tree, on which was crudely printed 'Bishop's Lane', headed back into town.

★ ★ ★

Alvin wandered about the kitchen. After opening and closing several cupboard drawers, he found the one he was looking for. He chose the longest knife from among several — a butcher knife. Holding it up, he ran his gloved thumb and forefinger along its steel blade. Yes, he thought, this would do just fine. In case she was not alone when she came back. He would use it on her, too, if he had to, though he had something much more appropriate in mind for her.

32

Lieutenant Mike Oldfield was in his office with Artie Wood, their computer man, going over the printout an excited Artie had brought in to him yesterday.

Over the past ten years too damn many women were murdered in a similar method to Gail Morgan and Cindy Miller, but, happily, if you could call it that, only *four* on this list had also had their faces painted up to look like clowns. Two of the women were murdered in California, one in the west end of Boston, with the latest victim being found late last spring in a wooded area just outside Augusta. No connection had ever been made.

Two names. Two Jane Does, including the one in Augusta.

The creep got around, all right. Mike wouldn't be in the least surprised if there were more victims out there — victims who would never make their way into anyone's computer, whose bodies would never be found. Hookers. Runaways. Mike suspected there were more than even he could imagine.

'I need everything you can get me on these women, Artie,' Mike said to the bespectacled man who looked more like a college freshmen than the twelve year veteran he actually was. 'See if we can find a thread to link them.'

'They're all similar physically,' Artie said, raising an eyebrow, shrugging. 'All blond.'

'More. I need more, Artie. Concentrate on the two identified women. Get back to me. Thanks,' he called to his colleague's disappearing back.

Artie gone, Mike leaned back in his swivel chair, laced his hands behind his head and stared grimly at the spot on the ceiling where a leaky roof had, over time, sketched a pretty fair map of Italy.

Ellen's phone call was still nagging at him. It had left him feeling a little bewildered. She'd sounded so short, like she was angry at him for something. Maybe he shouldn't have kissed her, not that he thought he could have stopped himself. Come to think of it, she really didn't kiss him back. Maybe he'd missed something. Did she think he was getting too familiar, coming on too strong? Trying to take advantage of her vulnerable state of mind? Was she right? Damn it, I've been out of circulation too long. Except for Angela (and the verdict wasn't in on that, yet), he didn't know how to act around a woman anymore, unless it was in connection with his job.

And who the hell was Sam? He knew he was acting like a jealous schoolboy, but he couldn't seem to help it. Did he imagine a woman as attractive and as bright as Ellen Harris would have no other man interested in her besides him?

No, he wasn't that big a fool.

Well, at least, she isn't alone.

He turned his attention to Cindy Miller.

Why hadn't the creep painted her?

Three possibilities came to mind: one, that she didn't fit in with some *special* criteria he had. Two, there hadn't been time. And three, and this seemed the most likely to Mike, this particular prey simply lived too close to home.

The chair squeaked as Mike swiveled around to face the window from where he could look directly across the street into the public library. He could see people moving about inside, could even make out the QUIET PLEASE sign on Miss Danfield's desk.

Mike made a careful pyramid of his fingers, rested his chin there. His gaze ventured beyond the two-story sandstone structure to the radio tower that disappeared into the milky grey sky, and farther still to the misty hills that marked the county's boundary. *Where are you, you sick son-of-a-bitch?*

Anger churned in his gut.

Sighing heavily, he swiveled slowly back around, his hand going involuntarily out to cover the names on the page — a strangely protective gesture, made unconsciously. But these women were far beyond anyone's protection.

How many more before they caught him?

If they caught him.

He called his daughter at home. 'Are you okay, honey?'

'Yeah, fine. Mrs. Balena's teaching me how to make divinity fudge. Then we're going to watch *Gone With The Wind* — it's her favorite. Why? Anything wrong?'

'No, no, nothing wrong, sweetheart. I just wanted to — tell you I love you.'

'Yeah, me too.' She sounded embarrassed. 'Bye, Daddy.'

He sat motionless for several minutes, then thought, *To hell with Sam*, and dialed Ellen's number. He needed to talk to her, tell her what they'd uncovered, and the connection to her sister. He wasn't looking forward to it. He also needed to find out if there might be other connections. While Mike had a strong feeling some of the victims were chosen at random, he didn't believe they all were.

He let it ring six times before hanging up. They'd obviously gone out, probably to dinner. Another twinge of jealousy made him annoyed at himself.

There was a light rap on his door and Gabe Levine entered. Officer Levine was a tall, loose-jointed man with a hawk-like face and a deceptively lazy way of moving. He set a blue and silver bow, sealed in a clear, plastic envelope down on Mike's desk. 'An Edie Carr brought this in earlier. She cleans over at the McLeod Building. She said the bow was on a gift the Miller woman bought for her mother — a *painting*. It was for her birthday. Said she found it behind the toilet bowl when she was washing the floor.'

'What's the significance?' Mike asked, picking it up.

'The painting seems to have vanished. The mother never got it.' Levine produced his notepad, thumbed back a couple of pages. 'The Carr woman said she saw the gift herself on the same night Cindy Miller went missing.' He referred to the notepad. ' 'It was standing against the copier. I didn't actually see the painting because it was wrapped, but Cindy said it was a farm scene, said her mom grew up on a farm. It was her mom's birthday the next day, don't you see.' '

Levine was the only man in the department who wrote out all his interviews verbatim, even to capturing the speech rhythms. The practice (or compulsion) had proven valuable on a couple of cases Mike could recall. That it would help crack this one was probably too much to hope for.

'Could she be mistaken about the time?' he asked.

'Nope,' Levine said adamantly. 'Everyone in the office saw the painting that day. Said she bought it from an off-the-street salesman a couple of days earlier. Apparently, they get a lot of sales people walking in, hawking everything from office equipment to pots and pans.'

'Anything else?'

'Yep. He had a mother of a scratch down one side of his face. Joked about being attacked by a Siamese cat his favorite aunt gave him for his birthday.'

'No name, right?'

'Right. But we collected a bunch of business cards; they're being checked out.'

'What about the private eye?' Mike asked, even though he'd all but dismissed him as a serious suspect.

'Matchett? Nothing. We'll keep an eye on him, though. From what the Fisher woman said, he just *looked* at Cindy, mostly, made her feel uncomfortable. She had a cute figure, apparently liked to show it off.'

Mike got a vision of Angela in her too-tight

sweater and vowed to lose the damn thing as soon as he got home. He was grateful to Mrs. Balena, their upstairs neighbor who kept a motherly watch on Angela when he wasn't around. She was widowed, and Mike was only too happy to pay her generously for her time. Her good soul they got for free.

'Anything else, Lieutenant?'

'Nothing I can think of. Phone calls still coming in on that composite?'

'Five hundred odd so far. Like we're running an open line game show. People calling in sure it's their boy-friend, ex-husband — lots of those — brother-in-law, the guy next door. We're chasing down every lead, no matter how weird.'

'Good. You never know when we could get lucky. Any mention of the sketch bearing a resemblance to the salesman with the scratch?'

'Nope. In fact, the Fisher woman — she's sort of a self-appointed spokesman for the entire office — said it was very definitely *not* him.'

'Okay, that's it, then. Keep me posted, Gabe.'

'You got it.'

As soon as the door closed, Mike tried Ellen's number again.

Still no answer.

The ringing telephone had Alvin's own nerves screaming. He'd cut the damn line except whoever was calling would probably get suspicious and the next thing he knew cops would be bursting in here.

Where in hell was the bitch?

In the very next second, he heard a car pull into the yard. Heard the motor cut to silence, a door open and shut. Keeping well back, he peered out of the upstairs hall window.

He recognized the blue Sunbird as hers. He watched her walk around to the passenger side, open the door. Seeing a dog hop out sent alarm racing along his nerve endings.

On closer inspection, he saw that the mutt was small and mangy-looking — nothing to worry about. Nothing he couldn't take care of.

Alvin withdrew into the shadows.

33

Sam's leash hooked over her wrist, Ellen struggled into the house with the two bags of groceries she'd purchased at the supermarket, containing mostly dog food. She bumped the door shut with her hip, kicked off her boots.

In the kitchen, Ellen deposited her burden on the table, peeled off her gloves and set about getting Sam's supper prepared while the little dog sat on his haunches, watching her every move, tail beating a happy rhythm on the floor.

Filling one bowl with water, the other with food, she set them on the floor by the fridge. 'There you go, fella. Just soft stuff for now. Eat up. But not too fast, okay? You don't want to get sick.'

She needn't have worried. Sam ate hungrily, but with a touching dignity. Ellen was already in love with him. 'Good dog. Later, we'll get you cleaned up. You'll feel a whole lot better after you've had a bath.' Not at all sure how Sam would feel about that, she left him to enjoy his meal in private.

Remembering to relock the front door, she started up the stairs.

★ ★ ★

Mike was standing at the bathroom mirror, holding his shaving brush in midair, but rather than his own face, it was Ellen's he was seeing, as she'd looked when he told her her sister was dead. He mentally blinked the image away, as he'd had to look away from her terrible anguish that day. Hearing her cries from the back seat, so primal and raw they tore at him, he'd been more than a little grateful her friend, Myra, was in the back seat with her to offer comfort.

Not that she'd taken any.

Not that it was the first time he'd ever had to break lousy news to someone. Generally, though, it was to a parent whose kid had wrapped his car around a telephone pole, or o.d.'d on drugs. It was a part of the job every cop dreaded.

This wasn't New York, but they had their share of crimes just the same, mostly break-ins, assaults, but a few murders over the years. And last spring there was a suicide — a husband and father of two drove out to the edge of town, parked the car and blew his brains out. No one knew why. Mike saw his widow in town from time to time.

Splashing warm water on his face, he toweled it dry, slapped on a little shaving lotion, winced in the mirror. He glanced at his watch. It was 8:25 p.m. He'd been home twenty minutes.

'Angela, honey,' he called out. 'Give Mrs. Balena a call, will you? I've got to go out for a while.' To hell with phoning; he'd just drive on out there. Maybe there was some problem with the line.

'No one's home, Dad,' Angela called back after a minute. 'Oh, I forgot, she's at her gourmet cooking class. She always gets home around nine-thirty.'

Damn! Wednesday. Right. Well, he'd just have to wait. Maybe he would try her number again.

Mike slipped his slate blue shirt from its hanger on the door-hook and put it on, frowning in the mirror as he buttoned it. Ellen needed to pick up the pieces, go on with her life. But he knew she wouldn't be able to even begin to do that until her sister's killer was found.

He prayed for the break that would make it happen.

Evansdale was a decent little town, mostly, nestled on the banks of the Penobscot River, a good place, to raise your kids, he'd always thought. He'd wanted to keep it that way. He remembered while working for Jack Seeley over on High, pumping gas, just a few

271

months out of high school, how he'd waited on the edge for the letter that would tell him whether or not he was going to be accepted into the police academy. He could have told you the exact number of rust spots on the green mailbox at the end of their driveway.

Would it all be for nothing?

Mike went into the living room. Angela was sprawled on the sofa, talking to one of her friends on the phone. He glanced anxiously at his watch and picked up a magazine.

He'd give her exactly fifteen minutes.

*   *   *

Tossing her coat and bag on the bed, Ellen changed into her jeans and an old shirt she wouldn't mind getting doused. An icicle clung to one leg of the jeans; she plucked it off. These jeans used to be snug, now they hung on her. A dull ache was starting at the back of her head. 'It's been a long day,' she sighed aloud, sagging down on the bed.

Her hand went out to absently smooth a wrinkled pillow sham. Through the window sheers, she could see the dark branches of the tree outlined against the darker night. After a moment, she got up and started for the bathroom, intending to take a couple of aspirin.

The phone rang.

She turned back. Tensing, she picked up the receiver. 'Yes.'

'Is this Ellen Harris?'

'Yes,' she answered warily.

'You don't know me, Mrs. Harris,' the woman said. 'My name is Ruth Miller. Cindy Miller was my daughter.'

Ellen felt an instant shock of empathy, mingled with resentment. 'Oh.' She swallowed against a sudden lump in her throat. 'I'm so terribly sorry about your tragedy, Mrs. Miller. I think I have some idea what you're going through.'

'I know you do, dear. That's why you're the one I wanted to talk to. They told me at the clinic you were taking some time off. I got your number out of the phone book. I hope you don't mind.'

'No, of course not,' Ellen lied. Her headache was getting worse.

'I have to talk to someone. I don't seem to be coping very well. And I must, for the sake of my little grandson, Jody. He keeps asking for his mother, asking when she's coming home. It just tears at my heart. I know he's picking up on my own state of mind, too. He cries all the time. He doesn't sleep or eat. I don't seem to be able to help him. I can't help myself.' Her voice broke.

'Mrs. Miller, I'm sorry, but I'm not the one to . . .'

'Oh, please don't refuse me,' she said, sobbing in earnest now, 'I know you have your own troubles, dear, and I hate to bother you, but . . .'

When Ellen hung up, she'd reluctantly agreed to see Ruth Miller the following afternoon. She didn't have any idea how she was going to help her. To paraphrase Mrs. Miller's own words, 'she couldn't help herself.'

But neither had she been able to bring herself to turn her back on the distraught woman.

Ellen snapped on the bathroom light, understanding for the first time that whatever happened, she wouldn't be going back to the clinic. Paul had made that impossible, but she couldn't blame Paul. She knew that it was her own doing that she got involved in the first place.

She stood looking at herself in the mirror. Her eyes looked enormous, her cheekbones too prominent. No wonder Mike had been moved to feed her lunch.

Something drew Ellen's gaze upward, to the circle of moisture on the mirror. The size of a half-dollar, it was evaporating even as she watched, becoming smaller and smaller. At first, the implication of what she was seeing did not register. And then it did, raising the hairs on the nape of her neck, slamming her heart up into her throat.

Someone had stood in this very spot just seconds ago. It was his breath on the glass she was seeing.

Licking suddenly dry lips, Ellen turned her head slowly, and saw what she had failed to see when she'd entered the bathroom.

The shower curtain was fully drawn.

Now she could see the faint silhouette looming behind the beige plastic. Her mind flooded with terror. *No . . . no . . . mustn't panic.* This was the moment she had waited for, had deliberately brought about. Except she had planned to have a gun in her hand. For the first time, it was not within easy reach. It was in her bag, on the bed. She had to get to it! *Please, God, let me.*

Her eyes riveted on the shadowy figure behind the curtain, she took silent backward steps, reached behind her for the doorknob, found it. Slowly, she turned it, pulled the door open a few inches. But she was too late. Suddenly, the curtain whooshed open, and he was standing there, grinning at her, the steel blade glittering in the bathroom light, poised above his head. 'Looking for me?'

She screamed.

With a lightning-quick movement, she was out the door and into the hallway before he could clear the tub. Sam was bounding up the stairs, barking wildly, growling, hackles raised.

'No, Sam,' she cried out, but even, as she said it, Sam had leaped at the throat of the man standing in her bathroom doorway. She could only watch in shocked horror as the knife arched through the air and plunged into Sam's body. The little dog let out a wail of pain that sounded uncannily human.

Her mind reeling with grief and helpless rage, Ellen watched through blurred vision as the man pulled the bloody knife from Sam. She heard the wet sound it made coming out.

Then he was grinning up at her. A death mask grin. Cold, cruel eyes. Narrow lips. Jagged scar down one side of his face. *You can't help Sam now. Get the gun. Try to save yourself.*

She bolted for the bedroom, slammed the door shut, but before she could get it locked, he rammed it, and she went flying across the room. She landed hard on the floor. The wind was knocked from her. She couldn't move. *You have to. Get up, damn you! Get up!* Gasping for breath, she struggled to her feet. Her heart was thumping in her breast like a small, trapped bird.

He was standing between her and the bed — between her and the gun. Mike needn't have worried about her being capable of killing him. She would shoot this monster before her without batting an eye, except she didn't think she was going to get the chance. There was no way to get to the gun save going through him, and she'd be joining Sam very quickly if she tried that.

He took a couple of steps toward her, his big boots making small thuds on the wooden floor. He moved with deliberate slowness, his expression mocking her. She was backed against the dresser. Her gaze involuntarily flickered to her bag, on the bed. She looked away, but too late. He'd already seen where she was looking.

Sauntering over to the bed, he picked up the bag, opened it. He turned it upside down, spilling the contents out onto the cream-colored spread. Smiled. Palming the gun, he held it out to her. 'Is this what you want?' His voice was soft. 'Come and get it.' He chuckled low in his throat, a mad, thoroughly evil sound that sent ice crystals racing along her spine. It was a laugh she'd heard only once before — over her phone line.

He dropped the gun into the deep pocket of what looked to be army camouflage coveralls.

Standing beside the bed, the light from the lamp on her nightstand cast half his face in shadow, highlighting the side bearing the scar.

A fairly recent scar. *Fragments of skin and blood were found under her fingernails.* Ellen knew intuitively Gail was responsible for the scar. She had clawed his face in her desperate struggle to live.

It was like a sign from beyond the grave. She could almost hear her sister's voice: *Fight him, Ellen! Fight him! Don't let him win this time.*

She reached behind her on the dresser for something to hit him with, her hand fumbling briefly before closing over the handle of her blow dryer. At the very instant he lunged at her, she brought it around with every ounce of strength she had, catching him squarely across the side of the head.

He stopped cold, letting out a grunt of pain and surprise. The knife clattered to the floor as his hand flew to the spot where she'd struck him. Blood was running between his fingers, over the back of his hand. He gave her one crazed look of fury before he staggered, half-falling on the bed.

She glanced at the knife on the floor, but it was too close to him, and he was already getting to his feet. Dropping the blow dryer, she sprinted past him into the hallway, (and tried not to look at Sam) and down the stairs, sneakered feet flying. She stumbled once, almost hurtling herself the rest of the way, but she managed to clutch onto the bannister and regain her balance.

Even before she hit the bottom step, she could hear his boots thumping heavily down the stairs behind her, could hear the string of obscenities defiling the air.

Her eyes focused on the front door directly in her path, but she knew she wouldn't have time to unlock it. Even if she did, she'd freeze to death without a coat. Running on past, she fled into the kitchen where she yanked open the knife-drawer, inadvertently bringing the whole thing crashing to the floor. She bent to grab a knife, but before she could pick it up, his boot slammed down on her wrist. Ellen cried out as agonizing pain shot up her arm and into her shoulder, buckling her knees. Blackness threatened. *No! You can't faint! You mustn't. You'll never waken.*

Far away, she could hear a phone ringing.

★ ★ ★

Mike hung up the phone. He checked his watch for the fifteenth time in twenty minutes. 8:45 p.m. A sense of urgency was growing in his gut.

He paced the living room. Sat down. Picked up a magazine. Tossed it. Got up again. Ten minutes later, he called the station. 'Did they get that unmarked car back out to Ellen Harris' place?'

'On its way.'

He muttered an oath, hung up. It should have been there hours ago. He checked his watch again. 8:55 p.m.

Angela came into the room. 'Daddy, it's okay if you need to go out. You're real worried about Ellen Harris, aren't you? You think the bad man will go after her, too.'

He started to lie, changed his mind. 'I'm not real easy about it, Angela, to be honest.'

'You really like her a lot, don't you?'

He grinned at her. She looked so serious, so grown up. 'Yeah, I guess I do, pumpkin.'

'Do you love her?'

He tousled her hair. 'Don't be so nosy.'

'You *dooo*,' she sang. 'I can tell. Well, you better go, then. I can wait right here until Mrs. Balena gets home. I'll lock the door and I promise I won't answer it to anyone. It's only twenty-five minutes more, for heaven's sake. Hardly that, now. I'm not a baby, Daddy.'

'No. No, you're not, sweetheart. You're sure not a baby.'

'Well, then. So go already. I'll be fine.'

'I'm sure you're right, Angela. It's your dad who'd have a problem with that.' He dialed the station again. 'I think I'll just make sure they go up to the house and check on her as soon as they get there. I'll wait for Mrs. Balena.'

Hands propped on her boyish hips, Angela rolled her eyes in mock exasperation.

34

He was straddling her, pinning her beneath him. She tried to fight him, to push him off, but he was too strong. His mouth mashed down on hers. She jerked her head away, but he gripped a handful of hair and forced her head still.

She was totally helpless now, unable to move. She could smell the wave of sourness coming off him, mingling with the odor of stale beer. He brought his mouth down again.

No! No, you bastard. I'll die first!

The instant his mouth touched hers, Ellen clamped her teeth down on his lower lip, bit down until she tasted blood. She fought the urge to gag.

Frantic as a speared fish, his hand wound tighter in her hair and he smashed her head against the floor in an effort to make her let go. With their mouths joined, his own head could only follow up and down with hers, teeth and noses striking together.

Pain exploded in Ellen's skull. Still, she hung on. And then his hands were around her throat, his fingers digging into the soft flesh, squeezing the breath from her. There was a roaring in her ears, a burst of color behind her eyelids. Her lungs on fire, she released his lip, noisily gulped in air, her chest heaving.

Looking up into his face, so twisted with hate and savagery, so utterly devoid of humanity, Ellen knew she was going to die. She waited helplessly for the final violation before he killed her.

And then she remembered him dropping the gun into his pocket. Maybe if he was distracted, she could . . .

But Alvin had lost all interest in raping her. Now his rage demanded a more immediate satisfaction. He began to beat her, pummeling her face and body with his fists as he vented his fury. Ellen tried vainly to protect herself, but in the face of such a brutal onslaught, her own small fists were as pesky moths flying against a screen door.

One of the blows smashed into her cheek, and she heard the bone crack and echo inside her head.

After that, she heard nothing at all.

35

Myra hung up from talking to the kids. It was 9:30 p.m. She didn't like Joey being up an hour past his bedtime, but she didn't voice her opinion. They were having a good time at Grandma Thompson's, and she guessed once in a while wouldn't hurt. They'd be home on Sunday.

She was about to dial Ellen's number again, thought better of it. She might just put her off. Maybe she was deliberately not answering her phone. Myra'd made the mistake of respecting her wishes and leaving her on her own after Ed died, and now she was doing it again. To hell with that. They'd just drive on down there. Ellen was the first person to put a hand out to someone else, but when it came to herself, she had too damn much pride, and a stubborn streak a mile wide.

Carl was warming up the car. Myra did a quick trip to the bathroom, and grabbed her coat.

★　★　★

284

Under darkness of night, unobserved but for a crescent of moon slipping in and out of raggy clouds, Alvin made his way across the frozen field, his prey draped over his shoulder. He aimed the flashlight low.

Even dead weight, she was much lighter than he'd expected. No trouble for him.

Nevertheless, when two minutes later he reached the small clearing in the woods where he'd parked the van, he was panting heavily. Sweating despite the cold.

His head hurt where the bitch had struck him with the blow dryer. His tongue probed his torn lower lip. He spat blood.

As he dropped her limp body to the ground, her arms flung outward as if in supplication to the heavens.

He was looking down at her when he heard the mournful call of a loon in the distance, mingling with the sighing of the wind in the trees.

Alvin looked nervously around him. Again, the loon's cry echoed on the night, causing his skin to crawl inside his clothes. Had the wind grown stronger? Despite the cold, he was now sweating profusely. Was it possible she could summon Satan's forces to save her? To destroy her enemies? She was a witch, after all. Hadn't her voice come to him in the night, wakened him?

No! No, I am the powerful one!

Hearing a car motor, panic gripped him. Picking her up off the ground, he threw her roughly into the back of the van. Her body struck the metal floor with a heavy thud. Closing the doors, he jumped into the van and sped off.

★ ★ ★

Where Cutter's Road met the main road, Officer Gabe Levine, sitting in the passenger side of the unmarked car that had been dispatched to Ellen Harris' house, barely noticed the dark Ford van going in the opposite direction.

36

Standing on the front step, Myra pressed the doorbell a second time. She could hear it ringing inside the house. Still no answer. 'I don't get it,' she half-whispered to Carl. 'She's got to be home. Her car's in the drive.'

'Maybe she's asleep.'

'You don't think the bell would wake her?' she said, almost angrily.

'She could have taken a sleeping pill.'

Yeah, Myra thought. *And she just might be passed out drunk in there. 'I developed a bit of a problem after Ed died.' Damn, why did I listen to her?* 'Let's try the back door,' she said finally.

'Maybe we should just let . . . '

But Myra was already racing around to the back.

She was about to knock on the door. Seeing it slightly open, an alarm went off inside her head. She opened it the rest of the way. 'Ellen?' she said softly, stepping into the brightly lit kitchen. She froze. 'Oh, my God! Oh, my God, Carl!' she breathed.

Stepping past her, Carl took in the macabre scene — the knife drawer on the floor, knives scattered everywhere, the bloody handprint on the white enameled, lower cupboard door, all the more horrible in the stark light of the room. 'Don't touch anything,' he said hoarsely. 'I'll call the police.'

The words were no sooner said when the doorbell rang sharply, followed by an urgent pounding on the front door. 'Mrs. Harris? Police! Are you all right in there?'

★   ★   ★

9:55 p.m.

Mike had just pulled in behind the dark green Chevy, was getting out of his car when a wild-eyed Myra Thompson flung the door open, screamed hysterically at them, 'She's dead. He's killed her. In — in the — kitchen.'

Ignoring Carl Thompson's attempt to clarify his wife's statement while at the same time trying to calm her, Mike burst past them all into the house, the small entourage at his heels.

He stopped at the kitchen door, braced for whatever horror might confront him. After a moment, he turned to look at Myra. 'Where?' His voice was hard.

'I didn't mean *Ellen* was here,' she said,

valiantly trying to get herself under control. 'But — look . . . '

She was pointing to the bloody handprint on the door. 'It's not hers,' he said, his voice softening a little. 'It's too large to be Ellen's.' He didn't want to ponder what that might mean.

He noted the two bags of groceries on the table, her kid gloves on the counter, the small pile of mail on the table, the untouched cup of tea. He stepped into the room, bent and picked up a Polaroid snapshot lying on the floor by the table leg. He already knew what its subject would be. It was the sort of thing those bastards did — part of the buzz.

But it was himself he was really blaming. He should have told her sooner. He'd had his reasons, of course. Unfortunately, they weren't working for him right now.

He gazed down at girl in the photo, felt sick at heart. No wonder she'd sounded so cool when she phoned him. He knew now it was hurt and anger he'd heard in her voice. She'd trusted him, and he'd betrayed her by not giving her the full truth.

He prayed it hadn't cost her her life.

Handing the photograph to Levine, who slipped it into a clear envelope and sealed it closed, Mike said to Carl and an equally ashen-faced Myra, 'Did you two go anywhere else in the house?'

'Only to answer your knock,' Myra said in a high, tremulous voice. 'We came in the back way. The door was open.'

'He must have left just minutes before we all got here,' Gabe put in. 'It's a damn cold night out, and the kitchen's still warm.' With that, he headed into the living room, gun drawn, just in case he was wrong and the killer was still in the house.

Mike glanced down at the manila envelope on the table, at Ellen's name printed in the same red-inked, block lettering as on the note she'd shown him. Noting the lack of a postmark, he took a last quick look around the kitchen, saw what he'd missed on first scan. Two bowls on the floor by the refrigerator, one filled with dog food, the other with water. A leash lay on top of the fridge, blue loop handle hanging down. Something else began to dawn on him, then — something that made him silently curse his own stupidity. Motioning to the other officer to remain with the Thompsons, Mike headed into the hallway and up the stairs, his own gun drawn, his shadow bounding up the wall beside him.

Reaching the top of the stairs, he saw the small pool of blood by the bathroom door — followed its trail with his eyes to what he assumed was Ellen's bedroom — the door was party open. Horrible visions flooding his mind, he closed his eyes and gripped the bannister.

'You okay, Lieutenant?' Gabe whispered, coming up soundlessly beside him, touching his shoulder.

Mike nodded, mentally shook himself. *Get a grip on it, Oldfield. You're a cop, dammit! Do your job!* So far he'd been a royal screw-up. Slamming a door on his personal feelings, leaving Gabe to check out the rest of the upstairs, Mike went into the bedroom.

He saw the contents of her bag spilled onto the bed, noticed the pack of cigarettes. He'd never seen her smoke. The gun was gone. No surprise. There was another bloody handprint on the bedspread on the bed closest to the dresser. The blood-spattered blow dryer was on the floor.

The trail of blood leading from the puddle in the hallway disappeared under the bed. Mike got down on his hands and knees and peered into the dark, narrow space. Glazed eyes flickered open to look pitifully out at him.

'Sam?' he said softly.

The dog lay unmoving, but managed a faint whimper in response.

By lying flat on the floor on his stomach

291

and inching forward, Mike was able to reach in far enough to get his hands behind the dog and ease him out from under the bed. He could feel the small body growing cooler as the life ebbed from it. The dog's fur was matted with blood; he was trembling, starting to convulse.

'He's in shock,' Mike said to Levine, who'd just returned from checking out the closet. Both men had put their guns away. 'He's lost a lot of blood. We've got to get him some help.'

'A little late,' Gabe said, staring down at the limp form, wondering why in hell the lieutenant was worried about a damned mutt. Clearly, the dog was history. 'He's dying,' he said. 'He knows it, too. It's why he dragged himself under the bed.'

'Have someone rush him to a vet, anyway,' Mike said sharply, getting to his feet and looking around for something warm to wrap the dog in. 'And get on the phone and have them set up roadblocks. Tell them to get some back-up out here.'

Levine wasted no time executing Mike's orders. ' . . . no way of knowing, Captain,' he said into the mouthpiece. 'The back door was open. He could have chased her out into the woods; maybe she's out there now, hiding, hurt. Or he could have taken her with him.

We don't know at this point.' It was at that moment that Gabe remembered the van he and Olsen had passed on their way out here.

He would have staked his career on it that Ellen Harris was in the back of that van.

37

Downstairs, while rookie police officer Doug Olsen took off for town with Sam, who had slipped into unconsciousness and might even be dead, Mike further questioned Carl and Myra Thompson. He wasn't getting anywhere. Myra was too upset to be of much help, and he wasn't even sure what questions to ask.

As he slipped the envelope the photograph had come in into a larger one, it occurred to Mike that the F.B.I. would have to be brought in. That they had a serial killer on the loose was no longer in question, if it ever was. Except now they had a clear DNA match from semen taken from three of the victims, which also matched up with blood and skin found under Gail Morgan's fingernails. He'd gotten the call as he was leaving the house.

'Maybe you should take your wife home, now,' he said quietly to Carl Thompson, who was trying unsuccessfully to comfort his wife, looking none too stable himself. 'There's nothing more you can do right now. I'll come by when we're finished up here.' To Myra, he said, 'We'll find her. I promise you. I know it's hard, but try not to worry.' His words sounded hollow in his own ears.

Nodding gratefully, Carl led the sobbing woman away from the scene that spoke louder than any words ever could of the horror that had befallen their friend.

They had just pulled away when half a dozen squad cars came screaming up to the front of the house, lights whirling, casting the entire area in hellish light.

Within minutes, flashlights were darting like giant fireflies through the woods. Men shouting to one another — joining Mike's own anxious voice in calling out Ellen's name.

It was forty-five minutes later that far more subdued and silent men came traipsing back across the field. Though they had found the spot where they figured the van had been parked, evidenced by broken branches, flattened brush, a fresh tire track in a patch of snow the rain hadn't washed away, they had not found Ellen.

That fragile thread of hope Mike had clung to was broken. She had not escaped her attacker.

The train of squad cars long gone, Mike and Gabe were rechecking the house, taking notes, bagging evidence. 'Why do you think he took her?' Gabe said, returning from upstairs and coming into the kitchen. 'Why didn't he just rape and strangle her like he did the others?'

'Because he's got something special in mind for her,' Mike said quietly, looking around almost numbly for that important piece of evidence he'd missed — something that would tell him where he took her. 'She publicly challenged him.' He sagged into a kitchen chair. 'He'll make her pay for that.'

Gabe cleared his throat. 'Well, at least we know she's not dead. There would be no reason to . . . ' The phone rang. Gabe snapped up the receiver. 'Yeah, this is Levine.' He listened. Mike knew by his expression it was not good news. He was right. No van with an abducted woman inside was found. They were in the process of taking down the roadblocks.

Mike glanced at his watch. 12:10 a.m.

After a moment's pause, Levine said wearily, 'We were too late. He had too good a head start.'

Mike thought: they were too late getting an unmarked vehicle out here; I was too late getting out here.

'There were a few specks of mud on the bottom of the tub, Lieutenant. He was probably standing behind the shower curtain when she came into the bathroom. And I plucked out a couple of cigarette butts floating in the toilet,' Levine added, as if this would surely cheer Mike up. 'Not her brand.'

'Pall Mall, right?' Mike said dully.

Levine shrugged, gave him a funny look. 'That'd be my bet. He came in through her bedroom window — climbed the tree. There's a fresh gouge in the wood where he shoved something under the frame to break the lock.'

Mike laughed.

Levine looked startled.

'Sorry, Gabe. You did a great job. We've got more solid clues here than you'd need to get through three mystery weekends. And we've got nothing.'

Gabe took a step toward him, hawk-eyes studying him from beneath bushy eyebrows. 'Hey, Lieutenant, if you don't mind my saying so, you don't look too good. You can tell me to mind my own business, but this wouldn't by any chance be something more than just a case for you, would it?'

Mike nodded. 'Yes, Gabe,' he said, his voice carrying all the weight he was feeling. 'I guess you could say that. She set herself up as bait to draw him out,' he went on quietly, staring down at his hands. 'We should have given her better protection. If she'd been a cop, we would have stuck to her like velcro.'

'Jeez, I'm real sorry, Lieutenant. You know, you're right about that. But we'll find her. We will,' he said, repeating Mike's own promise to Myra. A promise that sounded just as hollow as when he'd made it.

Both men fell into an uneasy silence.

38

'Do either of you recall seeing a strange van in the area, lately?' Mike asked. He was sitting at the Thompson's kitchen table, sipping tea Carl had made. Myra sat across from him beside Carl, clutching her cup with both hands. She had calmed down considerably. Now she just looked numb.

'No,' she said in a small voice. 'Carl drives a company van when he's working, but other than that . . . why, do you think he took her away in a van?'

'We're pretty certain of it. This is a dead end road, and one of our officers remembered passing a van headed into town on their way out here — passed it right where the main road begins.'

'And he didn't get a license number?' Carl asked incredulously.

'Unfortunately, no. There was no reason to. We weren't on the lookout for a van, then. We didn't know Ellen had been taken.' He turned his attention to Myra. 'What about the note, Mrs. Thompson? Was there anything about the note that rang any bell for you — the printing, the choice of words . . . ?' He was grasping at straws, but you never knew when something would click — something that could break a case wide open. Glancing at the colorful drawings pinned with magnetic daisies to the front of the fridge door, Mike found himself wondering what sort of pictures a child who would grow up to be a psychopathic killer would draw.

'What note?' He turned to see Myra looking blankly at him.

'The one that maniac slipped under her windshield wiper.'

'Ellen didn't tell me about any note. Oh, my God . . . ' She lowered her head into her hands. Carl smoothed her hair, his face anxious.

It seemed odd to Mike that Ellen hadn't confided something like that to her friend. Wouldn't it be natural to expect . . .

'My wife hasn't been feeling too well, lately,' Carl said, picking up on Mike's thoughts. 'Ellen probably didn't tell her about the note because she didn't want to upset her further.'

'Oh, Carl,' Myra said, looking up at him almost sympathetically. 'That might be part of the reason, but the truth is, though Ellen was a wonderful friend to me, she never really let me in. Well — maybe she was starting to. It was like she couldn't trust the whole way.

Other than Ed, the only other person she was really close to was her sister, Gail.'

Ed was her late husband. He had bought her the gun, Mike thought, taught her how to use it. It was gone from her bag. Somehow, Mike didn't think it was in Ellen's possession. What Myra said fit in with the little he really knew about Ellen. He wanted more than anything to have the chance to know her better. And he would. He damned well would! He held to the belief, which was really a prayer.

'I'm not going to keep you folks much longer,' he said. 'I know how hard this is — how exhausted you both are. Just a couple more questions.'

'Ask as many as you need to,' Myra said, 'if it will help you to find her.'

'Thanks.' Mike smiled wearily. 'Right now we're going at this from several angles. Trying to trace the van is one. We're following up on every phone lead. We're also attempting to establish a link between the victims, and, subsequently, their killer. Clearly, time is not on our side.' Repressing a sigh, Mike glanced down at his notes. 'I don't suppose either of you were acquainted with Cindy Miller?'

Carl looked surprised at the question. He glanced at Myra. To Mike he said, 'No. I did meet her, though. I told Myra about it. I was

301

installing a couple of phones in Anderson's Insurance over at the McLeod Building. She showed me where they wanted them, and then she seemed anxious to get back to the guy who was in there selling paintings. If I'm not mistaken, I think she bought one.'

Mike stroked his jaw, for a moment saying nothing, just staring off into space. 'No,' he said finally. 'You're not mistaken. She bought the painting for her mother's birthday. Mrs. Miller never got it. In fact, no one's seen it since the night Cindy was missing. You didn't happen to notice a scratch on this guy's face?'

'Sure. You couldn't miss it. It was real nasty — looked infected. Said a cat scratched him.'

Maybe not a cat, Mike thought. Maybe not a cat at all. 'Did you happen to see the police composite on T.V.? Or in the paper, Mr. Thompson?'

'It's Carl, Lieutenant. Sure I saw it. I'm pretty sure it wasn't the same guy, though. Why? Did anyone in Anderson's Insurance think it was?'

'No. No, they didn't, actually.' Odd, Mike thought. Very odd. His brow furrowed in concentration as a new path began to present itself to him. Vaguely at first, then with definite clarity. He would see where it led. 'I don't suppose,' he said, looking from one to the other, 'you hung onto that particular newspaper?'

A few minutes later, Myra was moving cups and teapot to one side and spreading the paper out on the kitchen table. All three stared down at the artist's sketch of the man A.J. Brooker had identified as the one who was in the Shelton Room just a couple of hours before Ellen's sister was murdered.

Mike was watching Carl intently.

'It doesn't look anymore like him than it did the first time I saw it,' Carl said flatly.

'Take your time, Carl. Look closer.' Mike's voice was quiet, weighted with urgency, hope. 'What if he didn't have the dark glasses on? And what if he had shorter hair, thinning?' Mike asked, recalling Gabe's written description. 'Not curly.'

Carl looked at it a moment longer, then, shaking his head, said, 'No. I don't think so. Anyway, I'm not that imaginative. Someone would have to draw him like that for me. Maybe then . . . oh, and what about the scratch? In this sketch,' he said, tapping the drawing with his index finger, 'there are no marks on his face.'

'There wouldn't be,' Mike said. 'The doorman saw him *before* he murdered Gail Morgan.'

39

'C'mon to bed, honey,' Carl said, laying a hand on Myra's shoulder. 'Try to get a little rest. They'll call if they find out anything.'

'I can't. You go ahead if you want to. I'll just sit here on the sofa — I'll lie down if I get sleepy.' She knew she wouldn't. She couldn't close her eyes without seeing that bloody handprint sliding down the cupboard door, without imagining . . .

Even now she could hear Ellen's voice on the phone telling her about the skin and blood they found under Gail's fingernails. And now the same monster who murdered Gail had Ellen. *Oh, please, God, help her!* Maybe it was too late. Maybe she was already dead.

Her thoughts raced.

Why didn't she ever see Jeannie Perry again? Why had she not once thought of her in all this time until she spelled out her name on the Scrabble board? It didn't make any sense. She offered to be her friend. God knows, she could have used one back then.

304

She was so pretty. She got her to stop crying. She was grateful to her. She clearly remembered feeling grateful. And why in hell was she mixing up thoughts of Ellen with Jeannie Perry, as though they were somehow connected? What could they possibly have to do with one another?

A 'Suffer the Little Children' picture slid up on the screen of her mind. A lamb in the picture. *Silence of the Lambs* was playing at the Paramount. She and Ellen feeding the pigeons, laughing. A brown van circling the square. A man looking out at them.

Did I really see that? Or did Lieutenant Oldfield plant the suggestion in my head. What did it all mean? Nothing, Myra. Absolutely nothing. Except that maybe you're finally losing what's left of your little mind.

She stared at the mute phone.

Please, please be alive, Ellen.

40

I'm in the hospital, she thought. I got hit by a car. My schoolbooks flew everywhere. She had to tell someone to get them for her. Someone said they tried to get her mother to ride in the ambulance, but they couldn't wake her up because she was too drunk, and no one could find Daddy.

'Do you know your name, dear?' the woman said. 'No, don't move, honey. Just lie still.'

'I'm Ellen Sarah Morgan,' she heard herself say. 'And I'm eight years old. I didn't cross against the light, honest.'

'It's not your fault, Ellen. Now don't try to talk anymore.'

Why was it so cold? Why didn't Mommy come? *I hurt, Mommy. I hurt so bad.*

And then the hurt faded as the darkness slipped over her again.

41

Back at the station, Mike studied the printout Artie handed him, though Artie had already related the information. 'Okay. So, we've got 147 registered vans in and around Evansdale,' he said. 'Let's start eliminating.'

'Son-of-a-bitch,' Gabe muttered, shaking his head. 'If only I'd thought to get the damn license number.' He was leaning against the wall by the door, arms folded. 'I can't even tell you for sure what color the van was.'

'You did say it was dark.'

'Yeah — maybe dark blue or black.'

'Strike all light-colored vans, Artie. New model?'

'Uh, no. Possibly eight, ten years old. Smooth running, though. Well-maintained.'

'Toss all vans four years and newer,' Artie said before Mike could open his mouth. 'That oughta trim 'er down pretty good.'

Mike thought about the profile Ellen had put together for him. She'd written that the killer might be driving an 'old car,' further on suggesting a van. Probably with lots of miles

307

on it, tinted windows.

What else? Mike picked up the now bulging folder from his desk and slid out the stapled, yellow sheets, flipped back a page. Reread: *He could have a job that takes him around the country. That way he can travel wherever he chooses without arousing suspicion. A salesman, maybe? He's likeable on the surface, has learned to mimic appropriate behavior. May live by himself or with his mother. Despises women, perhaps starting with her. Reason can be real or imagined. Addicted to pornography, the more violent the better. A loner except when he's working.*

Other general stuff. Mike slid the pages back into the folder, wondered heavily how different the profile might be if, at the time Ellen compiled it, she'd been in possession of all the facts. Maybe it wouldn't be any different.

Running a hand through his hair, Mike looked around at his equally bleary-eyed colleagues. Everything that could be done was being done. Now they could only wait and hope for a break. 'Let's get some shut-eye, guys,' he said. 'We'll meet back here at . . . ' He looked at his watch ' . . . six-thirty.'

'Tonight?' Olsen piped up.

Mike didn't trust himself to answer.

'This morning, 'old son,' ' Gabe said, playing on the name 'Olsen,' and grinning wryly at his newest wet-be-hind-the-ears partner.

★ ★ ★

It was exactly quarter to four when Mike slipped his key into the lock and let himself into the house. Mrs. Balena was asleep on the sofa, snoring softly. He hated to wake her, but she'd be more comfortable in his bed, anyway. 'Sorry I'm so late,' he whispered, getting out of his jacket. 'I've got to go out again in a couple of hours. Can you stay?'

'No problem.' She stifled a yawn, rose on one elbow. 'Oh, a man called while you were out — just after midnight. He said to give you a message. It was a very weird message, Mike. I wrote it down, but it's not that hard to remember.'

'Oh?' He felt a cold dread in his gut. 'What was it?'

'He just said, 'Tell the lieutenant, 'Ding-dong, the witch is dead.' ' '

Mike's breath caught somewhere in his chest and stayed there. He couldn't seem to expel it. After a moment, he said, 'What else?'

'That's all. Just 'Ding-dong, the witch is dead'. Then he laughed.'

42

4:05 a.m.

'Ellen — it's time to wake up, Ellen.'

The voice seemed to come from far off, but she knew it was the doctor. She wanted to do what he asked, but her eyes felt swollen shut. They hurt. Everything hurt. 'I'm Ellen Sarah Morgan,' she whispered again, running her tongue over dry, bruised lips. 'Where's my Mommy?'

'She's not here, Ellen. She's abandoned you. Your mother's no good, just a drunken whore.'

Instant tears welled behind her lids. Why would the doctor say something so mean? Mommy drinks sometimes, but she's not the bad word he said. She could hear the wind howling outside. I'm so cold. Why doesn't someone cover me? Gradually, Ellen became aware of the smells in the air — not the medicinal ones of the hospital, but old, musty smells — sort of the way her grandmother's attic used to smell, except for the cold. Soon, Ellen grew conscious of the hard floor beneath her, unrelieved by the thin, stinking blanket she lay on. She was curled on her side. She tried to move her hands, felt the rope bite into her flesh. Her hands were bound behind her.

Everything came rushing back to her now, like a train speeding through the night to its destination. There was no way to stop it. She was not a child suffering some minor bruising and a broken leg from a confrontation with a car, and this was anything but a hospital.

'Do you know me?' Horribly soft-spoken words uttered from the darkness, chilling her with a deeper, far more malicious cold that had little to do with the temperature. He had sensed her return to the present.

She tried again to open her eyes. This time, out of small slits, she peered into the inky blackness. She heard a faint 'click' and suddenly his face was floating above her, glowing, disembodied, a nightmare jack-o-lantern come to life.

She tried to scream, but no sound came.

And then, realizing he was holding a flashlight under his chin, grinning down at her, she began to cry. You bastard. You cruel, sick bastard.

He laughed as though she'd spoken the words aloud. 'It's a joke, Ellen. Just a little joke. What's the matter? Don't witches have a sense of humor?' He snapped off the flashlight, instantly returning them both to darkness.

She felt his fingers brush her cheek. She winced. The entire side of her face throbbed with pain. 'Please — please don't hurt me anymore . . .'

He removed his hand. 'I'm not going to hurt you, Ellen,' he said, sounding wounded at being misunderstood. 'Do you need to use the bathroom?'

This new, gentle tone left her feeling confused. Was it another 'joke'? 'Yes, please,' she whispered. It didn't hurt as much to speak if she remembered to open her mouth just a little. She ventured farther. 'Would you untie me?' Even if he agreed, which was unlikely, she didn't know if she'd be able to walk, or even to stand. But she had to try. Ellen knew she was badly hurt, but at least she was still alive.

She didn't question why.

'Yes, Ellen, of course I'll untie you. You just lie still now. You must be very cold. There's a bad storm brewing. I'll bring you some blankets.'

But he'd promised to untie her so she could use the bathroom. Where was he going? Had he brought her to his house? It didn't feel like a real house where people lived. Ellen lay listening to the hollow sound his boots made on the wood floor. Finally, she could no longer hear them. She tried to tune in to other sounds that might give her some clue as to where she was, but other than the odd creaking sound, and an ominous scurrying in the wall, there was only the raging of the wind outside.

The wind sounded so close. She felt strangely as if she were at the center of the storm. There were no windows, so the walls must be very thin. No insulation to muffle the sound. Perhaps she was in an attic, after all. Or a barn.

Ellen started as his voice leaped out of the darkness. 'Is Lieutenant Mike Oldfield your boyfriend, Ellen? Is he the man you lay with?' The hard edge was back in his voice, all pretense of gentleness gone.

'No,' she said, her heart racing with the fright of hearing him so unexpectedly, and sense of her complete helplessness. He must have tiptoed back. Why? Where did he think she could go in her condition? Aside from being tied up.

'Are you sure? I found a scrap of paper beside your telephone with his name and number on it. And I've seen you with him — once through the window of a restaurant.

I've also seen his squad car parked in your driveway. Pretty damning evidence, Ellen. I don't much like being played for a fool.'

Ellen said nothing.

There was no answer.

43

Mike collapsed on the sofa, closing his eyes for maybe twenty minutes, then he showered and shaved, drank two cups of black coffee and was back at the station by six-fifteen.

'We're on the right track, finally,' he said the instant Levine walked in the door. 'It just hit me — so damned simple I don't know why we didn't make the connection before.'

'What, Mike? What connection?'

'It *is* the guy who sold her the painting. He's our killer. He's the one who has Ellen.'

Levine shrugged. 'Maybe . . . '

'No maybe about it, Gabe. It's why he took the painting. Who else would take it? It wasn't valuable as a piece of art. No, he took it, okay. For one obvious reason. It links him with Cindy Miller. An irrational, impulsive action. A mistake. We need a name, Gabe. We need to find out who this guy works for.'

By seven o'clock Mike had in his possession a newly wrought artist's drawing of the man A. J. Brooker saw in the Shelton Room on the night Gail was murdered — this

315

time without the dark glasses, or longish, blond curly hair. Mike's foot hard on the gas pedal, the cruiser went screaming out to Cutter's Road, parting traffic all the way.

Carl Thompson needed only one look before he said, 'You were right, Lieutenant. That's him, okay. Maybe not exact, but close enough. That's definitely the guy I saw in Anderson's Insurance selling oil paintings.'

Mike laid a grateful hand on Carl's shoulder. 'Good man. Carl, you didn't happen to hear anyone call him by name? Or maybe mention the company he worked for?'

'No. But I knew a fella once who was into the same line of work. Sold paintings all over the country. Did okay, too, according to him. I think he sent his orders along with his check to some post office box he saw in an ad. They'd ship the paintings to him. He got to keep everything over and above what he paid.'

Damn, Mike thought. Ferreting out some shady, if not downright illegal operation in God knows where could take weeks. He didn't have weeks. If that phone call Mrs. Balena got last night was on the level, maybe he had no time at all.

'I'm just making a pot of coffee, Lieutenant. Care to join me?'

'Uh, no thanks, anyway, Carl,' he said to the big man in the brown rumpled robe, whose own face spoke of a hell of a long night. 'Smells tempting but if you don't mind, I'll take a raincheck. I'm going to try and confirm your I.D. with the staff at Anderson Insurance. Not that it's absolutely necessary, but it can't hurt. How's your wife coping?'

Carl shook his head, ran a hand through his thinning hair. Sighed. 'Not so good. I gave her something to help her sleep. She blames herself. She figures if she'd insisted on staying with Ellen, this wouldn't have happened.'

'If she'd insisted on staying with Ellen,' Mike said soberly, 'we might very well be looking for Myra, too.' He didn't add that they probably would have found her — at least enough of her to bury. Shame instantly followed a twinge of envy Mike felt because the woman Carl Thompson loved was upstairs, safe in her bed.

While Ellen — where was Ellen?

* * *

Carl was pouring himself a cup of coffee when Myra came into the kitchen, her eyes quietly questioning.

'I thought you were asleep, honey,' he said, automatically reaching into the cupboard for another cup. 'Lieutenant Oldfield was here; he asked about you.'

'I thought I heard someone talking. Anything . . . ?'

'He brought out a new composite. It *was* the same guy I saw in Anderson's Insurance selling paintings.'

'Oh.' She looked frightened. 'Carl, let's go and get the boys from your mother's. I want them with me.'

'Why?' He set their cups of coffee on the table. 'Myra, they're fine where they are. They'll be home on Sunday.'

'Carl, you don't understand. I . . . '

'Myra, listen to me.' He placed both hands on her shoulders, leveled his eyes at her. 'You don't need anymore to cope with,' he said gently. 'And this is definitely not the best place for the kids right now.'

Knowing his wife, he waited for further argument, but her face seemed to crumble before him in defeat, and she moved into his arms, laying her head wearily against his chest. 'You're right, Carl. Of course you're right. I just feel so scared. So damned helpless.'

He stroked her hair. 'I know you do, honey. We all do.'

After a moment, she asked, 'Where do you think she is right now, Carl? Where do you think he's taken her?'

Carl didn't answer.

Myra really didn't expect him to.

44

When Ellen was fairly certain that he had really gone, she tried to calmly assess her injuries. Her eyes were swollen nearly shut. Her face felt as if it had met dead on with a mack truck. She could taste blood inside her mouth. But the real pain was centered in her left cheekbone. She knew it was broken.

She attempted to make a fist with her right hand, remembering trying to grab the knife off the floor and his boot coming down. She winced as scalding pain shot up her arm. Waiting a few seconds, she breathed deeply, and repeated the action. Then again. Badly bruised, she concluded, but probably not broken.

Now her legs. They were bound at the ankles. She inched them toward her along the floor, and out again. Other than the fact that her feet felt as though they were encased in blocks of ice, her legs seemed to be working properly. But then again, she hadn't tried to stand on them.

There was probably not a square inch of her upper torso that wasn't covered with bruises, but Ellen didn't think anything else was broken, but she couldn't be certain of that. For all she knew, she might very well be bleeding to death internally even as she lay there. Well, there was not much she could do about it, if she was.

Except to try and get away — to find help for herself.

Think, she commanded herself. *Think*.

Okay. He's tied me so I can't escape, but he didn't tape my mouth which has to mean he's not worried about anyone hearing me if I should try to call for help — or if I scream. And since the walls don't seem to be insulated and I would certainly be heard, there must not be any nearby neighbors.

She tested the strength of the ropes binding her hands. Though the pain in her right hand punished her, it was not so bad that she couldn't stand it.

Her hands stilled as she heard his footsteps returning. Moments later, she felt him kneeling beside her in the darkness, smelled him the way one might smell a beast in the instant before you saw it. Feeling his hands sliding down her arms, her entire body and soul recoiled from his touch. Cringing inside herself, bracing for some new assault, Ellen went limp with relief when she felt him untying her hands as he'd promised.

'Do you want me to help you undo your jeans, Ellen?'

'What? No, I — you said . . . ' she stammered.

'You thought I was going to take you out of here, didn't you? No, I don't think that will be necessary. I've brought you a bedpan. It belonged to my Aunt Mattie, but she won't be needing it anymore. I've even warmed it for you. And there's a roll of tissue on the floor beside you.'

'Please, I . . . '

'There's no need to feel embarrassed, Ellen. I'm used to this sort of thing. I took care of my aunt's more 'delicate' needs for a long time.'

'It — it's not you,' she said, trying to speak clearly through barely parted lips. 'It's me. I don't think I could go if you were standing here.'

For a long moment, he didn't speak, and Ellen was terrified that she'd angered him. Then, 'Very well, Ellen. If you think you'd be uncomfortable with me here, then of course I'll leave you.'

'Thank you.'

'You won't try to get away, will you?'

'No. No, I promise.' Her voice sounded almost childlike.

'Good. Because if you did, I'd have to hurt

you some more,' he said with chilling softness. 'And I don't think you'd like that.'

* * *

It was next to impossible to maneuver in the darkness, especially with her bad hand and her ankles bound, but finally Ellen managed to wriggle her jeans and panties down. Lifting herself onto the bedpan, she had to bite her lip to keep from crying out against the knives of pain that attacked her body from every direction. When the pain leveled off a little, she forced herself into a sitting position. Despite the cold, the effort left her bathed in a clammy sweat, her heart racing wildly in her throat. She was sure she was going to be sick, but thankfully, after taking a couple of deep, slow breaths, the feeling passed.

It was humiliating to have to pee with him listening, but he might not oblige her by untying her hands next time, and she did have to go. Badly.

To hell with modesty.

* * *

He seemed to sense when she'd righted herself, or else he could see in the dark, which wouldn't have surprised her. 'Okay?' he said, his voice coming from a mere few feet away.

'Yes. Except I'm freezing.' Exhausted, Ellen was more than willing to lay her head back down. She needed to rest. She needed to feel stronger so she could escape this madman.

Taking the bedpan away, he returned shortly to cover her with blankets. As he tucked them around her, his hands lingered momentarily on her thighs. Ellen held her breath, letting it out again when he took his hands away.

'Comfy?'

'Yes, thank you.' She was too grateful for the warmth the blankets provided to worry about their disgusting smell.

'I used to do this for my mother,' he said, almost fondly. 'Sometimes she'd wake up in the morning with a bad hangover and I'd cover her up and bring her aspirin. Later, she'd call for her tea and cigarettes. She'd smile at me when I took them to her. Sometimes, she'd take me into her bed.'

Ellen thought the safest comment was none at all.

'I know what you're thinking,' he said sharply, ' . . . but it wasn't like that. I was just a kid. She was my mother. We didn't do anything.'

'No, of course you didn't,' she said quickly.

'I know that. It was just that I was thinking of my own mother, and how I used to do the same thing for her. That can be a lot of responsibility when you're young. A lot of unfair responsibility. It can make you feel resentful.' Perhaps, she thought, if she could establish a common bond between them, he would feel more favorably toward her and let down his guard. Then she would have a better chance of getting away.

'Did you?' he asked.

Encouraged, Ellen replied, 'Yes. Lots of times.'

He laughed. An ugly sound. 'You think you know what it's like to be me,' he said, yanking her arms hard behind her and beginning to retie her hands. He gave the rope a final jerk so that it dug into her flesh. 'You uppity bitches don't know anything. You need to be taught.'

'Are you going to kill me?' Her voice was childlike in her ears, barely audible. She knew the very question might set him off, but the not knowing, the wondering when his damn chain would snap, was worse. Why had he brought her here? Why hadn't he just killed her back at the house?

When he answered, his tone was back to being perfectly reasonable, almost pleasant. 'No, of course I'm not going to kill you. I'm not going to do anything at all to you — unless you misbehave. Now. You must be hungry, Ellen. I'll make you some lunch. How about some nice, hot soup?'

'That would be fine. Thank you. Please, can't you loosen the ropes just a little? They're cutting into me. I can hardly feel my fingers.'

Giving a mock sigh of exasperation, he said, 'You're getting spoiled, Ellen. You girls do tend to spoil easily. But all right, just a little.'

While he was busily granting her request, she ventured into a little deeper water. 'Can you tell me where we are? Where you've taken me?'

His hands stilled momentarily on the ropes, and she tensed. But there was only the slightest hesitation before he answered, 'Why not? It's not like you're going to tell anyone, is it? You're in a home for wayward girls. You've been a very bad girl, Ellen.'

And then she felt the slightest tug on her scalp and heard the snip of the scissors as he cut off a large chunk of her hair.

45

Every available man was working double-time trying to find out who belonged to the van Officer Gabe Levine had seen coming from the direction of Cutter's Road just minutes after Ellen was taken. Artie had narrowed the list of possible vans in and around the area to forty-seven. After dividing said list between several officers and handing out copies of the new composite, Mike took off for Anderson Insurance.

It was close to noon when he returned with a unanimous 'yes.' The man in the sketch was indeed the same one who had been in there selling paintings just a couple of days before Cindy Miller was reported missing.

No one had anything new or helpful to report. He managed to engender a few shrugs and some stupefied looks. It was as though they'd hit an invisible wall. Mike wished to hell solving a case could be as easy as they made it look on television. In fact, police work came down to slogging through endless details, talking to endless people, paperwork. Sometimes you got lucky.

This didn't seem to be one of those times.

The day dragged on. The odd phone call was still trickling in — drying up quickly. Mike's frustration grew.

At least getting around wasn't going to be a problem. They'd gotten a few inches of snow during the night, but nothing like what had been forecast. All he'd needed was a major storm to shut the town down.

It was three in the afternoon when F.B.I. man Frank Burgess arrived on the scene. Wearing horn-rimmed glasses and dressed like an ad for Brooks Brothers, he looked more like a Wall Street broker than a detective.

He seemed a decent enough sort, though, not at all heavy, which Mike had half-expected. Mike filled him in on what they had so far.

'*Ding-dong, the witch is dead*,' Frank Burgess repeated, gazing ceilingward. 'That's from *Sleeping Beauty*, isn't it?'

'*The Wizard of Oz*,' Mike said. 'My daughter had a small role in the school musical last year. Do you think it contains some sort of code — a riddle?'

'It's possible, but I doubt it. Probably no more complicated than that it just popped into his head, struck his fancy. Hard to believe, isn't it, that raving psychotics were kids once, too? I don't think he's killed her yet, either, though I know that's what the message implies.'

'Why is that?' *Please let him be right.*

'He wouldn't have phoned your house. He wants your attention, Lieutenant. He wants you to know he exists, that he's a force to be reckoned with. My guess is that you'll be hearing from him again, and soon. Interesting, isn't it, that he perceives her as a witch? With the others, it was important to show them up as fools, which is obviously why he painted them to look like clowns.'

'He didn't with all of them,' Gabe said, with a trace of belligerence. He was leaning against the wall beside the door, lighting up a cigar. The acrid smell permeated the air in the small room. He blew out smoke, looking defiantly at the F.B.I. man. 'Mind?'

'Yes, as a matter of fact, I do.' He grinned. 'Makes me crave one. I've been trying to kick the habit. You make a good point, though, Gabe,' he said easily, defusing the momentary tension with a slickness that sent him up a couple of notches in Mike's estimation. 'It's true, he didn't paint all of his victims. Probably just those who most closely resembled the object of his hatred.'

'His mother,' Mike said, thinking of Ellen's sketched profile.

'It usually is, but not always. Maybe just

some girl who turned him down at a crucial point in his life — at a moment when the whole world seemed against him. Maybe he failed a class in school, got fired from a job. Stuff we can all relate to at one time or another. The trouble with killers is that they have to blame someone else for their problems. The hatred builds. After awhile it needs to find release. So they become human predators. Sometimes they don't even hate anymore. They just do it because it's fun.'

'Welcome aboard, Frank,' Mike said, putting out his hand. 'We can use another good man on this case.' He meant the welcome genuinely, but he also thought it was important to set the tone. Bruised egos had no place in this investigation. This was Ellen's life they were dealing with.

'Thanks, Lieutenant. I appreciate the vote of confidence. Look, you're the one familiar with this case. You know the woman. Why do you think he perceives her as a witch?'

Mike shrugged. 'Because he's a maniac. I don't know, maybe because in the beginning Ellen was the one doing the stalking. She went a little nuts after her sister was murdered. Maybe she scared him.'

Frank Burgess nodded. 'Where are you with the van situation?'

Mike told him, not that there was anything

to tell. 'We're also running the new composite on the five o'clock news.'

'Sounds to me like you've got everything pretty well in hand.'

'Not everything. Look, if you can come up with any — '

'Got something for you, Lieutenant,' Artie said, poking his head around the door. His shirt sleeves were rolled to his elbows, a thatch of hair fallen over one of his lenses. 'One of the victims we turned up in California was a native of Evansdale. Name of Tracy Betts. She worked at a club in L.A. called the Phoenix as an exotic dancer. The murder happened nearly ten years ago.'

'Family still living here?' Mike asked.

'Scattered. Father took off when she was just a kid. According to the club's manager, there was a brother who's probably in jail someplace, had a few run-ins with the law. He also remembered that Tracy had a mother back here — said she was in a nursing home. But don't bother to question her.'

'Why not?'

'Alzheimer's. She could also be dead by now.'

'Christ.'

'There must be friends who remember her,' Frank Burgess interjected. 'Old school-mates, teachers, neighbors. Lieutenant, instead of trying to tie in all the victims, maybe it would be a good idea to focus on just a couple of them — two that he painted — this dancer — what was her name?'

'Tracy,' Artie frowned, raking his hair out of his eyes. 'Tracy Betts.'

'Okay. Zero in on Tracy Betts and Gail Morgan. Look for the link between those two. Go back to when they were kids. Find out who taught them in kindergarten, where they went to summer camp, if they did. That stuff's not too hard to dig up.'

'What about Gail Morgan?' Gabe said. 'Pretty damn hard to ask family about her when her only living kin is the one we're looking for.'

'That's okay, Gabe,' Mike said quickly. 'I'll take care of that part of things. You and Olsen concentrate on the Betts girl. Any problem with that?'

'No problem,' Gabe said just a trifle sulkily, mashing out his cigar stub in the battered brass ashtray Mike kept on his desk just for him.

'Good man. Then let's do it.'

When Gabe and Doug Olsen were gone, Frank Burgess said, 'Hope you didn't mind my stepping on your toes, Lieutenant. Sometimes when we're too close to an issue, we get to feeling a little like that fellow who jumped on his horse and rode off in all directions.'

Mike didn't miss the wry, perceptive smile behind the horn-rimmed glasses. It was not devoid of sympathy.

46

Matilda Bishop's dining room served mainly as her office during the time she ruled over the Evansdale Home for Girls. Everything remained exactly as it had been for all those years. Tall, wooden cabinets, now laden with dust, housed files on every girl who had ever been incarcerated there, which included snapshots Matilda took herself of each new arrival. The photographs were for police identification in the event of a runaway, which was rare. Matilda kept a tight rein.

Alvin had already been through the files on numerous occasions. Ellen Harris had never been an inmate. Just her younger sister.

Twelve of the files had 'inactive' printed in red block letters on the front covers. Alvin's own way of keeping track, as well as providing him with an amusing private joke.

Clippings of stories on some of his victims over the years were spread across the dining room table, some now yellowing. Sliding a brief writeup on Cindy Miller aside, he picked up the article that had first drawn his attention to Gail Morgan. Actually, it was her picture he had noticed. So different from the snapshot in the folder, yet vaguely familiar.

He turned the article over and reread yet one more time about the planned demolition of the home, which was scheduled for nine in the morning. When he first read it, it was as though someone had slammed a boulder into the pit of his stomach. After awhile, he got used to the idea. It was time to move on, anyway. Things were getting a little too warm for his liking. He'd find a new 'secret' place.

Last night he'd been worried the storm might postpone things — an awkward turn of events — but he needn't have sweated. On this morning's news they said the burning of the Evansdale Home for Girls would go ahead as scheduled.

Ellen Harris would burn with it.

Soon you'll be together, he told the girl in the picture.

*   *   *

Out in the kitchen, Alvin took a match from the metal container hanging on the wall, struck it on the top of the stove, then held the flame to the ends of the hair he'd cut from Ellen's head.

The sickening smell of burning hair rose in the air, making Alvin reflect how in the old days, long before he was born, they burned witches at the stake. The tradition held a certain appeal for him. Of course, a public burning would have been far more exciting, but since that was impossible . . .

In the meantime, Alvin thought, shaking out the match, slipping the hair into an envelope, then going into the pantry and taking down a tin of tomato soup from the shelf, it was important to keep her alive.

Later, driving down the narrow, winding road past the grey building that would by this time tomorrow be nothing more than a pile of ash and debris, he told himself that she would be all right for a little while. She wouldn't be in any shape to try to escape.

He'd made sure of that.

47

No more than a half hour could have passed between the time he left taking a hank of her hair with him, and when he returned with the soup, which was neither 'nice,' nor 'hot.' It also had a funny taste, but Ellen was famished and ate it to the last spoonful. She even munched soundlessly on the crackers which were so stale she couldn't hold back an image of tiny black inhabitants scurrying through the box they'd come in.

Why had he taken her hair? Surely not for ransom. Though she'd like to think there were a couple of people out there who valued her, no one she knew had any more money than she did.

After she'd finished eating, he attended to her more 'delicate' needs, then covered her with more blankets.

He had not spoken a word during the entire process, and instinct warned her to follow suit.

Within minutes of his leaving, her lids began to grow heavy, her limbs lethargic, and she knew she'd been drugged. No doubt something else his aunt no longer had any use for.

She fought hard to stay awake, but she was helpless against the swirling blackness that kept rushing over her, pulling her down and down, Myra's voice following . . . '*Last night I dreamed I was back in the home and Miss Baddie had me tied to a chair . . . chopping off all my hair . . . great chunks falling on the green tile . . . so awful . . . just so damned real, Ellen . . . so real . . .* '

48

'I'm going out for a walk, Carl,' Myra said pulling on her boots. 'I need to think.'

'I'll go with you,' he said, immediately putting down the newspaper and reaching for his coat on the door hook.

'No, please,' she said more sharply than she'd intended. 'I need to be by myself for a little while. It's still light out. I won't be long.'

★ ★ ★

Her boots made no sound on the newly fallen snow. Though it was not yet dark, there was already a sprinkling of stars in the sky. As she walked along the road, she could see her breath in the frosty air. A light wind stirred the trees on either side of her. In the distance, a train whistle sounded.

There seemed to be a stillness in the air — a waiting.

Burying her hands deep in her jacket pockets, Myra trudged the mile to Ellen's house, her steps slowing as she approached. She went a little ways into the driveway, touching Ellen's car as she passed it, as though in some way the gesture might transfer into touching Ellen.

She stopped and gazed up at the house. The yellow police tape was across the door. It had always been to her such a warm, welcoming house. But now, no light glowed in any window. No outside light was on.

Soon, the house would be swallowed up in darkness.

For how long?

★　★　★

It had been dark in the cellar too, though there was enough light to see. Remember? One of the girls sent you down to fill up the basket with potatoes. She said it was your turn. You didn't want to go. You were afraid, but the tall girl's hands were at your back, pushing you toward the door. You had no choice. She was one of Miss Baddie's spies.

Something happened, then. What was it? You went down the stairs. Remember? You were carrying the basket. You had just stepped onto the bottom step. What did you see, Myra? What did you hear? Hear it now! See it again! She squeezed her eyes shut, hunched her shoulders forward.

'Myra?'

She whirled around, her hand leaping to

her breast. 'Christ, Lieutenant! You scared the hell out of me.'

'Sorry.' He flung the passenger door open. 'Hop in. I'll give you a lift back. I wanted to talk to you, anyway.'

He didn't sound sorry. 'About what?' she said stiffly, settling into the seat beside him, still shaken from the fright he'd given her.

'Ellen. I need to talk to you about Ellen. What do you know about her childhood, Myra? She must have talked to you about it.'

'I told you, she didn't let me in.' That wasn't entirely true, she realized now. Ellen had confided in her. Just not easily. And she'd be damned if she was going to betray her confidence, especially when she couldn't see how it could possibly help them find her, or the sick creep who took her.

The instant the cruiser pulled into the yard, Carl was out the door. 'Myra, honey, are you all right?'

'I'm fine,' she snapped. 'For God's sake, Carl, stop fawning.' The moment the words were out, she apologized. 'The truth is, I'm not all right. My head feels like it's coming apart. I'm going upstairs to lie down for a while. I'm sorry I can't help you, Lieutenant.'

When she was gone, Mike explained to Carl why he was there. He'd no sooner finished when the phone rang.

'It's for you, Lieutenant.'

It was Gabe. 'Some kid just delivered an envelope addressed to you. It's got the same red printing as on the other stuff.'

'Open it.'

After a pause, during which Mike could hear paper tearing, Gabe said, 'It's a lock of hair. Kind of reddish gold. Feels silky.'

Mike closed his eyes. After a pause, he said, 'Any note?'

'Uh, yeah. Says, 'A little keepsake, lieutenant. Enjoy.' Sorry, Mike.'

'Who did the kid say gave him the envelope?' His voice had a ragged edge. His shoulders felt as if they belonged to a very old man.

'Some woman with red hair wearing a long, black raincoat. She approached him as he was coming out of the library. Offered him two bucks just to run the envelope across the street. There's something odd about the hair, Mike. The ends are singed. You can smell it.'

What have you done to her, you bastard?

'Anything else?'

'Nope. We ran into a major snag with the vans. We got one guy who runs a delivery service with a fleet of ten. He says he's hired a lot of people to drive for him — maybe thirty, forty — over the past couple of years. I guess the pay sucks.'

That's not the only thing, Mike thought miserably. The only bright spot he could find to focus on was Frank Burgess' theory that the killer wouldn't be bothering to taunt him if Ellen was already dead.

But maybe Frank Burgess didn't know everything.

'You look like you could use a drink, Lieutenant. I've got some first-rate scotch I've been saving. Now, I don't want to corrupt the Evansdale Police Department, but . . . '

'I'm officially off-duty,' Mike said. 'And I'd be mighty grateful.' He'd never felt so close to bawling since he was eight years old.

Carl had just taken the bottle out of the cabinet when the phone rang. Carl passed him the receiver. It was Gabe again. A woman had driven in from Southfield and was waiting in his office to see him.

'She says she thinks she knows who the killer is, Lieutenant. She caught you on tonight's news broadcast and won't talk to anyone else.'

'Does she sound legit?'

'Does to me.'

'I'm on my way.'

'Right. In the meantime, while Doug is pouring over some old city directories looking for past neighbors of the Betts', I'm taking off for a bite to eat. We had a couple of leads, but . . . '

'Another raincheck,' Carl said when Mike hung up the phone. A statement, not a question. He was standing with a regretful smile on his face, an unopened bottle of scotch in his hand.

'Sorry,' Mike said, heading for the door.

'No problem. But I'm gonna hold you to it when this is all over.'

'I'd like that.' He turned. 'Carl, I — uh, don't want to sound like I'm suggesting anything as dramatic as a curfew, but I don't think it's a real good idea for your wife to be walking this road by herself right now.'

'Neither do I. I was just about to go after her when you drove up.'

Mike nodded. 'I really do need to ask her some questions about Ellen, Carl. About her and Gail's childhood.'

'I won't pretend to understand the significance of that, but I'll talk to her. If she knows anything at all, we'll give you a ring.'

* * *

Gabe sat at his favorite table in Papa Bear's — by the wall facing the door. Officer Gabriel

344

Levine was by nature a people watcher, and with the exception of a bus station or an airport, a bar was the best place to do it. Though right now, pickin's were slim. He was one of a half dozen customers in the place. Two guys at the bar, three more — lawyers maybe — at a back table.

The T.V. was on with the sound turned off. 'Matlock.' Gabe couldn't stand the guy. Maybe if he didn't yell and holler so damn much. Even with the sound off, you could tell he was raking someone over the coals.

When his order of a beer and the house specialty — roast beef — arrived, he felt himself starting to relax a little, his thoughts slowing down. This case was making him nuts. He could only imagine what the lieutenant was feeling. Gabe was married to someone he had loved a lot once — for about ten minutes.

He hoped the woman from Southfield really had something solid. They were overdue for a break.

Gabe had decided the F.B.I. could have sent them worse then Frank Burgess, even if he didn't buy all that crap Burgess had spouted about why serial killers did what they did. That was the trouble with today's world. We're trying so hard to analyze the bastards, we can't see what's right in front of our eyes. They're just plain bad.

Any dog breeder could tell you bad dogs are born into a litter. Why do we think people are any different?

Gabe cut into his roast beef. Tender as a mother's touch, depending on who your mother was. He didn't frequent the tavern, especially if it was busy, but he did manage a meal here from time to time. The food was edible, but it was the atmosphere that drew him. It was sort of like being in a warm, pleasant cave.

And no one gave him any bullshit about his cigars.

'Hey, Johnny,' the bartender bellowed, which was Jake's natural way of talking, and Johnny his name for any young fellow he didn't know, 'That's a good color lipstick for you — matches your eyes.' Setting the beer down in front of the man in the plaid shirt, he let out a loud guffaw, and went on wiping the already clean counter, cleaner.

Jake Pappas was the owner and operator of Papa Bear's. He had stubbly iron-grey hair and the look of a man who likes his booze, though Jake happened to know he hadn't had a drink in more than ten years — he just served the stuff.

'Told the bitch to blot,' the man mumbled,

346

plucking a napkin from the metal holder.

Jake laughed again. 'Wouldn't kid a kidder, would you, Johnny?'

Takes all kinds, Gabe thought, continuing to eat his meal.

49

The woman sitting in Mike's office had introduced herself as Victoria Grey. She was nervously playing with the gold signet ring on her finger. Mike guessed her to be in her late thirties. She was attractive, brown-haired, maybe ten or fifteen pounds overweight. She was wearing a loose-fitting suit to hide the fact. Her eyes were hazel, intelligent.

'I want to say right at the start, Lieutenant Oldfield. I can't be absolutely certain it was the same person I taught in my grade ten class. That was a very long time ago. I was hardly more than a girl myself, then. Not much older than my students.'

'Duly noted,' Mike said. 'Go on.'

'The first artist's sketch they ran on television and in the papers meant nothing to me, you understand, but this one . . . anyway, the boy I remember . . . he was an odd boy with a very definite mean streak. He had disturbing eyes. Liked to bully the little ones. His poor mother — Lili, her name was — seemed unable to control him. I called her in for a conference on a few occasions. She seemed actually frightened of him. She was

very pretty in a tired way. Blond. Exception-
ally blond. I perceived her, perhaps unfairly,
as not the brightest person around, and
certainly too generous for her own good, but
she did seem to me a decent soul. I believe
she tried.

'She told me she was a high-school
dropout, herself, that she'd gotten pregnant
at sixteen and had waitressed most of her life
to support herself and her son. I got the
impression she was lonely, and maybe liked
men — the wrong sort, of course — and
strong drink, a little too well.'

Mike hadn't heard the term 'strong drink'
since his grandmother was alive.

Trying to contain his impatience, he said,
'Something other than what you've told me,
Miss Grey, must have happened to make you
think this person is going around killing
women.'

He felt her bristle. 'Yes. I'm coming to that.
Please bear with me, Lieutenant. This isn't
easy for me.'

'Of course. Sorry. Please — take all the
time you need.'

'Thank you.' She let out a long, shuddering
sigh and Mike heard its underlying sadness.
'There was a girl in my class that year by the
name of Debby Fuller. Debby was cute and
bubbly — a cheerleader type. A nice girl. She

had a wild crush on this boy. Some girls are drawn to dangerous types. Anyway, I watched him play cat and mouse with her for weeks. And one afternoon out in the parking lot, I saw her get into his car. I wanted to call out, to warn her, but they were already speeding away. She probably wouldn't have listened, anyway.

'I didn't see her or the boy for — oh, two or three weeks after that. Actually, he never returned. The family moved away, I have no idea where to. Debby came back to school a much quieter, timid girl. There were bruises on her face and neck — faded, but I could still see them. Perhaps because I half-expected to see them, because I looked for them. I know I should have gone to the authorities, but I didn't. I was just so relieved to have that terrible boy gone from my class, from my life. I always knew he'd come to no good end.'

The woman looked drained, paler than when she'd begun her story — which Mike suspected she'd told for the first time. He also suspected it was not the whole story. Her memory was too clear.

'I think any doubts you may have had about the composite are gone now, aren't they, Miss Grey?' Mike said quietly.

She nodded.

'Do you remember his name?'

'Of course.' Her voice was barely audible. 'It was Alvin Raynes.'

After a long silence, Mike laid his hand on the woman's shoulder. 'Debby wasn't the only one who suffered at the hands of Alvin Raynes, was she, Victoria?'

She shot him a surprised look, seemed about to challenge his implication. Then she lowered her head into her hands and began to weep.

* * *

Alvin remained at the bar just long enough not to appear in too big a hurry to take off. He'd been looking in the mirror behind the bar when Jake made his comment about the lipstick. He was in plain clothes, but Alvin could always smell a cop.

Now, as he drove toward the outskirts of town, it took all his concentration to keep his foot easy on the gas pedal. Once, he saw lights flashing behind him and came close to panicking until he realized the lights were on a tow truck.

It was that witch. She was still doing it to him — making him mess up. Like she'd made him take that painting back after he'd killed the Miller girl. And now, tonight, taking off the wig and coat, then forgetting to wipe off the lipstick. How could he have forgotten that?

He knew how.

He wouldn't wait for the fireman's torch. Morning was a long way off. He'd finish her off himself — tonight.

The decision made, he began to feel calmer. He was also feeling a warm buzz from the three beers he'd had and thought he might just have a little fun, first, sample a little of what the lieutenant was getting. He began to grin, thinking about it. And then he wondered if her boyfriend had gotten the little souvenir he'd sent, yet, and what he thought about that.

After a few minutes, he let his thoughts drift back to the cop at the bar. Alvin had been careful to keep his back to him, not to let him get a look at his face. He might start putting two and two together, though he doubted it. Cops were generally pretty stupid. Besides, Alvin didn't think he looked anything at all like that artist's drawing they were showing on T.V.

Though it did resemble, just a little, he thought, his Aunt Mattie.

Dear Aunt Mattie.

He could still hear her laughing when he would ask if there was any mail for him, any phone calls. 'What did you expect from that tramp?' she would say of her younger, prettier sister.

After a while he stopped asking.

He'd been planning to stay with his aunt just until it was safe to go back home. But when he phoned his mother about a week after he got there, the operator told him the phone was disconnected. That's not possible, he said. There must be some mistake. Try again. And then two days later he got his letter back marked 'address unknown.'

Like the old joke: *Every time I leave the house my parents move.*

The heat was rising up in him, the vein in his forehead beginning to pulse the way it always did when he thought about her.

Caution forgotten, Alvin clutched the steering wheel and lowered his foot on the gas pedal.

The van shot forward.

50

Ellen drifted in and out of the grey zone between sleep and consciousness. Someone was calling out to her, urging her to wake up, to get away. *Hurry, Ellen! Hurry!*

Gail? She forced her eyes open and was met with a deeper, almost palpable darkness. Her head felt as if it were packed with gauze, and her mouth tasted faintly of chemicals.

She lay very still and waited for her memory to tell her where she was. She felt disoriented. She couldn't remember. She tried to move her hands and felt them trapped behind her. Panic seized her.

In the next instant, memory rushed down on her like an avalanche, and with it the horrible knowledge of where she was and why she was there. The city was going to burn down the Evansdale Home and he intended her to perish in the fire.

She tested the ropes binding her hands, and felt encouraged. They were not as tight as before. Ignoring the pain and stiffness in her right hand, and her raw, bleeding wrists, Ellen began systematically to work at the ropes. Ten minutes later, she slid one hand free and then the other. Trying not to breathe too loudly, she gently rubbed the circulation back into them, and quickly undid the ropes around her ankles.

She was free. It had seemed almost too easy. Was he close by, waiting, amused at her pathetic attempt to get away?

She strained to listen, but there was no sound but her own breathing now, not even the wind.

Outside the cocoon of blankets, she was shivering with the cold. It seemed to reach right inside her bone marrow. Dressed in just a cotton shirt and jeans, clothes she'd changed into to bathe poor little Sam, she knew she'd last maybe fifteen minutes out in the open.

First things first, Ellen.

Which meant trying to stand up.

After a couple of unsuccessful attempts to get to her feet, she finally made it. Her legs were shaky, and there was nowhere she didn't hurt. Beads of perspiration broke out on her forehead, but she managed, by leaning against the wall, not to sink back down to the floor.

Waiting a couple of seconds, she took a tentative step in the direction she'd heard him leave.

With no light to guide her, her hands held

out in front of her like a woman newly blinded, she took maybe a dozen steps before she felt the wall in front of her. Yes, she thought, this is where his footsteps begin to fade. She moved her hands over the rough wood, testing, touching — until a section of wall gave beneath her hands.

A door.

She stepped through, and knew at once by the musty smell of old clothes that she was inside a closet. Her guess was confirmed by a rattling of wire hangers as her shoulder brushed against them. Further exploration brought her in contact with a couple of cloth coats still hanging on the rack. She pulled what felt like the larger of the two from its hanger and put it on. It was snug across the shoulders and the sleeves were too short, but as far as Ellen was concerned, it was as welcome as a luxurious mink.

Slowly opening the closet door, she peered into the hallway. By the shaft of moonlight coming through the tall window at the end of the hall, she could see faintly.

Every silhouette was a beast crouching, ready to pounce.

No, not a beast. Just a high-backed chair, an old trunk. *Calm down. Easy. You can do this, Ellen. You can get away.*

Warily, she stepped into the hallway. She

held her breath. Objects came gradually into clearer focus as her eyes adjusted to the semi-darkness after the total absence of light. She could make out the doors leading off the hallway on either side.

The stairway was to her right.

She was about to descend the stairs when she heard the heavy thud of boots on the lower floor. For an instant, like a deer caught in the glare of headlights, she froze, her mind flooding with panic. Quickly, she ducked into one of the rooms.

By now she was soaked in perspiration, her body screaming in pain. Her heart was hammering so hard it seemed as if at any second it might fly straight out of her body.

Unable to take another step, she sank to her knees and began dragging herself past the three remaining iron-framed beds into the farthest corner of the room, where moonlight did not reach. Huddled there like a frightened, wounded animal, trembling inside the moldy coat she clutched about her, she tried to make herself as small as possible.

And listened.

And waited.

Thump!

Yes. He was coming up the stairs. She pressed her back hard against the wall and felt the cold pouring through.

Thump! Thump!

He was nearly at the top now. She sensed something different in his step. A calculated slowness. Measured. Anticipating. He was coming for her. She knew it as she knew her own name.

He was coming to kill her this time.

51

Myra sat on the edge of her bed staring at her reflection in the mirror as if it were one not familiar to her. In a way, it was a stranger she was seeing. There were gaps missing from her life — whole chunks she couldn't remember. This thing with Jeannie — why couldn't she remember anything more about Jeannie? She was sure they'd been friends. What happened to her? And what did it have to do with Ellen's disappearance?

What did I see in the basement?

I'm trying too hard. Just let the memory come, Myra. Let it come. She closed her eyes.

Suddenly, she was back in the Evansdale Home sitting with the other girls at the dining room table. They were having breakfast. Miss Mattie has come into the room. She is tall and frightening in her black dress. Her long face is hard beneath the red wig. Her voice sharp. 'I have distressing news. The new girl, Jean Perry, has run away. The police are combing the countryside looking for her. She is a worthless girl and you will all forget about her. Her name is not to be spoken on these premises. She is not to be discussed either among yourselves, nor with anyone else. Any girl caught disobeying will answer to me.'

I watched her go out of the room, heard the whisper of her black skirt, saw that stiff, unyielding back and I knew she was lying. Jeannie had not run away. But I obeyed the order. I forgot about her. For all these years I forgot about her.

And then Myra remembered something else. A few days before Miss Mattie's announcement, Jeannie had told her a secret — an important secret. One that had frightened both of them. What was it? But all she remembered of the secret was the fear she saw on Jeannie's face when she was telling it.

'Myra? Are you all right?'

She turned to see Carl standing in the doorway. 'No, Carl,' she said, her hands going to her head. 'I really don't think I am.'

★ ★ ★

They now had a name to go with the face. APB's were issued around the country for serial killer, Alvin Raynes. Law enforcement agencies were in close contact with one another, cooperation at a maximum. In Augusta, Alvin's name showed up on a computer. At sixteen, he'd been charged with rape with violence. Later the charges were dropped. The girl said she'd lied, that she'd consented to have sex with him. Mike didn't think so.

By all accounts, they should have apprehended Alvin by now. The problem was they still had absolutely no idea where to look. He wasn't in the city directory, had never applied for a credit card, not even a driver's license, which had to mean he was operating under an alias. All efforts to trace him fizzled out.

They were back where they started. Which was exactly nowhere.

He rose from his desk, his hands clenching and unclenching. He paced. He sat down again.

Frank's analogy about the guy who jumped on his horse and rode off in all directions didn't really fit Mike. He felt more like he was running in place.

Gabe had managed to track down an elderly landlady who had once rented a flat to the Betts. A copy of his notes were in front of him on the desk. Mike reread them, thinking he might have missed something important.

'That wretched old devil made all their lives miserable. No summer camps for those two children, no sir. They were lucky to have shoes. He used to beat those little tykes unmercifully — and he didn't spare no rod on his missus. It's probably why the poor woman's head went bad. He was a mean drunk, Ralph Betts. It was a happy day when he left; too bad he did it too late. The children were in and out of foster homes half the time cause she wasn't able to look after them properly. I heard the girl — Tracy — took off for greener pastures as soon as she was old enough. Pretty little thing. I don't believe the boy fared too well — a lot like his father. Like they say, 'The apple don't fall too far from the tree'.'

Mike wondered if Ellen or Gail ever spent any time in foster homes when they were kids. He picked up the receiver and dialed the Thompson's number.

Myra had a raging migraine, Carl said. He gave her a couple of sleeping pills and she was dead to the world. He said he'd ask her when she woke up and call him back.

Mike hung up. Sighed heavily. He knew the suicide rate among cops was high. He wondered what the statistics were on those who simply descended into madness.

52

She heard him going into the closet, heard the faint rattle of hangers, then the inner door open. Any minute now he would discover her gone. Now was the time to run, but she knew she wouldn't make it halfway down the stairs before he'd be on her. If her legs could even carry her that far.

She brought her fingers to the left side of her face. She could no longer feel it. It felt as if it were pumped full of novocain. Both eyes throbbed with pain, but she could deal with that.

Her only hope was that he would think she was already on the road and race after her. Then she might have a chance.

At a sudden thud against the wall, Ellen's fist flew to her mouth to stifle her cry.

* * *

Alvin had already begun to smile in anticipation when he felt for her beneath the mound of blankets on the floor. The smile was stillborn. At first, he couldn't believe she wasn't there. He tossed the blankets aside, kicked angrily at them. Switching on his flashlight, he walked the full distance around the passageway and back again.

She's gone. The witch is gone! He muttered an obscenity, kicked at the blankets again, smashed his fist against the wall.

He made himself calm down. He had to think. She couldn't have gotten very far, could she? Not in the shape she was in. Unless she'd taken off as soon as he left. But she couldn't have. He'd given her enough dope to keep her out for hours.

Alvin started to go after her, had his hand on the door leading into the closet, about to push it open when he stopped. Slowly he walked back to the place where so many years ago he'd made the nail hole in the wall.

Flicking off the flashlight, he brought his eye to the hole.

He scanned the room. The 'Suffer the Little Children' picture still hung on the wall, crookedly now.

At first, he'd thought the dark form huddled in the far corner of the room was no more than shadow — until the shadow moved.

Slowly, the smile returned.

Oh, this was good. Very good. Excitement rippled through him. It had been so long since he had played this game.

So very long.

★ ★ ★

What was he doing in there? He should be rushing down the stairs after her by now. At that moment, she heard the closet door creak open, heard his footsteps out in the hallway. *Oh, please, go down the stairs. Let him go down the stairs.*

But he didn't. His footsteps were coming toward the room — slowly — coming closer.

Hugging her knees tight to her body, she pressed herself deeper into the corner, ceased to breathe.

Please, someone help me. Oh, God, please.

Someone did try to help you, Ellen. Someone tried but you wouldn't let them. You thought you could handle this all by yourself, just like you always think you can do everything by yourself.

And suddenly there was no more time for self-chastisement, or anything else. He was filling the doorway, grinning in at her helplessness. He stepped into the room.

'You were a bad girl, Ellen,' he said. 'And now you have to be punished.'

She knew an instant of raw terror, and then, as though some greater force had

365

intervened, all fear left her, replaced with a feeling of uncanny calm.

He was walking toward her, in no hurry, savoring the moment.

'You murdered my sister, you bastard,' she said, positioning herself for maximum leverage. She had nothing to lose. She was going to die anyway. Might as well get a little satisfaction.

'Yes. And now it's your turn. When do I start paying, Ellen?' he mocked. 'Remember, you said I was going to pay? I was asleep and your voice woke me. That was how I knew you were a witch. And then you said it again on television. I was in a bar. You were looking straight at me. I knew you could see me. So — when do I start paying, Ellen?'

Come a little closer, you crazy piece of slime, and you'll find out. She planted her palms firmly on the floor on either side of her. Come on. Just a little closer.

He closed the gap between them. He was towering above her, now. His fingers curved, moving toward her. 'When do I pay, Ell — ?'

Right now, you bastard! Summoning every ounce of strength she possessed, she brought her legs up with the precision of a Parisian dancer, her feet smashing straight into his groin.

For a split second, nothing happened. It

was like watching a freeze-frame on film. And then his mouth opened like an impaled fish trying to scream, and he dropped to his knees in front of her, clutching himself.

Ellen scrambled past him, but before she could get to her feet, his hand shot out and clamped around her ankle. She tried frantically to kick it away, but his fingers only gripped her ankle tighter. And then her free ankle was trapped in his other hand and she could do nothing. His strength was born of madness, and Ellen had used up what little strength she'd had left.

He held her like that for several minutes, neither of them moving, his breathing raspy in the silence, chorusing with her own. Finally, he recovered enough to draw himself up. Yanking her onto her back, his hands went immediately for her throat, his rigid thumbs pressing into the soft part, squeezing the breath from her. The face above her was distorted with rage.

'I'll come back,' she managed to choke out, desperately trying to pry his thumbs away. 'You know I have powers.'

The ploy came out of nowhere. For a brief, horrifying moment she didn't think it was going to work. Then she felt him hesitate, felt his fingers loosen on her throat.

He drew back.

She sensed his fear, seized on it. 'I'll haunt you,' she whispered hoarsely. 'I'll haunt you till the day you die. And you'll die screaming.'

He looked long at her. Then, without a word, he rose to his feet. His movements were stiff, and she knew he was still in some pain, but she was helpless to take advantage of it. The next thing she knew, she was being dragged feet first from the room out into the hallway, her head striking the door casing, on through to the closet. Here he dropped her legs just long enough to open the door, and in the space of a breath she was back behind the wall and he was snapping her hands behind her, tying them roughly, hurting her.

Next her ankles.

Finally, she couldn't move.

'Oh, no, please,' she cried as she tasted what had to be a filthy scrub rag, but her plea was cut short as he jammed it into her mouth. She gagged. Tried to work it out with her tongue, but couldn't.

'There,' he said, clearly satisfied with his work. He was standing over her, breathing hard. 'You won't escape this time. You'll die like you were meant to — in hell. The flames will make sure you won't be coming back.'

He left her then, to return maybe ten minutes later. 'Here. I've brought you a present.' He shone the flashlight on the small, rectangular clock before setting it on the floor where she could see the green, glowing numbers. It was 12:45 a.m. 'I don't mind if you take it with you,' he jeered. 'The radio doesn't work anymore, anyway. The fire is set for nine in the morning. I thought you might enjoy the countdown. In the meantime,' he said, covering her with the blankets, tucking them in around her, 'we don't want you to freeze to death in here, do we?'

This time he didn't return.

For a long time, Ellen lay awake in the darkness, tears glistening in the glow of the clock. From time to time, she would try to work the gag loose with her tongue, but this only resulted in making her stomach heave, though she did manage every so often to shift her position a little, to work her hands and feet enough to keep the blood circulating.

I should have let him kill me. All I've done is postpone the inevitable. I'm sorry, Mike. I'm such a fool. She envisioned his face, those warm, sensitive eyes, the smile that made him seem younger. She felt the sweetness of his lips on hers. So much there. Sadness, humor, an innate sense of justice — qualities she would have enjoyed exploring further. She would have liked to have met Angela.

So many things she wanted to do, now that

369

it was too late. Open a private practice. Be a better friend to Myra. *Dear Myra — I've failed you. I've failed Gail, too. Now that monster will be free to go on raping and murdering other innocent women.*

Through the long agonizing hours, sometimes Ellen was awake, sometimes she dozed fitfully. When she was awake she watched the numbers on the clock change, and listened to her own measured breathing. When she slept, she dreamed.

In one dream a little boy was sitting at her kitchen table, sobbing hysterically, while beside him, her hand resting on his blond head, a woman kept saying over and over, 'He doesn't sleep or eat. Can you help him? Can you help him?'

In another dream, Gail was standing on a stage in front of a microphone, wearing a skimpy green jacket, her hands drawn up inside the sleeves. She was singing, but no sound was coming out. Her face was contorted in panic. Ellen tried to comfort her, to tell her it was all right, but she kept backing away, and then she was flying backward through space, growing smaller and smaller until at last she was no more than a tiny doll-like figure at the end of a long tunnel. Ellen could hear her faint shout, 'Is anybody here?'

I'm here. Wait, Gail. I'm here.

'Hello?'

Ellen opened her eyes. She looked in terror at the new numbers on the clock. 8:31 a.m.

It was morning. Nearly time.

'Anybody here?' came the shout again.

Not Gail. A stranger's voice. It must be a fireman. He's come to check out the building, make sure no one is trapped inside before they start the fire. Hope soared in her. She could hear him walking, could feel the slight vibration of his boots on the floor, just outside the wall. Just a few feet from her.

I'm here! Behind the wall. Oh, help me, help me, please. The screams were inside her head. Like in her dream of Gail, no sound came. Again, she tried to work the soggy rag from her mouth, but it was no use. She struggled against the ropes binding her hands, uncaring that they were cutting into her flesh. She was beyond pain.

His footsteps were fading. She could hear him leaving the room, going back down the stairs. *No! Oh, don't leave me here to die. Please!*

When she could hear him no more, a black shroud of despair settled over her.

Silent tears fell.

53

Alvin started at a loud pounding on the back door. He'd been finishing off a beer, was just about to leave to watch the show. He knew a moment of panic until he looked out the window and saw the fireman's uniform. No sweat.

He opened the door, smiling pleasantly.

'Morning,' the kid said. 'You seem to be the only neighbor around here. Just wanted to inform you the old Evansdale Home's going up in a few minutes. We didn't want anyone to be alarmed at the sight of flames.'

'I did know about it, but thanks, anyway. I'm Al Bishop. It's a good thing you're doing. Kids could get trapped in there, set the place ablaze with cigarettes or whatever the hell they're smoking these days.'

'Yeah. You've been in there yourself, huh, Al? I followed your footprints over here. Otherwise, I wouldn't have known anyone lived around here.'

'My aunt ran the home for years,' Alvin said easily, closing the door and walking back with him. 'I was just checking to see if there was anything left in there belonging to her.'

As they trod across the snowy field, the fireman kept a breathable distance between them. The guy smelled.

Damn near as bad as the house he lived in.

54

Myra was soaking in the tub, her eyes closed when Carl called through the door, 'The lieutenant called last night while you were asleep. He wanted to know if either Gail or Ellen ever spent any time in foster homes when they were kids. I knew *you* did, but I didn't think that had any bearing.'

Why would he want to know that? Why in hell weren't they out there looking for her? 'No,' she said. 'I don't think so.'

Hearing Carl's receding footsteps, Myra slid deeper into the warm, sudsy water until it lapped at her chin. Just the echo of her migraine remained. She closed her eyes again. *She's not dead. I know she's not. I can feel her helplessness. She's in a dark place . . .*

Dark place . . .

She was suddenly back in the home, descending the steep, narrow stairs leading into the cellar, one hand on the rough, splintery railing, the other holding the basket the older girl had thrust at her as she pushed her toward the door. 'It's your turn to bring up the potatoes for dinner, lard-ass, scaredy-cat,' she'd brayed, 'so just go do it.'

She hated going down to the cellar. It was so spooky down there. There was a lot of old junk — stuffed chairs, lamps — covered with dust-laden sheets. Sometimes she imagined something moving under one of the sheets.

Dirty, yellow light came from a naked bulb hanging on a string from the ceiling beam, casting pools of light everywhere.

I had just stepped onto the floor, was about to go to the potato bin when I heard something — noises, like a baby kitten mewling, coming from the far end of the room, over by the boiler. I was frightened. I ducked behind the stairs, hid there, crouched down low . . .

'Don't, oh, please, don't . . . '
Jeannie.

Do something! Scream! Help her, Myra. But she couldn't. She was too afraid. Her heart was pounding so hard she was sure he would hear it.

After a few minutes, it got quiet. So very quiet. The man stood up and turned around . . .

Now Myra remembered the secret.

*   *   *

Carl was on the phone with Mike when Myra came flying down the stairs, dressing on the

375

run, hair dripping. 'I heard him killing Jeannie,' she cried, bursting into the room. 'I heard her struggles. I was hiding behind the stairs in the cellar.' The words rushed from her, tumbling over one another. 'He didn't see me. But I recognized him. It was Miss Baddie's nephew, Alvin. All the girls talked about how creepy he was, hanging around outside the fence all the time. When he was gone, I slipped back up the stairs. I couldn't look at her. I knew she was dead. She didn't run away like they said. I blocked it all out — all these years. That's where Ellen is, Carl. I know it. That's where he's got her.'

'Where, Myra, what are you — ?'

'The *home*, goddamit, Carl,' she screamed in frustration. 'The Evansdale Home for Girls.'

'Hey, take it easy, honey. What makes you think — ?'

'Hurry! We have to hurry! Tell Mike! They're burning it down this morning!' She was putting on her coat, getting into her boots. 'What time is it?'

Carl glanced bewilderedly at his watch. 'Quarter to nine.'

'Oh, my God! The fire is set for nine o'clock.'

Before Carl could utter another word,

she was out the door.

Seconds later, the door burst open again. 'The third floor, Carl. Tell him there's a false wall on the third floor!'

But Mike had already hung up.

55

Ellen could hear faint shouts, people calling to one another. She had ceased her struggle, begun to pray. At the faint smell of smoke, her eyes opened. It was 8:50 a.m. They had started. *No! It's not time.*

Had he set the clock slow?

How long did it take to burn to death? Maybe she would be overcome with smoke first and wouldn't feel the fire.

Yes, please God — that wouldn't be so bad. Let me be already dead when the flames find me.

She closed her eyes, and began again to pray.

★   ★   ★

Outside, a small crowd had gathered on the scene. Across the road, along the shoulder, a line of cars stretched back maybe a quarter of a mile.

Though most of Evansdale's residents knew of the scheduled burning of the home, had noted exactly when it would happen, a few, like Myra, had a special interest in its fiery demise.

'Oughta go up like a tinderbox,' one of those women in the crowd said now, with a bitter note of glee. 'Gonna be some fireworks. Should of brought the camera.'

The fire was already in progress when Mike's cruiser screeched to a stop. Flinging the door open, he leaped out. Before anyone could stop him, he'd grabbed up an air-pack from the back of the nearest firetruck. Ignoring the angry shouts of the fireman behind him, he raced inside the building.

The boards had been ripped off the doors and lower windows and arranged on paper close to the cellar walls at strategic points. Most of the fire, thank God, was still contained in that area, but it was spreading fast.

'Ellen,' he called out, strapping on the apparatus. He made a quick search. She's not here. They would have found her. After peering inside an old vegetable bin, he bounded the stairs to the first floor, his steps echoing through the empty building. He searched the rooms, flinging doors open, calling out her name.

He bounded to the second floor. Was Myra wrong? Was it only wishful thinking that Ellen was here?

He ran through the rooms. Not here. The

smoke was getting thicker, pouring up the stairs. He clamped on the mask, took a few gulps of air while making his way to the top floor.

He checked the rooms on either side of the hallway. Not there. Then he saw the door just past the stairs. He opened it. Smoke rushed in, too thick to see through, now. He felt for her in the closet, felt behind the single coat that still hung there.

Bright orange flames were licking around the door casing at the bottom of the stairs. He could feel their heat. He stood helplessly, fighting panic. 'Ellen!' he bellowed. He coughed and gasped for breath as the smoke seared his lungs. 'If you're here, please answer me. Ellen!'

He clamped the mask back over his face as the flames raced up the stairs toward him.

Outside, a murmur of awe and fear rose up from the crowd as a lower window popped, then another. Flames leaped out, the old wood crackling and snapping like the sound of paper being crumpled. The acrid smell of smoke was strong in the air.

Myra stared up at a third floor window. She's behind the wall, Mike. Oh, please, let him find her. Let them both get out safe.

Jeannie had told her about the wall, had said she was writing in her diary when she heard someone laugh. Later, she found the tiny hole and peered through . . .

★ ★ ★

'Ellen!' Mike called. The fire was traveling faster than he'd anticipated. The flames were getting closer. His hands tingled. The hair stirred on his head. *I have to get out of here. I have to go now. Ellen's not here. Myra was wrong.*

Thump!

At first he thought he'd imagined the sound. He listened. It came again, louder this time. THUMP!

Ellen had managed to maneuver herself into a position where she could hit her feet against the wall. Hearing Mike's voice had given her back the will to fight, to survive. She kicked at the wall. Feeble kicks, the best she could do. Again. The heat was rising up through the floor boards. She was lathered in perspiration. She couldn't breathe. Her lungs were already on fire. She pressed her face into the blankets.

She could feel herself slipping. Sinking. *No! Not now. Hang on.* At last, she worked the gag free, spat it out. 'M-i-i-k-e . . . '

Ellen! My God, she's behind the wall. There had to be a way in there, but he'd

381

never find it in this smoke, and with the fire so close.

Taking a backward step, he drove his foot against the wall. Nothing. Again. Harder. On the third try, his foot broke through. Wood splintered. Two more solid kicks, and he'd made a hole big enough to begin feverishly tearing with his bare hands at the chunks of plaster, the laths, oblivious to the punier fire of jagged wood and nails.

Though it seemed forever, it was mere seconds from the moment he heard her scream until he was climbing through the opening and scooping her limp body up in his arms. Through a hell of blinding, choking smoke, he staggered with her to the window at the end of the hallway and placed her on the floor. No time to give her air or untie her. The flames were at his back.

He tried to raise the window. It wouldn't give. *Oh God, we're not going to make it.* He thumped the heels of his hands against the frame. Tried again. The window shot up. Cold air rushed into his lungs.

The firemen were below, holding the net. People were screaming up at him, motioning him to jump.

Quickly, he gathered Ellen up again, and without letting himself think, he tossed her out the window.

When he saw her land safely, he climbed over the sill and jumped.

As he hit the net, a loud cheer went up in the crowd.

★ ★ ★

It had been too many years, and Myra had not recognized the tall man in the plaid jacket, his cap pulled low, standing at the edge of the crowd. His shoulders were slumped forward, his hands buried deep in his pockets. Now, he took them out and began to move slowly away.

Ellen and Mike lay side by side on the ground, the medics working over them. Ellen had regained consciousness. Seeing *him*, she pushed the mask from her face, pointed a trembling hand. 'It's him, she said in a weak, raspy voice. 'It's him.'

He'd seen her look in his direction, saw her hand go out, but before anyone could react, he broke from the crowd. To the horror of those watching, he rushed inside the burning building, choosing a fiery death over captivity.

A stunned silence ensued as flames shot high, as an explosion of sparks gave the promised show of fireworks. Within minutes, the building was a towering furnace, collapsing in on itself with a shuddering groan.

Mike, black with soot, his hands blistered and raw, eyebrows singed, rode with Ellen to the hospital. She had slipped into unconsciousness after her tormentor had run into the building.

As the fire completed its destruction, the ambulance wailed through the streets of Evansdale, while behind them a great, eerie glow lit the morning sky.

★　★　★

For one brief moment, Alvin imagined he saw his Aunt Mattie's face emerge from the wall of flames — elongated, melting, hollow-eyed. And then her gnarled, fire-drenched hands were reaching out for him. 'Welcome to hell, boy!' she hissed.

He screamed. And screamed.

★　★　★

Later that day, police searched the house and found the stash of souvenirs which would tie Alvin in with several unsolved murders. They found the files marked 'inactive.' They also found Aunt Mattie. An autopsy would later confirm she'd died of starvation.

Jeannie Perry's remains would never be found.

56

It was the early afternoon of her third day in the hospital. Ellen was propped up in bed watching the news on the 12 inch television. She still hurt everywhere, her throat was raw, her face battered, including a hairline fracture to her cheekbone. But the doctor had assured her the bone would knit nicely on its own. The bruises would fade. Soon she would be as good as new.

Maybe physically, she thought. But she knew it would be a long time before she slept in a room without a light on.

After listening to a little of the commentary about her ordeal, about Alvin Raynes, alias Bishop, she snapped the set off and wondered what sort of childhood could produce such an evil monster.

She'd believed him when he said nothing happened when his mother took him to her bed. His words had held a ring of truth. But she knew there were more subtle forms of seduction. Had he wanted his mother sexually? Had shame and confusion planted the seed of hatred that would soon include all women?

No. That explanation was too pat, too easy. She knew plenty of people who survived horrible childhoods — Myra, for instance, even herself and Gail — and managed to grow up into decent human beings.

All thoughts of Alvin Raynes slipped away at the sight of Mike standing in the doorway, holding a vase of pink roses, so many they nearly obscured his face. She knew he'd been here before, but she'd been pretty well out of it, and the memory had a dream-like quality.

'Hi,' he said, looking at her with something close to reverence. 'Do you know, you are without doubt the most beautiful woman I have ever seen.'

Her heart was doing a fluttery little dance in her breast. 'Then you must have been holed up somewhere for a very long time,' she joked, in a voice still raspy, still not her own. 'The roses are gorgeous. Thank you.' She took in the blue sweater beneath the open overcoat, the grey slacks. The neat way they fit. He was even more handsome than she remembered. Had she thought him handsome? Yes. She just didn't know it then.

'You're welcome.' He set the roses on her night table, drew up a chair to her bedside. 'How are you feeling?'

He smelled nice, of shaving lotion and

winter. 'I've been better, but they tell me I'll live.'

'Oh, I brought you some cigarettes,' he said, taking the pack from his pocket. 'I think this is your brand.'

'Are you kidding? Do you think I would ever again willingly inhale smoke?'

He grinned, dropped them back into his pocket. 'Good girl. I'll give them to one of the guys.'

'Oh, Mike, look at your poor hands. You could have been killed. I'm so sorry. I was such a fool. I should have accepted your offer of a policewoman. I should have phoned you the second I got that photograph of Gail in the — '

'Shh.' He touched his fingertips to her lips. 'You're here. You're alive. That's all that matters.'

'You saved my life.'

'As much as I'd like to take the credit, it really belongs to Myra. She told me where to find you.' He related the story to her.

Poor Myra. She'd been so traumatized by her father that her young mind couldn't cope with any more, and so she blocked the murder out.

Until Ellen needed her to remember.

She thought then of the little dog leaping at Alvin's throat to protect her, of the

387

knife . . . 'I wish Sam had been as lucky,' she said sadly.

'Sam? I'd say Sam was very lucky.'

She looked at him, afraid to hope. 'What do you mean?'

'He'll be okay. He lost a lot of blood, and it was pretty dicey there for a while, but the vet says he'll make it. He's a tough little guy. Another fighter. Oh, by the way, my daughter, Angela is anxious to meet you. She thinks you're a major celebrity.'

She smiled. 'I can't wait.'

'Neither can I,' he said, bringing his face down to meet hers, kissing her gently, sweetly. But she could feel his restrained passion, and was pretty sure they weren't talking about the same thing.

★　★　★

Just outside Houston, Texas, in the back room of a truck stop called Jack and Lil's, a too-blond, slightly frowsy, middle-aged woman sat puffing on a cigarette and dabbing at her eyes as she watched the news on the black and white television.

And wondered where she went wrong.

We do hope that you have enjoyed reading this large print book.

Did you know that all of our titles are available for purchase?

We publish a wide range of high quality large print books including:
Romances, Mysteries, Classics
General Fiction
Non Fiction and Westerns

Special interest titles available in large print are:
The Little Oxford Dictionary
Music Book
Song Book
Hymn Book
Service Book

Also available from us courtesy of Oxford University Press:
Young Readers' Dictionary
(large print edition)
Young Readers' Thesaurus
(large print edition)

For further information or a free brochure, please contact us at:
Ulverscroft Large Print Books Ltd.,
The Green, Bradgate Road, Anstey,
Leicester, LE7 7FU, England.
Tel: (00 44) 0116 236 4325
Fax: (00 44) 0116 234 0205

PLAIN DEALER

William Ardin

Antique dealing has its own equivalent to 'insider trading', as Charles Ramsay finds out to his cost. Offered the purchase of a lifetime, he sees all his ambitions realised in an antique jade cup, known as the 'Loot'. But as soon as the deal is irrevocably struck he finds himself stuck with it like an albatross around his neck — unable to export it without a licence, unable to sell it at home, and in a paralysing no man's land where nobody has sufficient capital to take it off his hands . . .

NO TIME LIKE THE PRESENT

June Barraclough

Daphne Berridge, who has never married, has retired to the small Yorkshire village of Heckcliff where she grew up, intending to write the biography of an eighteenth-century woman poet. Two younger women are interested in her project: Cressida, Daphne's niece, who lives in London, and is uncertain about the direction of her life; and Judith, who keeps a shop in Heckcliff, and is a divorcee. When an old friend of Daphne falls in love with Judith, the question — as for Cressida — is marriage or independence. Then Daphne also receives a surprise proposal.

SEARCH FOR A SHADOW

Kay Christopher

On the last day of her holiday Rosemary Roberts met an intriguing American in the foyer of her London hotel. By some extraordinary coincidence, Larry Madison-Jones was due to visit the tiny Welsh village where Rosemary lived. But how much of a coincidence was Larry's erratic presence there? The moment Rosemary returned home, her life took on a subtle, though sinister edge — Larry had a secret he was not willing to share. As Rosemary was drawn deeper into a web of mysterious and suspicious occurrences, she found herself wondering if Larry really loved her — or was trying to drive her mad . . .